Record Store Reckoning

RECORD STORE RECKONING

A DARCY GAUGHAN MYSTERY

J.C. KENNEY

First published by Level Best Books 2022

Author Photo Credit: Amy Pangburn Photography

First edition

ISBN: 978-1-68512-066-5

Cover art by Level Best Designs

This book was professionally typeset on Reedsy.
Find out more at reedsy.com

This is for Aidan and Lorianne, who, to borrow a phrase, sure have the music in them. And to all members of the Ball State University School of Music, past, present, and future. Thanks for keeping the music alive!

Praise for Record Store Reckoning

"*Record Store Reckoning* is a rockstar debut for the Darcy Gaughan Mysteries."—Sarah E. Burr, author of The Trending Topic Mysteries

"A unique whodunit, with visually descriptive narrative, engaging dialogue and a small-town feel."—Dru Ann Love, Dru's Book Musings

Chapter One

When she was twenty-three and drumming for the all-girl punk band Pixie Dust, people said Darcy Gaughan wouldn't live to see thirty. She didn't care what they said. She was too busy pounding the skins hard and the bottle even harder. She was going to live forever.

Then she got hurt.

If someone had told her back then that tearing a ligament in her elbow would end her drumming career and save her life at the same time, she would have laughed in their face. Followed by a swig of whiskey and a few choice curse words directed at the commenter for good measure.

And then thrown a drumstick at them.

As present-day Darcy pulled on a T-shirt bearing the logo of the seminal, all-girl rock band *The Runaways*, she chuckled at how much things had changed in a decade. Instead of traveling the world to play for audiences from Anchorage, Alaska to Zagreb, Croatia, she was a general manager of a record store in Marysburg, Indiana. Instead of basking in the roar of an adoring crowd in the thousands, she was helping customers one by one discover music by artists from Audra McDonald to Warren Zevon, and everything in between. Instead of burning the candle at both ends with a bottle right beside it, she was stone-cold sober and living a simple, uncomplicated life.

Her story had been filled with more twists and turns than a treacherous mountain road, but she'd managed to hold on tight enough to avoid careening off a cliff and plummeting into oblivion. Sometimes, like right after the band fired her, that connection had been little more than a fingernail. She'd never lost it, though. Now her handhold was steady and strong. The current gig was way different from what she'd imagined growing up, but she was still around and part of the show that was life.

When the lights went down at the end of the night, that was what mattered. Still being part of the show.

"Day one thousand, eight hundred and twenty-six, buddy." She scratched the gnarled ear of her cat Ringo as she slipped the AA token into a jeans pocket. Today marked five years of sobriety. It would be an amazing day. One to remember. Darcy was sure of it.

"My how time flies. Ready for a celebration breakfast?"

Ringo jumped from the bed, landing on the hardwood floor with an ungraceful sounding *thunk*. After stopping long enough to lick a paw, he limped out of the room. He'd shown up on Darcy's doorstep one stormy October night. Soaked to the skin and bleeding, it didn't take a genius to know he wouldn't last the next twenty-four hours without some help. So, she did what others had done for her. She took him under her wing, got him medical care, and gave him a safe place to stay.

Three and a half years on from that memorable evening, Ringo was fat and happy, if not exactly fleet of foot, or paw, anymore. The rough-and-tumble tomcat had been through more than his fair share of close calls, but he was a survivor.

Same as his adoptive mom.

Darcy scooped some fancy food out of a can, tossed in a kitty treat in honor of the day, and got him fresh water. While the feline attacked his breakfast, his human glanced at the clock on her tiny microwave. It was a little after eight. That gave her plenty of time to stop for a doughnut and a cup of coffee before she had to be at work.

"Later, skater. No wild parties while I'm gone," Darcy opened her back door. She knew better to be hurt by her cat ignoring her while he ate.

Once outside her tiny abode, she took a minute to soak in the surroundings while she pulled her sandy brown hair into a ponytail. Under a cloudless pale blue sky, the buds on the sycamore and maple trees were popping open. The grass was taking on a vibrant shade of green. A pair of red squirrels made a racket as they chased each other up and down and around an oak tree in the corner of her yard.

Even though the house was small, only eight hundred square feet, the location was priceless. It was nestled at the confluence of Mary's Creek and the White River, forming the southwestern tip of the community of Marysburg, Indiana. The triangle-shaped lot was ringed with trees, which gave Darcy a much-desired sense of privacy. The fifty feet of waterfront property served as a constant reminder that life is in a constant state of change. She couldn't change the past, but the future held too many possibilities to count.

Originally built as a fishing cabin, Darcy's century-old home had been vacant for twenty years when she bought it. The roof leaked, the floorboards sagged, and the water heater belched forth as much rust as hot water, but the price had been right. Four years after buying the heap, much work still needed to be done, but the roof shingles were solid, the gleaming hardwood floors were level, and the tankless water heater made for endless long, hot showers.

And she'd done all the renovation work herself.

She hopped in her rusting, decades-old jeep and crossed her fingers before keying the engine. Rusty, as she lovingly called it, had been lacking in the reliability area in recent weeks.

"Come on, dude. If you turn over, I promise to take you to Liam's for a tune-up." The engine fired up on the first try. In celebration, Darcy tossed a salute to the photo of Go-Go's drummer Gina Schock taped to the dash, then did a little drumroll on the steering wheel with her fingers.

It was another sign the day would be one to remember.

She waved to Ringo, who'd moved to the kitchen windowsill, and rumbled out of the driveway, leaving a trail of gravel dust behind her. With the stereo blasting Joan Jett's "Bad Reputation," she headed for the heart of Marysburg for breakfast.

Between the creek to the north, the river to the south, and a busy thoroughfare to the east, the town of Marysburg, like Darcy's property, had a roughly triangular shape. Locals said it was shaped like one slice of a pizza that had been cut into eight equal pieces. The community had originally served as a wealthy suburb of Muncie, Indiana, the home of Ball State University, which lay ten miles to the northeast. Nowadays, Marysburg was home to funky shops, unique restaurants, and a handful of bars that thrived on the influx of dollars from the university crowd.

Some members of the older generation didn't care for the bohemian vibe Marysburg's business district had. Darcy loved it. As she rolled to a stop in front of Perfect Pastries, a bakery owned by her friend Jenna Washburn, there was no place on Earth she'd rather call home.

When Darcy turned off the engine, it made an attention-grabbing *bang*. A cloud of acrid blue smoke then floated from the tailpipe. Recognizing fate should be tempted only so long, she called her buddy Liam Simmons at Marysburg AutoCare and scheduled a service appointment.

Darcy was stubborn and took pride in living life on her own terms. She wasn't foolish, though. Rusty needed help, not unlike like she had years ago. It was encouraging to have both her head and her heart in a good enough place to take care of other things besides herself.

The bell above the bakery's door rang when Darcy entered. The *jingle, jangle* was a happy sound, one that matched her mood.

"Hey, girlfriend." Jenna, bedecked in her signature blue and white checked apron, waved. "Welcome back. I've got a spot here at the counter with your name on it."

As Darcy settled onto a chrome stool with a red, vinyl seat, her blonde-haired friend put a ceramic mug, a brushed aluminum tea kettle, and a package of Constant Comment tea on the counter.

"My fave. Yum. What's the royal treatment for?" Darcy dropped the tea bag into the mug.

Jenna grabbed the kettle's handle and poured for her. "Today's a big day. Thought you deserved to celebrate. Now, close your eyes."

Jenna had been there when Darcy hit rock bottom. She'd opened her spare bedroom, and her heart, when Darcy had nowhere else to go. She understood the day's significance as well as anybody did.

Darcy squeezed her eyes shut. In addition to following her friend's directions, doing so helped keep the tears at bay.

After a few seconds, Jenna took Darcy's hand. "Okay, now open."

A lump formed in Darcy's throat when her gaze landed upon a chocolate-covered croissant. Five birthday candles, each one a different color of the rainbow, had been stuck into the pastry. They had tiny, blinking lights at the top to simulate flames. Her vision became blurry with tears, but she managed a laugh, thanks to the adorable candles.

"Happy birthday, anniversary, sobriety day, or whatever you want to call it."

"I like sobriety day. Let's go with that." Darcy laughed again and wiped tears from the corners of both eyes with a napkin. "Five years. Wow. Hard to believe it's been that long. Some days it feels like yesterday that you and Eddie picked me up from rehab."

She removed the candles, one by one, turning each one off with a flourish, as if to signify the passage of the time.

"You should be proud of yourself. It's a huge accomplishment." Jenna took a drink from an aluminum water bottle she always had close at hand.

"Yeah. Not gonna lie. It *does* feel good." Darcy tore off an end of the croissant and put it in her mouth. It practically melted on her tongue. "Oh my God. This is the best thing I've ever eaten in my life."

"Thanks. It's a new recipe. Thought I'd try it on you before I risked offering it to any customers." Jenna winked and glided to the other end of the counter to fill a burly young man's coffee cup.

Darcy was halfway through the croissant when her friend returned. "I bet The Bahamas were amazing. I want to hear all about it."

Jenna never asked people to do things, she told them. In a friendly way, of course. She'd once informed Darcy it was a result of growing up with three younger brothers who were tougher to corral and a herd of cats. When Darcy asked her if she used the same approach to keep her husband, Bogie, in line, she declined to answer.

She didn't deny it, either.

"Best vacation ever. Six days of nothing to do but sit on the beach all day, then go dining and dancing all night." She weaved side to side on her stool to simulate a dance she'd learned.

"Nice." Jenna raised her eyebrows in appreciation. "I thought you didn't like to dance, though."

"Well, the resort had a salsa dancing instructor with moves like Jagger and looks like Anthony Ramos." Her cheeks pinked up at the mention of Dwayne, the instructor. "He made it easy to give it a try."

"Girl, I am proud of you. Mixing it up with a dude straight out of a romance novel. Well done."

Darcy laughed and they exchanged a high five. "Get your mind out of the gutter. He was professional at all times. A true gentleman."

"The way your brown eyes are sparkling right now, I'll bet he was." Jenna flashed a wicked smile.

"Besides," Darcy took a drink of her tea, "there were more than enough women lavishing him with attention. I had a deeper relationship with Pablo."

"Oh, really." Jenna dragged out the words as she leaned closer. With her elbow on the counter, she propped her chin on her hand and raised her eyebrows. "Do tell."

"He was young, handsome, and had a smile that could light up a concert hall. He read poetry to me and tended to my every whim."

"Poetry. Wow." The breathless response told Darcy all she needed to know about what Jenna thought.

"Yep. He was the pool waiter who brought me lunch and my umbrella drinks. Nonalcoholic, of course. When I asked him about the daily specials, he read from the menu like he was reciting something from Stevie Nicks or Maya Angelou." Darcy put her hand over her heart. "It took my breath away."

"Ugh You tease." Jenna threw a napkin at Darcy as she straightened up. "Don't lead me on like that."

"You walked right into it." Darcy stuffed the last of the croissant into her mouth and washed it down with the remaining tea. "Duty calls. New inventory for Record Store Day should have started arriving last week. I can't wait to see what we've gotten in so far."

Record Store Day was to independent record stores what Black Friday was to large retailers. Lots of special merchandise, tons of excitement, and customers lined up out the door. As the general manager of Marysburg Music, it was Darcy's job to make sure store operations ran with the steady reliability of a Neal Peart drumbeat all year round, but especially on Record Store Day.

It was the job of Eddie Maxwell, Darcy's boss and the owner of Marysburg Music, to make sure the store had the inventory to keep customers coming through the doors all year round, even more so on Record Store Day. Together, they'd formed quite a power duo.

"Stop by the house after work. I invited a few friends over for cake and ice cream in your honor," Jenna said.

When Darcy promised she would, Jenna pointed a finger at her. "If you got any new import or limited-edition ABBA records, let me know. Price is no object."

"Will do." Darcy gave Jenna a fist bump and headed out the door.

The record store was only three blocks from Jenna's shop. While it seemed wasteful to drive the short distance, Darcy didn't want to take up a prime spot in front of the bakery. Besides, from time to time, Eddie had asked her to take a drive to pick up someone's personal record collection he'd purchased.

Since she'd been gone for a week, it wouldn't be a surprise that he had a few trips lined up for her. Darcy had learned, sometimes the hard way, it was important to expect the unexpected.

A few minutes later, she was parked in her usual spot behind the store, right next to Eddie's black Subaru Forrester. As she got out of the jeep, Darcy a long look at Rusty. It, too, had been black at one time. The years had taken their toll, leaving the vehicle in its current dull, sun-bleached gray condition. But, like her in so many ways, it was a reclamation project worthy of some TLC.

"You're a good set of wheels." She gave it a friendly pat. "I'll give you a nice, long wash this weekend. Pinky promise."

Darcy couldn't deny the pang of disappointment that ran through her as she walked past Eddie's car. She'd been hoping to get to work first to show him the week in the Caribbean sun hadn't turned her into a slacker beach bum. They'd joked before the trip that he wouldn't be surprised if she never came back, instead choosing to live the rest of her days in tank tops, cut-offs, and flip-flops, playing percussion instruments for tips.

The thought *had* crossed her mind once or twice, but Darcy was happy with her life, and her job, in Marysburg. She was content. Besides, given all that Eddie had done for her, she owed the man. The thought of leaving him high and dry was a nonstarter. Not even for a carefree, island lifestyle right out of a Jimmy Buffett song.

After all, he was the one who literally found her passed out in the gutter a stone's throw from Champions Sports Bar on a frigid March night five years ago. He'd taken her home and made sure she didn't die from hypothermia or from choking on her own vomit.

The man had worked with Jenna to get Darcy into rehab, then made sure she had a job when she came out six weeks later. A few months after that, when Jenna needed Darcy's room for a baby on the way, Eddie moved her right into his spare bedroom. Not a single time did he utter a harsh word at her. The only things he gave her were kindness and support.

Darcy literally owed Eddie her life.

And would do anything to repay him.

She strolled to the front of the building, drumming a tune on her thigh as she passed a row of windows decorated with concert posters. Even though Eddie was inside, the door was unlocked only when the store was open for business. Marysburg was a safe community. But when it came to protecting the merchandise, especially the expensive collectibles, Eddie didn't take chances.

Which was why Darcy found it odd that the door was unlocked when she inserted her key. With a dash of trepidation niggling at her, she went inside.

"Eddie? You back there?" The store was dark. A sliver of light came from under the office door in the back. Everything else was in shadow

When no response came, the hair on the back of Darcy's neck rose to attention. Eddie kept the door open when customers weren't around. It was easier to move inventory in and out of the stock area that way.

Something was off. Like listening to a 45 at 33 speed kind of off.

The door closed behind her with a soft *thunk* as she stepped inside, prompting her to let out a little *eep*. She called out again but was met with only the low-level hum of the HVAC system pushing warm air through the store.

She put her hand on the light switch. After taking a deep breath to steel herself against being grabbed by a bad guy in a mask, like from the old *Scooby-Doo* cartoons, she flipped the switch to the *on* position. The LED lights flared to life, bathing the room in a warm yellow glow.

All was still.

Maybe a burglar was in the back of the store. Her skin broke out in goosebumps at the frightening thought. She made her way toward the office on her tiptoes, for some reason afraid of making noise.

The scene was all wrong. Surely, a robber would have tried to make an escape or whack her over the head by now. The only other explanation must be Eddie. He was in good health but was also on the other side of seventy. Had he suffered a heart attack or a stroke and couldn't respond to her calls?

"Hey, Boss. I'm back." Darcy put her fingertips on the office door and pushed it open.

Eddie was seated behind the desk in his leather executive chair. His eyes were closed, and his head was leaning to one side as if he'd fallen asleep. It wouldn't have been the first time he'd crashed while hard at work.

Darcy let out a shaky laugh. "Stupid paranoia."

Then a nauseating coppery stench filled her nostrils. The unmistakable smell of blood.

"Eddie!"

In the blink of an eye, she was by his side. A stain the color of brownish maroon covered the left half of his lime green polo shirt. His right hand lay on top of the stain in a futile attempt to stop obvious bleeding. It was covered in blood, too.

As understanding that Eddie wasn't asleep hit Darcy, the world swam before her eyes. To keep from passing out, she grabbed the corner of the desk with both hands and sucked in as much air as her lungs could take.

The instant the spell passed, she dropped into the guest chair and called 9-1-1.

"I need help. My boss is dead."

Chapter Two

Too overwhelmed to do anywhere else, Darcy was staring at the acoustical ceiling tiles when a man's voice registered in her stunned brain. It was Paul Gerard, a local cop. A real by-the-book kind of guy, but he was also a huge Green Day fan, so that made up for some of his nit-picking nature.

"Darcy Gaughan? It's Marysburg P.D."

"Back here." She tried to swallow, alarmed by the tremble in her voice. "I'm not armed."

Seconds later, he appeared in the doorway, all six feet four and two hundred, fifty pounds of him. His service firearm was trained on Darcy. Once she raised her hands, he holstered his gun, evidently satisfied she didn't pose a threat. After taking a few moments to assess the scene, he donned surgical gloves and pressed his fingers against Eddie's neck to check for a pulse.

"Is he…" The lump in Darcy's throat made it impossible to say more.

Paul's brown eyes had softened by the time he turned toward her. "I'm sorry. He's gone."

He removed his gloves and spoke into his police radio, requesting additional officers and a crime scene investigator.

Darcy closed her eyes to keep from breaking down and weeping. Even with them squeezed tighter than a drumhead, hot tears escaped along with the brutal realization that there was nothing to be done.

Eddie Maxwell, Darcy's teacher, mentor, and savior, had breathed his last breath.

Before she realized what was happening, someone had whisked Darcy out of the office and planted her on the stool behind the cash register.

"Right. I need to get the store ready to open. Thanks." She got to her feet, her knees wobbly from the devastating events. She needed something to do. Something she could grab and hold onto for dear life so she didn't drown in a sea of grief.

"Take it easy, Gaughan." Marysburg Detective-Sergeant Kaitlin Rosengarten eased her back onto the stool. "You've had a shock to your system. We needed to move you so we can begin our investigation. The store's not opening today."

"But—"

"No buts." The detective took a small notebook from her pocket. "My team has a lot of work to do here. The more you cooperate, the sooner we'll be finished."

As if on cue, a police officer with bulging muscles under his uniform shirt, and short, dark hair walked past them. He had a black nylon bag with all kinds of zippers and pockets slung over his shoulder. Darcy had watched enough cop shows to recognize an evidence collection bag when she saw one.

She rubbed her forehead. "Any chance this is a nightmare I'll wake up from soon?"

"Sorry." The detective popped a mint into her mouth. "This is all too real."

With broad shoulders and dark brown eyes that could make a saint confess to a crime, Detective-Sergeant Rosengarten personified authority. Salt and pepper hair that was pulled back into a tight bun made her look older than she was. In fact, she was only two years older than Darcy.

Despite the pasted-on smile, the woman was not a friend. They'd had a handful of run-ins during Darcy's drinking days. Back then, Darcy had made Kaitlin's life as a patrol officer difficult. Even with five years of sobriety in her pocket, she sensed Kaitlin wasn't likely to put much stock in what she said.

At least that gave Darcy an idea of where she stood. Even the slightest hint of indecision meant Kaitlin would try to toss her in a cell and make every attempt to forget all about her.

"I need to call my coworkers." Darcy pulled her phone from a back pocket. "I don't want them hearing about this through the grapevine."

She'd take things one step at a time. One minute at a time. The same as during her early days of sobriety. She'd done it then. She could do it now.

Kaitlin put her hand over the phone's screen. "Give me their numbers. I'll have an officer contact them."

Despite a desire to lash out at the cop, she shrugged and scribbled down the phone numbers for the store's other employees. Thanks to things like call-offs due to illness and last-minute schedule changes, she'd committed the numbers to memory.

"Charlotte Ryan, Hank Greenbaum, Izzy Preston, and Peter Douglas." Darcy ran her fingers through her hair with one hand as she handed over the piece of paper. "I don't know what we're going to do without Eddie."

Kaitlin furrowed her eyebrows as she studied the list. "That's it? Only four people?"

"Two of them are full-timers. I work full-time, too. Eddie works," her voice caught in her throat, "worked more hours than me. We have each other's backs. We didn't need anyone else."

Officer Gerard approached. That made three on the scene. With a population a tad shy of eleven thousand, Marysburg wasn't a big city. The twenty-strong size of its police force was reflective of that. The cops on hand made up a good chunk of those who were currently on duty.

"The primary scene's secure, Detective-Sergeant." He pointed toward the office, where black and yellow police tape warned all not to cross. "Other than the staff from the coroner's office, I don't want anyone entering the store. We'll look for evidence out here when we're finished with the primary scene."

"Good. Get someone to manage crowd control. We'll have onlookers here in no time."

Kaitlin flipped open the notebook as she turned her attention back to Darcy. "Tell me your whereabouts for the last twenty-four hours."

Darcy bit back a snarky response. The cops should be looking for Eddie's killer, not wasting time by peppering her with questions. Acting surly with the police wouldn't bring back Eddie, though. She closed her eyes until the churning in her gut settled down. Then she took a deep breath.

I can do this. For Eddie.

"I was out of town until yesterday. My flight landed in Indianapolis a little after five. I got home around six-thirty and spent the rest of the day doing laundry and hanging out with my cat."

Normally, the drive home from the airport took Darcy ninety minutes. She missed Ringo so much, the journey had taken only seventy-five. Once she'd hit the highway, the speedometer's needle never dropped below eighty. She'd said a little prayer when she pulled into her driveway, thanking the powers above that she didn't get caught in a speed trap.

And for making sure Rusty's engine didn't blow up.

Kaitlin raised an eyebrow but refrained from commenting on Darcy's speeding. "Can anyone verify this?"

"As a matter of fact, yes." Darcy fished around in her purse until she found the airport parking receipt. A quick glance at it as she handed it to Kaitlin confirmed she exited the parking lot at five twenty-five.

The detective perused the document. "And what time does the store close on Sundays?"

"Six." Once again, the hair on the back of Darcy's neck rose to stand at attention.

"Can anyone confirm when you got home?"

Darcy's cheeks got hot when she realized where the line of questioning was going. She hung her head in shame at the memory of a falling-down drunk Darcy taking a swing at Kaitlin during an arrest six years ago. The alcohol was in control of her then. It wasn't now. She looked the cop in the eye and placed her palms on the cool glass countertop.

"The neighbor girl, Halle Birch, looked after Ringo while I was gone. She stopped by around eight to return the key I gave her."

"We'll talk to her to confirm that. What about today?"

Darcy recounted her morning from the time her alarm went off until she made the 9-1-1 call. "You can call Jenna right now. She'll vouch for me."

"We'll see." Kaitlin gave her a half-smile, as if to send the message she didn't believe a word Darcy had been saying. "Do you know who was working with the deceased yesterday?"

The deceased? Darcy's blood began to boil. Eddie deserved better than to be referred to in such a cold, offhand way. He'd been a good man, and not only to Darcy.

"The deceased has a name. Eldred Maxwell. He was known to one and all as Eddie."

Kaitlin raised an eyebrow. "Who was working with Mr. Maxwell yesterday?"

"According to the schedule," Darcy pulled a piece of paper from a corkboard mounted behind the register, "it was Charlotte and Peter. He left at four. She worked until close and signed out at six-fifteen."

The detective tapped her pen on the counter as fast as a speed metal drummer. The continuous *tat, tat, tat* grated on Darcy's nerves. And both of them knew it. Darcy was in a better place now than in the past, though. She could wait as long as Kaitlin.

Eventually, the detective rubbed the back of her neck. "Any idea who would want to harm Mr. Maxwell?"

She shook her head. "Eddie spent his life helping people, making the world a better place. He was one of the good guys."

A flood of memories washed over her. Darcy had attended Ball State on a percussion scholarship. At the time, Eddie taught trombone. Every now and then, she'd drop by during his office hours to talk about the intersection of brass and percussion.

During her sophomore year, she formed Pixie Dust. Some people in the School of Music, including Darcy's percussion instructor, shook their heads at the time and energy she put into a punk band.

Not Eddie. He'd encouraged her to follow her passion.

Six months after she graduated with a degree in Music Performance, her band was headlining gigs at sold-out theaters across North America. In less time than it takes to potty train a toddler, Pixie Dust went from an idea to a contender for The Next Big Thing in the music biz. Darcy had been unprepared for the meteoric rise. To cope, she turned to the bottle. What started out as a single, harmless nightcap to help her fall asleep morphed into a monster that ruled her every waking moment.

For a while, she held it together.

Then came the injury.

Chronic pain in her elbow made it impossible to play. The only remedy was an extended period of rest. Between the alcohol abuse and the injury, she became a liability. Her bandmates chose not to give her the rehab time and fired her.

The constant ache from the injury left her depressed. The agony of being cut off from her creation destroyed her. Her answer was to drown herself with a bottle.

Eddie was the one who hauled her out of the abyss.

Darcy's trip down memory lane was interrupted when the evidence technician approached. "I think I found the cause of death, Detective-Sergeant. Thought you might want to take a look before we proceed."

Kaitlin pointed a finger at Darcy. "Everyone, even so-called saints, has enemies. I'll be back. While I'm gone, I want you to think long and hard about who may have done this. The more you cooperate, the better this will be for you."

A tension headache was extending its tendrils from the base of Darcy's skull upward. She stared at the schedule as she struggled to come up with the name of someone, anyone, who had a bone to pick with Eddie.

She was still drawing a blank when Kaitlin returned. The detective held a cell phone in front of her so Darcy could see the screen. "Do you recognize this?"

Darcy studied the photo. A long, thin object was in the center of the shot. At one end, a handle was covered with dozens of tiny stones of various colors. The gems encircled a photograph of the King of Rock and Roll, Elvis Presley. Clean edges tapered to a sharp point at the other end. It was an ideal tool for piercing and cutting open objects like envelopes and cardboard boxes.

A dark red sheen covered the blade portion of the object.

"Yeah. It's Eddie's letter opener. Is that what was used to kill him?"

"That remains to be seen. It was on the floor, underneath his desk. Any idea how it got there?"

Darcy looked at the photo again. The letter opener was one of Eddie's prized possessions. Eddie had met Elvis once and talked about it every chance he got. He'd told Darcy the story so many times, she could recount it, word for word, without hesitation.

The memory made her smile even as a new lump formed in her throat.

"No. He kept it on his desk. For display only. The only time he touched it was to tell his Elvis story."

"Which would help explain the sharp point." Kaitlin chewed on her lip then nodded. "I've got all I need from you for now. I'll be in touch if I have more questions."

"I'm free to go?" Cool relief washed over Darcy. Despite the awful circumstances, it was reassuring to know she wasn't going to be led away in handcuffs.

"Yes." The detective gestured toward an officer standing by the store's entrance. "It looks like a case of death by suicide. That's a call for the coroner to make, though."

After arranging to be notified when the police had finished their crime scene work, Darcy left the building on wobbly legs. Twice, she had to put her hand against the wall to stay upright. Once she was safely seat belted inside Rusty, her body began shaking like she was going through a severe case of withdrawal symptoms.

Suicide? The Eddie Maxwell that Darcy knew was the last person to commit suicide. He'd been in love with the record store, with the community, with life. Detective-Sergeant Rosengarten was wrong. This wasn't suicide.

It was murder.

To add insult to injury, Eddie's car sat without a sound to her left, like a loyal pet waiting for its master to come home. A wish that would never come to pass. He'd never drive it through town with the windows down and the stereo cranked up, jamming to the latest from Victor Wooten or another jazz artist. He'd never spend an afternoon off giving it his own bumper-to-bumper detail job.

Sometimes, life was so unfair.

Emotionally unable to go back inside, Darcy called the number on Kaitlin's business card. She kept the call short.

"Hey, just wanted to let you know that Eddie's car is parked behind the building."

"Thanks for the information. If you think of anything else, you know how to reach me." While Kaitlin's approach in the store had been gruff and borderline confrontational, her tone on the phone had been cordial, almost friendly even. The thank you had been totally unexpected, too.

Maybe Darcy's choice to volunteer information had made a good impression on the police officer. *I hope so. I could use all the good karma I can get.*

As Rusty's engine coughed to life, a new thought hit Darcy with enough force to take her breath away.

Regardless of the circumstances, her boss was dead. That meant her job was in limbo. What was she going to do now?

Chapter Three

Darcy had learned a lot during her five years of sobriety. One of the most important was that isolating herself in times of turmoil was a recipe for disaster. In the days when she was drinking, she usually responded to bad news by retreating somewhere behind closed doors with a bottle of some variety of grain alcohol her only companion.

Eddie's death wasn't bad news. It was devastating news of tsunami proportions. The only thing worse for Darcy would be losing her parents or sister. It would be so easy to drive home and curl up in the recliner with Ringo with a blanket over her head. The isolation would weigh her down, weaken her. She'd be making herself vulnerable to a lot of poor decision making.

No. Going home wasn't the answer.

She needed to be around people, especially her coworkers. They deserved to get the news from her, not some rando cop. She grabbed her phone off the passenger seat and dialed a number.

"Hey, Charlotte," Darcy said. "Look, something happened at the store. It's about Eddie. Can you meet me at the park shelter in fifteen minutes?"

A quarter of an hour later, Darcy was seated at a wooden picnic table, drumming a tune with two sticks she'd found on her walk from the parking lot. She stopped when the crackle of dead leaves signaled someone's approach.

"I got here as quick as I could," Charlotte said as she took a seat across from Darcy. Her cobalt blue hair was much shorter than the last time Darcy had seen her. The bob style flattered her high cheekbones and accentuated her greenish eyes.

"Love the cut. Don't think I've seen you with hair above the neckline before." Darcy smiled. She liked her friend's new look. Even with a broken heart, it was crucial to find the moments of joy in life and celebrate them.

"I finally gave Joey the boot for good last week, so I decided it was time for something different." Charlotte had been in an on-again, off-again relationship with Joey Fulton, the manager at the local credit union, for ages. Joey wasn't a bad guy but had gotten into fitness big time in the last year. Ever since, he'd badgered Charlotte about how he thought her hips were a little too wide or her arms were a little too flabby.

With a hug or encouraging word always at the ready, Charlotte was one of the kindest souls in Marysburg. The twenty-eight-year-old was patient and would tolerate a lot of things. Emotional abuse wasn't one of them. The woman was kind, but she wasn't weak. She could do better than her ex.

She also had an affinity for jazz.

She'd played trombone during her middle and high school years. That was when her love affair with classic jazz began. She performed in a couple of ensembles while in college, the music providing an ideal creative outlet to her accounting studies. These days, she was part of a quintet that performed on the weekends at the local brewpub.

Charlotte had been one of the record store's best customers and often hung out with Eddie, talking about jazz legends like Miles Davis and Ella Fitzgerald. When the chance to work with him came up, she dropped her well-paying accounting gig like a singer dropping the mic at the end of a show-stopping song. In the four years she'd been working with Eddie and Darcy, she'd never once mentioned having even a second of regret.

"That's awesome." Darcy gave Charlotte's hand a squeeze. "You deserve someone who cares about you for who you are."

While she'd made great progress on her own state of well-being in the last five years, Darcy wasn't ready for a serious relationship. She still had too much work to do on herself. Maybe someday, though.

"Someone like me, maybe." A gray-haired, heavy-set gentleman took a seat next to Darcy.

"If you weren't forty years my senior, I'd marry you tomorrow, Hank." Charlotte blew him a kiss. "Now, what's going on, Darcy. It's bad news, right? Especially since I was supposed to be at work at eleven."

Darcy took her AA token out of her pocket and squeezed it. There had been a lot of tough moments since she'd gotten sober. The bead of sweat that broke out on her brow forecasted that this one was going to be in the top five of tough moments.

"When I got to work today, I found Eddie in his office. He was dead."

The color drained from Charlotte's face. At the same moment, Hank let out a breathless, "What?"

"The police found his Elvis letter opener under the desk. It was covered in blood. Looks like he was stabbed in the belly." Darcy squeezed her eyes shut to keep the tears at bay.

Hank took Darcy's hand as he reached across the wooden table for Charlotte's. "How awful. Do they know what happened?"

"Not yet. The police said it looks like suicide. The front door was unlocked when I got there, which was weird. The whole set up doesn't make sense."

Darcy focused on the coin in her palm. If she looked at her coworkers, she'd lose the tenuous grip on the control she still had. The store needed a leader. She'd been second in command. With Eddie gone, that meant she needed to step up.

Hank let out a long, ragged breath. "I can't believe it. He was fine Saturday when I left. Said he had dinner plans with some school of music colleagues."

"He was in a great mood yesterday. We spent an hour working on the schedule for bands performing on Record Store Day." Charlotte hugged herself. "Do you know if the cops are going to notify his family?"

Eddie had an ex-wife and two stepsons, one of whom, Rafe, lived with him. Darcy wasn't a fan of Rafe. It wasn't that he was a horrible person or a criminal. She didn't like the fact he was slacker who had turned sponging off his stepdad a career.

Rafe worked fifteen hours a week at the local library. He claimed that a back injury from playing football in high school kept him from working full-time. Darcy didn't buy it. One time, she ran an Internet search for his alleged exploits on the gridiron. The search came up empty.

Despite his assertions, she thought he was lazy. End of story.

"My old buddy Detective Rosengarten is on the case, she said she'd notify next of kin. She's also supposed to be letting you both know so don't freak out if she calls. I'll get ahold of the kids as soon as school's out." Darcy liked to joke with Izzy and Peter, the store's high-school-aged employees, by calling them her kids since having children of her own wasn't in her plans.

"What do we do now?" Charlotte began chewing on her lower lip.

Darcy shrugged. She wanted to be honest, but she also didn't want Charlotte to worry.

Hank was retired from a job in the retail world. He worked at the record store because enjoyed it. Charlotte wasn't in such a comfortable spot. Her income and health insurance came from working at the store. She needed the job. Same as Darcy.

"Kaitlin promised to let me know as soon as they were finished at the store. I want to reopen tomorrow if you guys are good with that."

Hank and Charlotte nodded in unison. As they did, relief coursed through Darcy, just like the warm waters at the vacation resort pool had flowed over and around her.

The team would stick together and keep the store going. Darcy knew, like she knew every drum fill her hero Gina Schock ever played, that Eddie would be pleased.

The trio chatted for a while. At Hank and Charlotte's request, Darcy recapped her vacation. Then the conversation turned to Eddie, as each of them shared funny stories about their beloved boss.

By the time the meeting broke up, Darcy's heart was lighter, but she still wasn't ready to be alone. With no word yet from the police, she decided some chips-and-salsa therapy would see her through until she had to call the kids.

* * *

Like many of the businesses in Marysburg, Selena's South of the Border

Grill catered to the townsfolk during the week and the Ball State crowd at night and on the weekends. The owner, Nathan Echols, was a Marysburg native and BSU grad. Between his business acumen and his loyalty to the community, he'd kept Selena's running strong for over twenty years.

He'd also helped the fledgling Pixie Dust by hiring them to perform at the restaurant on Cinco de Mayo. Darcy had never forgotten that support and tried to repay it by visiting Selena's as much as possible.

The restaurant occupied the first floor of a brick-and-mortar building at the corner of Maple Avenue and Trout Street, in the heart of the Marysburg Business District. It was flanked on one side by a deli and on the other by The Big Bean, an independent coffee shop. A web services firm made its home on the building's second floor.

A maintenance man was power washing the restaurant's canary yellow awnings as Darcy approached. The bright color always lifted her spirits, calling to mind the long, sunny days and warm, firefly-filled nights of summer, her favorite time of year.

Spring wasn't a bad second choice, though. Today's forecast had called for a mix of sun and clouds, with a high in the mid-sixties. Not bad for the first week of April in Indiana. It was the kind of day that signaled winter was finally over and wasn't coming back for a long while.

Darcy liked Spring for another, deeply personal, reason. She enjoyed watching the grass turn green and the flowers bloom. Nature's annual rebirth reminded her of her own life. How, with things like hope and faith, a new start was never out of reach.

"Nachos and a soda. Nothing more." She took a deep breath as she entered the restaurant. The comforting aroma of seasoned beef and chicken welcomed her like an old friend. Any thoughts of booze were shoved aside by her growling stomach.

Evidently, trying to cope with the murder of her mentor and friend had created quite the appetite.

She rarely ate out by herself. It could get expensive, and Darcy had found she enjoyed the craft of cooking. Ringo rarely objected to beef and chicken scraps, so that was an added bonus. When she went out, Selena's was a safe place. The bartender, Thea Lewis, was one of Darcy's friends. They first met the night Pixie Dust performed at the restaurant and had since bonded over their love of Broadway musicals.

Once inside, Selena's customers could turn left for the dining room or right for the bar. Darcy chose the bar because that was where Thea would be.

"What's a girl gotta do to get a drink around here?" Darcy perched herself on her favorite stool, the one at the end of the bar farthest from the beer taps.

"Holy smokes, DG. I heard about Eddie. Is it true?" Thea filled a pint glass with ginger ale and garnished it with a lime wedge. At six feet tall and over two hundred pounds, the bartender cut an imposing figure. The platinum blonde buzz cut and tattoo sleeves covering both arms completed the don't-mess-with-me vibe. And hid the bruises that came from playing in a women's rugby league.

She was kind of a modern version of the fictional warrior Brienne of Tarth from *Game of Thrones*. That was a show that Darcy could *not* get enough of.

While the woman behind the bar might have looked intimidating, in fact, Thea was one of the friendliest people Darcy knew. She smiled easily, laughed out loud at the drop of a hat, and preferred hugs to handshakes.

"News travels fast." Darcy brushed a few strands of hair away from her eyes and stabbed a straw into her drink. "Yeah, afraid so."

It was bad enough Darcy had to cope with the death of her friend. It was borderline unbearable she seemed designated to be the official bearer of bad news.

It was enough to make a girl want a drink.

Almost.

"I, uh," Darcy placed her sobriety token on the bar in front of her. "I don't want to be alone right now."

"You came to the right place, buddy. Supreme nachos it is, then." Thea pushed a few icons on a computer screen behind the bar, filled a coffee mug emblazoned with Selena's smiling sun logo, then took a seat directly across from Darcy. The bartender's swift, graceful movements conjured images of

Eddie waltzing through the aisles of the record store as a Lena Horne record played.

"Thanks." Darcy took a long sip of her ginger ale. The cold liquid soothed her throat, but not her heart. "I can't believe he's gone. I keep hoping I'm going to wake up and all this'll be one big, horrible nightmare."

While she tossed the sobriety token between her hands, Darcy told Thea everything she could remember from the moment she arrived at the store. It hurt her soul that there was so little to say.

"I was originally scheduled to work yesterday. Eddie agreed to cover my shift so I could have an extra day of vacation. I can't help feeling if I would have been there instead of him, he'd still be alive end everything would be okay."

A server brought the conversation to a halt by putting the nachos and two plates on the bar. "Nathan says these are on the house. And he's sorry for your loss. He's tied up on a call or he'd have delivered the message himself."

Darcy's eyes welled with tears. "Tell him I understand, and I really appreciate it."

After he walked away, Thea pointed a crooked finger at Darcy. "You need to put any feeling of guilt out of your head right now. You don't think Eddie really killed himself, do you?"

"Nope. Absolutely not. The odds of him doing that are about the same as me going out on tour again." Darcy let out a long sigh as she reached for a sour cream-covered tortilla chip. "I feel so helpless right now. I don't know what to do."

"You did the right thing by coming here." Thea tapped the sobriety token with a closely trimmed fingernail. "For now, keep it simple. Take things one hour, one day, at a time."

When Darcy nodded, Thea fetched a dog-eared spiral-bound notebook from under the bar. They assembled a to-do list for Darcy while they munched on the nachos. By the time Darcy scooped the last blob of salsa onto a chip, the list of tasks filled up most of a page.

"This is good. I haven't made one of these since my early days of sobriety." Darcy ran her index finger down the list. There were twenty-three items in all, ranked from highest priority to lowest.

"This isn't too overwhelming, is it? I know you don't want to be sitting around at home, but you sure you can handle all this?" Worry lines crossed Thea's forehead.

It was a welcome reminder to Darcy that she wasn't alone in this tough time. Even though her family was hours away, she had friends only minutes away.

"I can do this. It'll help keep me on task. I can use it to focus on one thing at a time." Darcy tapped the top item on the list. "Like giving the kids the bad news."

* * *

A few hours later, Darcy, Izzy, and Peter were sitting at a corner table of The Big Bean. The devastating news had left the high schoolers in stunned silence. After giving them a few minutes to absorb the information, Darcy cleared her throat.

"I'll try and answer any questions you have." She took a sip of her green tea. The subtle floral aroma of the drink calmed her. Given that she'd just had to inform two bright young people their boss was dead, she needed as much help keeping calm as possible.

"Do you know about funeral arrangements? I want to be there." Izzy closed her eyes for a moment. When she opened them, they were cloudy with tears instead of the usual sparkling blue. She played saxophone in Marysburg High School's marching, jazz, and concert bands. She and Eddie had bonded over contemporary jazz artists like the singer and pianist Diana Krall and vibraphonist Sasha Berliner. As the child of a single mother, she needed the job to help pay for her music expenses.

"I'm sure Eddie's stepson will be handling it. I'll text you as soon as I know something."

"What about the store? I'm supposed to work tomorrow." Peter picked at his dreadlocks. It was something he did when he was nervous. Like Izzy, he was a musician and played bass in the school's jazz and basketball pep bands. His dream was to attend the prestigious Jacobs School of Music at Indiana University. Eddie had been helping him with that. The man's death was truly a shocking loss for both teens.

"Assuming the police finish their work today, we'll be back in business tomorrow. I'll do everything I can to make sure the store stays open. I think that's what Eddie would want."

Izzy and Peter nodded in unison.

"Yeah, that's what he'd want." Izzy gave Darcy a hug. "For Eddie."

"For Eddie." Darcy smiled and pulled Peter close so they could share a group hug.

After the kids were gone, Darcy asked for another green tea. She had a lot of questions to mull over. One question rose above all others.

The store had always been Eddie's dream. She wanted to keep that dream alive. How on Earth was she supposed to pull that off?

Chapter Four

Darcy awoke with a start, drenched in sweat, with a pounding like a bass drum behind her eyes. It was still dark outside, but she wasn't getting back to sleep any time soon. Horrific visions of ten-foot-tall blood-soaked letter openers chasing her through a maze of twenty-foot-high Alice Cooper album covers made staying awake way better than going back to sleep.

Ringo was curled into a ball at the foot of the bed, snoring away. Darcy breathed a sigh of relief that her nightmare hadn't awakened her fuzzy buddy. She'd lost track of the times she'd woken up, her throat as rough as sandpaper from screaming while still asleep, to find Ringo trying to help her escape from whatever monsters were pursuing her by pawing at her arm.

After wiping a line of perspiration from her brow, she slipped from under the quilt her mom had made for her and exited the bedroom. Eventually, Ringo would hear her messing about in the kitchen and join her for breakfast. That was a way better reason for the little guy to get up.

A bit later, Darcy stood on the step outside her backdoor, scrolling through her phone while Ringo chased a squirrel. There were reports from Muncie to Fort Wayne, even Indianapolis, about Eddie's death. They all said the same thing.

The man died of a single self-inflicted stab wound.

"They're all wrong, buddy." Darcy put her phone in the pocket of her hoodie. A breeze out of the north made her shiver. It was a reminder that April mornings in Central Indiana were often pretty darn chilly.

Ringo, who was now sniffing the bushes that lined the northern edge of

Darcy's property, stopped his investigations and ambled over to her. He sat, looked up at her with his big copper eyes, and gave her a *mrrow*.

"Exactly." She crouched down and scratched under the cat's chin, his favorite spot. Actually, one of many favorite spots. Ringo wasn't choosy. He relished every bit of attention Darcy gave him.

"There's no way Eddie killed himself. And even if he did, which I'm not saying is the case, stabbing himself would be a horrible way to go. It'd be worse than listening to a fifteen-minute prog-rock keyboard solo. There have to be a million ways to do it that wouldn't be so godawful."

Ringo bonked his head against her shin, then went and sat by the back door. Evidently, the feline thought there was nothing more about the topic to discuss.

If only that were the case.

Darcy was on her third cup of English Breakfast tea when the sun broke over the horizon, bathing her kitchen in a cheerful, yellow glow. Her mouth curled up on one end into a half-smile. As her therapist liked to say, it was a new day, with endless possibilities and opportunities.

The was in mid-sip when the rhythm of a Parliament/Funkadelic tune emanated from her phone to fill the room.

"Detective, what can I do for you?" Darcy kept her tone cheerful in the hope it would keep the conversation from devolving into a series of back-and-forth accusations.

"It's Detective-Sergeant. I wanted to let you know the cleanup crew is finished. You can open for business as usual. They'll send you a bill. Check with your insurance company to see if you have coverage."

When the police finished their evidence collection, they'd turned the shop over to a firm that specialized in crime scene and trauma cleanup. Despite Darcy's protests that she was more than capable of cleaning up the mess, Kaitlin had insisted she leave it to the professionals and go home and try to get some sleep. The gesture was kind enough, which Darcy now appreciated, even if her sleep had been filled with visions of Eddie covered in blood.

"Thank you, Detective-Sergeant." Darcy let out a sigh of relief. She needed order in her life. Getting back to work would help restore some of it. "Have you found anything that might change your thought that he..." Her throat closed up before she could finish the question.

"Took his own life? It's up to the coroner to make an official determination, but it looks like that's the case."

Darcy shook her head. Eddie'd been full of life. His slacker stepson Rafe was a pain in the backside, but Eddie had continued to support him with good cheer. The store was on solid financial footing. His love for good food, fine bourbon, music of all kinds, and his friends was legendary.

In short, there were no signs of someone at risk of taking their own life. Darcy knew those signs. Heck, she'd lived through them. Alcohol abuse, withdrawal from relationships, inability to get out of bed in the morning.

If she drew a Venn diagram showing Eddie and the indicators of suicide, the circles would be as far apart as Indiana is from California. She'd worked with the man for five years and known him for fifteen. If there'd been signs of trouble, Darcy would have noticed.

"But I knew Eddie. It doesn't make any sense." Darcy cringed at the desperation in her voice. Sounding like an injured squirrel wouldn't convince the cop on the other end of the line.

"I get it, Darcy. Mr. Maxwell meant a lot to you. You want someone to blame. It's a natural emotional reaction. I don't deal with emotions, though. I deal with facts. There was no sign of forced entry. There was no sign of a struggle. There was no sign of theft. The device used to take his own life was found at his feet. And had his fingerprints on it."

Darcy scratched her head. On the surface, it looked like an open-and-shut case. She'd watched enough episodes of the Caribbean-set mystery show *Death in Paradise* to know looks could be deceiving, though.

She snapped her fingers.

"What if Eddie knew his killer? That could explain why there weren't signs of a struggle or forced entry."

Kaitlin let out a long sigh. Evidently, she was ready for the conversation to be over. Even if Darcy wasn't.

"I'm sorry, but there's simply no evidence to support your suggestion. I think you need to let this line of thinking go. It's not good for you." The line went dead before Darcy had a chance to respond.

After counting to ten to calm herself, Darcy put down her phone. A huge problem like this needed to be broken down into small steps. She consulted the list she and Thea had made the previous day. The first order of business was to keep the record store open. People were depending on her.

It was time to get to work.

A little while later, Darcy pulled into her parking spot behind the store. Eddie's car was still there. The auto's presence was like a kick in the teeth. It wasn't enough that she had to deal with the fact that her friend was gone. She was going to be confronted with Eddie's death in ways she couldn't foresee.

The vehicle made her think of Rafe. She left a voicemail message asking if she could stop by after work to offer her condolences in person. There was more she wanted to discuss, but that would do for now.

* * *

Darcy's hand lingered on the handle while she gathered the courage to open the store's front door. It was as if stepping through the doorway would eliminate any hope that the past twenty-fours had simply been a nightmare from which she'd wake up in a minute. Going inside meant she was stepping into a concert hall-sized void created by Eddie's death.

She was in charge of Marysburg Music now. Not because she wanted to be. Because she had to be.

"Give me strength, Eddie."

Out of habit born from years of making the same move, Darcy entered the store and turned on the lights in one single, fluid movement. Once inside, even with the warm light cast from the LED bulbs overhead, she was hesitant to move. After a few minutes, she took a deep breath and stepped into the next chapter of her life. If any bad karma remained in the store, she'd exorcise it by working hard and making her mentor, her savior, proud.

She wandered up and down the aisles, breathing in the comforting, vaguely dusty smell of vinyl stored in sometimes decades-old paperboard covers. Her fingertips brushed against the record albums, drawing strength from each one she touched. An autographed copy of the Black Pumas debut album hung slightly askew on one wall. She straightened it. When she noticed a misplaced record, she returned it to its proper spot.

A few attempts at restoring order to an out-of-control situation.

Eventually, Darcy found herself at the door to the office. It was closed. She put her fingers on a black and white poster of Johnny Cash attached to it. An acoustic guitar was strapped around his neck. He was snarling and flipping the bird at the photographer. It was a classic shot that the Ball State students loved and had adorned countless dorm room walls over the years.

Eddie had treasured the poster's simple message of defiance. People told him he was too old to start a new venture. That a record store in the age of digital downloads and streaming music had a future the same as the dinosaurs. That hiring Darcy, an alcoholic with no everyday work experience, as his right-hand person was a fool's errand.

The man had proven the naysayers wrong. He knew something they didn't. Marysburg Music wasn't merely a retail operation. It was a celebration of music in all of its varieties. It was a gathering place where folks of all ages and from all backgrounds could immerse themselves in everything from Al Jolson and Bessie Smith to BTS and H.E.R.

Darcy knew it, too. And would do the same.

"Don't worry, Johnny. You're not going anywhere." She opened the door.

* * *

She was going through inventory that hadn't made it to the sales floor yet when a *knock* broke her concentration.

Hank gave Darcy a salute when she let him and Charlotte in. "Reporting for duty, Boss."

Both of her co-workers, no, her friends, had dark circles under their eyes. *Looks like you guys got about as much sleep as I did. Or didn't, really.* She kept the thought to herself and gave them both hugs.

"Like the mythical phoenix rising from the ashes, Marysburg Music is back in business. We've got a lot of work to do."

"I brought the fuel." Charlotte held up a travel caddy containing three tall drinks from The Big Bean. Wisps of steam rose from two of them. "Hot tea for you, hot coffee for Hank and iced coffee for me. Let's do this thing."

Darcy tasked Hank with checking whether a bank deposit was made after the store closed Sunday evening. When he confirmed it hadn't, she asked him to take care of it.

"Eddie told me he had someone coming in with records to sell," Charlotte said. "He told me to get going and enjoy the weather."

The cash hadn't been touched. Why not? Had Eddie not gotten to it when he was murdered? If that was the case, then who was the mystery record collection seller? She pulled her hair back into a ponytail. That question needed an answer.

While Hank was busy counting the money in the cash register, Charlotte made sure the inventory on the sales floor was tidy.

To show she wasn't afraid to do the dirty work despite her new role, Darcy swept the brushed concrete floors and collected the trash. Two other closing tasks that hadn't been done. On her way out the door to toss the trash in the dumpster, Charlotte stopped her. The woman nodded toward Hank, who was busy filling out a deposit slip.

"Since there was money in the drawer, it's logical to assume it wasn't a robbery, right?"

"Makes sense." Darcy massaged the back of her neck. The muscles there were tighter than a drumhead. "Helps the police's theory that Eddie took his own life, too."

"But you don't believe that." Charlotte's steely gaze made the woman's thoughts clear. They were of the same mind.

"No, I don't."

Their conversation was interrupted when Hank announced he had the deposit ready. Darcy's heart stopped when she looked in his direction.

"The White Album's gone." Darcy's day had taken yet another dark turn.

Hank looked over his shoulder. There was a bare spot on the wall where the store displayed its most expensive item. A few years ago, Eddie had gotten a deal on a pristine copy of The Beatles' 1968 self-titled recording.

Packaged in a plain white cover, the double album came to be commonly known as *The White Album*.

It had been valued at eight thousand dollars.

And it was missing.

"Holy smokes," Hank said as Charlotte dropped a curse word. "It was here last time I worked. I'm certain of it."

Alarm bells went off in Darcy's head. "Maybe it was a robbery, after all. Hank, make the deposit. Charlotte, finish prepping the store. I need to call the cops."

Detective-Sergeant Rosengarten didn't pick up when Darcy called, so she was forced to leave a message. Despite her desire to say the missing album was proof Eddie didn't kill himself, she stuck to the facts. By the time she ended the call, the tightness in her neck muscles had eased.

It was crushing that the store's most valuable item was missing. Yet another agenda item for her call with the insurance company. But hopefully, it also meant Darcy's instincts were on target. That thought kindled a fire within her.

Eddie's murder was not going to be swept aside. She'd see to that.

* * *

A few minutes before it was time to open, a crowd had already gathered outside. Darcy put her arms around Hank and Charlotte.

"Looks like we're going to have a lot of traffic today. This is still Eddie's store, so let's make him proud." She gave them each a fist bump.

"What do we say if people ask about him?" Charlotte tugged on her right ear. It was her tell, the signal she was nervous. Totally understandable, given the circumstances.

"Tell them the cause of Eddie's death hasn't been determined, but we hope to have answers soon."

"But," Hank glanced at the throng on the other side of the store's windows, "if the police are saying it was suicide, should we contradict them?"

"We're not." Darcy held up three fingers. "One, Eddie wasn't suicidal. We all know that. Two, the missing *White Album* complicates the police's theory."

"What's three?" Hank and Charlotte asked in unison.

Darcy rubbed her hands together as a pulse of electricity, fueled by a new purpose, spread through her. She straightened her spine to bring herself up to her full five foot, nine inch height.

"I'm going to find Eddie's killer."

Chapter Five

At eight o'clock, the normal closing time for a Tuesday, Marysburg Music was still packed as tight as the mosh pit of a Pixie Dust concert. Throughout the day, three types of people had spent time in the store.

The first was comprised of kind-hearted souls who wanted to pay their respects to Eddie. Darcy made a point to spend a minute or two with every person in this group, the majority of whom were friends of his and the store staff.

The second type were morbid busybodies who were only there to see where the man who owned the record store had died. Whenever one of them mentioned suicide, Darcy corrected them with a curt reminder that a final cause of death hadn't been determined.

The final type made Darcy cry happy tears. They were people who wanted to show their support for Marysburg Music with their pocketbooks. Within ninety minutes of opening, Darcy could tell the store was on its way to a sales record. At noon, she'd texted Izzy and Peter, asking them to come in as soon as they got out of school. At one, word about the crowds had evidently gotten out because Jenna arrived with sandwiches and drinks for Darcy and her team.

On three separate occasions, Darcy had sprinted to the office to haul out more used inventory to the salesfloor. It had been one whale of a day.

"Closing time, Boss. What do you want to do?" Hank dropped onto the stool behind the cash register and wiped a bead of sweat from his brow. Charlotte had run the register all afternoon until she said she couldn't see straight. Now, she, Izzy, and Peter were on the floor helping customers while Darcy bagged the sales after Hank rang them up.

"Let it ride. Just like a second encore. I want to make Eddie proud." While Darcy could only imagine what Eddie's thoughts would be about the day, she was bursting with pride and gratitude.

The store's high-water mark for single-day sales had been on Record Store Day two years ago. They wouldn't reach that mark this day. RSD was its own kind of musical event, after all. For a regular day, though, today was one for record books. Darcy made a vow that April 6 would always be a day to celebrate Eddie's life at Marysburg Music.

When she finally ushered the final customers out the door, it was nine o'clock. With a celebratory flourish, she pulled the string to turn off the "Open" sign and let out a long, cleansing breath.

"Amazing job, everyone." She wanted to say more but got a lump in her throat as tears welled up. She closed her eyes to keep from falling to bits.

While her eyes were still closed, someone put an arm around her, followed by someone else. By the time she opened her eyes, she was in the middle of a five-person group hug. There were no dry eyes to be seen.

But everyone was smiling, too.

"I think we did right by Eddie," Hank said.

Everyone nodded, then laughed when Charlotte joked that she was going to need a pain reliever for her fingers after ringing sales for six hours without a break.

Amid the feelings of solidarity, the group got busy with the daily closing tasks. Thirty minutes later, Darcy returned from dumping the trash and told everyone it was time to hit the road.

"You were rock stars today, even better than David Bowie's band on the *Let's Dance* tour. Go home and get a good night's rest." She pointed at the teens. "Tell your parents I apologize for keeping you so late. I promise it won't happen again."

"Beats doing homework. Right, Izzy?" Peter raised his hand for a high five.

"Truth." Izzy slapped Peter's open palm with an ear-ringing *whack*. "Come on. I'll give you a ride home."

After making the bank deposit, Darcy made a quick stop at home to drop off a stack of paperwork she needed to review and to fetch Ringo. Her body ached like she'd played a three-hour concert without a break, but her cat deserved some outside time after being cooped up all day.

Besides, a walk in the chilly night air would be good for both of them.

There was a second reason for the walk, though. She needed to see Rafe. In all the insanity of the past two days, she hadn't talked to him. Even to offer her condolences. That needed to change.

Even though the man was in his late thirties, he behaved like he was still in high school. He had no direction, no motivation, and had gotten by thanks to the kind heart of his stepfather, Eddie. That included letting Rafe stay, rent-free, in one of the two upstairs bedrooms.

As they approached the house where Rafe now lived alone, she set aside her feelings about the man. This visit wasn't about her. It was about Eddie.

She glanced down at Ringo. The feline sneezed, then gave his body an all-over shake. It was a funny-looking maneuver that always made Darcy chuckle. Hopefully, that was a portent of good things to come.

"Okay, buddy. I promise to play nice. What about you?"

Ringo let out a little *meow* and flicked his tail. If Rafe was nice to him, the cat would respond in kind. Hopefully.

The house was a two-story Cape Cod. Maroon shutters and exterior trim complemented the white brick exterior. The color scheme made Darcy think of Ball State University since the school's colors were cardinal and white. Fitting for a man who'd taught at BSU for twenty-five years.

A walkway made of red paving stones led from the sidewalk to the front door. A brass door knocker that looked like it belonged on the door of Ebenezer Scrooge in *A Christmas Carol* hung from the door at chest height. The curtains were drawn, obscuring an electric glow emanating from the living room. Despite the creepy door knocker, the home had a welcoming vibe, much of it due to the many days and nights Darcy spent there over the years.

The metallic *clack, clack, clack* of the knocker brought forth another *meow* from Ringo. The cat had been to this house many times and had learned its owner always had a treat for him.

Seconds seemed to drag into minutes while they waited. Darcy stamped her feet in an attempt to keep the evening chill away from her toes. Or maybe she was agitated about entering Eddie's home for the first time since his passing.

She was about ready to turn around when the deadbolt released with a scraping noise. Moments later the door opened. The silhouette of Eddie's stepson loomed in the doorway.

"Darcy. What up?" Between his height and pronounced girth, Rafe blocked most of the light coming from the house. It was impossible to read his reaction to Darcy's unannounced visit.

"I wanted to see how you're doing. To express my condolences." With her free hand, she flipped up the collar of her denim jacket. "Got a minute?"

Rafe stared at her, his hand resting on the doorknob. It seemed like even odds whether he would welcome her or slam the door in her face.

"Come on in." He stepped back and waved them indoors.

The sudden flood of light blinded Darcy for a few moments. While she looked at the floor to let her eyes adjust, Ringo took the lead and made a beeline for Rafe's vintage Air Jordans. Once there, he started sniffing at their host's spotless footwear like they were filled with catnip.

Darcy covered a grimace with her hand as she entered the home. The front room was a disaster area. She'd had seen her fair share of trashed hotel rooms while on tour. The scene made those places look as tidy as an operating room.

Unfolded laundry sat in a mound in Eddie's beloved leather recliner. Unopened mail had been tossed in a pile on the oak coffee table in the center of the room. A half dozen empty soda pop cans formed a loose perimeter around the mail, separating it from an empty pizza box.

Eddie had never been known as a neat freak, but he kept his home tidy. Rafe didn't share that trait. In any way. On top of the mess, the sight of the pricey shoes, that Eddie had undoubtedly paid for, made her blood boil.

Unsure of whether she was really welcome, Darcy stood close to a wall and wrapped her arms around her. The sooner she got through this, the better.

"I wanted to say how sorry I am about Eddie. For your loss, I mean." She clamped her mouth shut to cut off any blabbering.

"Yeah. A real bummer." Rafe dropped onto a couch half-covered with video games and grabbed a game controller. "This place is mine now, I guess."

For a second, Darcy wanted to throw a drumstick at the unfeeling jerk. Then she reminded herself that people grieve in different ways. Maybe Rafe was still processing everything. She'd give him another chance.

"I wanted to give you this." She handed him a key ring that held a fob for Eddie's car and a few other keys. "It's still parked behind the record store. Thought you might want to get it before someone vandalizes it."

"Cool." He tossed the ring onto the coffee table, where it slid off and landed on the carpet. "Hey, do you play Call of Duty? I'm part of a sick online group that plays it. A new game starts in a few minutes."

Darcy rolled her eyes. So much for second chances. This guy clearly didn't care about his deceased stepdad. And that gave her an idea.

"I don't want to interrupt your gaming. Do you mind if I go through Eddie's things? I thought I might try to find papers that are important for the record store."

"Like what?" He picked up his game controller.

"Insurance policy, financial records, a will. Things that might be relevant to the store."

"Why? You want to find out if you're in the will?"

Darcy closed her eyes and counted to ten. The man was more irritating than feedback from a messed-up sound system. Why Eddie had put up with the ungrateful louse was beyond her.

"Of course not. But the man owned a business, this house, a car, and who knows what else. If no will is found, everything will have to go through probate. Which will take a long time and won't be cheap. And the costs to pay that will come out of Eddie's estate."

Darcy didn't know whether a trip through probate court would be time-consuming or expensive. What she did know, or at least suspected, was that Rafe was counting on receiving a large inheritance from the man. The presence of a will might put a monkey wrench into those plans.

When Rafe chose to start his game instead of responding, she threw up her hands. "Come on, Ringo. Let's take a look around. See what we can find."

She was two steps away from Eddie's home office when Rafe shouted at her to stop. "I didn't give you permission to snoop."

"I'm not snooping. I'm trying to do what needs to be done." She ran a hand through her hair. "Look, the cops told me you're making funeral arrangements. That's a lot on you right now. Let me do this one thing for you."

He shook his head. "Yeah, I don't think so. I'll look for that stuff later."

Her shoulders drooping in resignation, Darcy returned to the front room. "Okay. Let me know if you find anything, okay? BTW, I'm going to keep the record store open. It's what Eddie would have wanted."

The last sentence was Darcy's challenge to Rafe. Without the store, there was no cash flow. The twerp wouldn't dare to cut that off.

"I'll let you know when the funeral arrangements are done. I still have to talk to my bro about it. And I know you're trying to help. I got this though, okay?" He waved goodbye at her, his gaze never leaving the TV screen.

With her visit so unceremoniously concluded, Darcy made headed outside. Ringo let out a little hiss when the door closed behind them.

"I know buddy. Eddie always treated you like a king. You can have a snack when we get home."

Darcy and Ringo stopped at the end of the walkway when he stopped to sniff at a bush for a bathroom break. While it was a juvenile thought, Darcy was proud of Ringo for going potty on a bush that now, more likely than not, would end up belonging to Rafe.

Then she had a more grown-up thought.

What if he was hiding something?

It wasn't out of the realm of possibility that Rafe knew exactly where the will was stored. The younger man had lived in the house since his mother and Eddie had gotten married, and that had been thirty years ago. Even after she died in a car crash, Rafe, who was in his late twenties by that time, chose to remain with his stepdad.

Three decades was plenty of time to learn where all of Eddie's important documents were kept. And to plan a murder. But why would Rafe kill his golden goose? Then Darcy recalled a piece of advice from almost every mystery she'd watched.

Follow the money.

If Rafe knew he was in line to inherit Eddie's belongings, maybe he got tired of living by the old man's rules and murdered him. That way, the house, business, car, and any other assets would go to him. To do with what he pleased. Good, bad, smart, or dumb.

It seemed plausible. Knowing Rafe the way Darcy did, any inheritance, even one in the hundreds of thousands of dollars, wouldn't last long. But Rafe didn't think about long-term consequences. He only seemed to care about his own immediate satisfaction.

That didn't bode well for the record store.

Another idea took off in Darcy's head. Maybe Rafe was the one who stole the Beatles album. Smart enough to know it might take a while to get his inheritance, maybe he killed Eddie and took the collectible as he left the store. Then, he could sell it and use the proceeds to tide him over until he got the keys to the inheritance kingdom.

That theory made a lot of assumptions. But, like a solid bass line, it gave Darcy's search for the truth a path to follow. It was the start she needed.

With Ringo's business complete and a roadmap in place, Darcy turned to head home. They'd only gone a few steps when a man emerged from the shadows. It was Claude Ewing, Eddie's neighbor.

"Evening, Darcy." The man lit a cigarette. "The missus doesn't let me smoke in the house. Sorry if I startled you."

"No. We were paying Rafe a visit. Ringo and I were about to head home."

Claude took a long drag on his cigarette, then blew out the noxious smoke as he nodded. A retired Marysburg firefighter, the man was well regarded around town. Darcy didn't know him well, though.

"How is he?" The ashes from the cigarette lit up his face with their fiery red glow.

"Hard to tell. Maybe he's keeping his grieving inside, but he doesn't seem too broken up about Eddie's murder."

Claude raised a bushy, gray eyebrow, but refrained from commenting on Darcy's use of the word murder.

"Maxwell was an asset to the community. I'm sorry for your loss." He chuckled. "It'll be a lot quieter around here. That's for sure."

Darcy smiled. Eddie had loved to entertain. One of his favorite slogans was *laissez le bon temps roule*. Let the good times roll. When he threw a party, which he often did, the good times rolled, indeed. Delicacies abounded, drinks flowed, and music played. The soirees often spilled into the back yard, where Eddie would lead impromptu jam sessions on his trombone.

There had been a couple of legendary Mardi Gras parties that ran into the wee hours of the morning and only ended when the Marysburg Police arrived.

Darcy had steered clear of Eddie's parties to avoid temptation. She heard about them, though. And could sympathize with a neighbor's unhappiness with the noise they produced.

Eddie had been her friend, though. She'd defend him until her own dying breath.

"He never meant to bother anyone. He just believed in living life to the fullest."

"I know. Most of the time he was a good neighbor." Claude took another drag on his cigarette, then dropped it on the sidewalk and rubbed it into the concrete with his boot. "I'm not going to lie, though. I'm looking forward to the peace and quiet. I'll keep an eye out to make sure Rafe's okay. Have yourself a good night."

With his hands in his pockets, Claude strolled toward his house, as if they'd had a conversation about the weather instead of about his deceased next-door neighbor.

Darcy shrugged and began the mile-long walk home, with Ringo bouncing along at her side. The cat was enjoying the trip, but something about the conversation with Claude bothered her.

She'd been raised that it was bad manners to speak ill of the dead. Even if Darcy didn't like someone who'd passed away, her parents had taught her the right thing to do was to keep negative comments about the deceased to herself.

Evidently, Claude didn't share the sentiment, which was fine. Different strokes for different folks, after all. But why bring up his unhappiness with the parties? Everyone in town knew how much Eddie meant to her. It was like pouring salt into a wound.

Darcy came to a stop.

Or was it something else? Was there more to Claude Ewing's problem with his former neighbor than met the eye? There had been plenty of folks murdered for reasons more trivial than hosting loud parties. Perhaps Claude Ewing needed looking into. To be thorough. Nothing more.

"I believe we've got two suspects now, Ringo." She scratched his ears and resumed their trek home. "We have some work to do."

Chapter Six

The following morning dawned clear and bright. The warm, golden glow of a new spring day woke Darcy before her alarm went off. Ringo was curled up, snoring away in his usual spot at the end of the bed.

"Did our walk wear you out, buddy?" Darcy scooped the cat up in her arms and snuggled him until his squirming got too much to contain.

She'd slept through the night without a single bad dream. That was rare occurrence.

Maybe it was the exhaustion from the intense day at work along with the walk. Whatever the reason for her well-rested state, Darcy sent the angels above a thank you. There was much to be done, after all.

The first thing on her agenda was to drop off Rusty at Marysburg AutoCare. As the jeep wheezed into silence in front of the garage, the manager, Liam Simmons, came out to greet her.

"I knew your wheels needed help." He waved an exhaust cloud from his face, the bluish haze obscuring his short, brown hair and hazel eyes. "I didn't know it was this bad, D. Be forewarned, I'm no miracle worker."

"Give it a rest, L. I'm a busy woman who ain't got time for extra drama." After tossing the keys to him, she scooped up the four-inch-high stack of mail and paperwork she'd ignored when she got home the previous evening. "A rolling stone gathers no moss, and all that kind of thing."

"I know." He put his arm around her and held her close for a moment, his chin resting on the crown of her head. The same as he'd done back in college whenever she was feeling low. "And I'm really sorry about Eddie. He was a good dude."

"Truer words were never spoken. And a forgiving one, in your case."

"You're never going to let me live that down, are you?"

They laughed. At one of Eddie's parties, after one too many mojitos, Liam had tried to play one of the host's trombones. Despite the fact air guitar was the only instrument he'd ever played.

"Why should I? The only things you got out of that stupid stunt were an embarrassing video that ended up all over social media and a bill to repair the damage you did to the horn."

"Come on. That video got over ten thousand views on Instagram." Liam gave Darcy a light punch on the arm. "Gave me my fifteen minutes of fame. Not bad for a no-talent grease monkey like me."

"Whatever." Darcy looked at her watch. The face looked like a drum. The hands resembled drumsticks. "I need to rock 'n roll. Tell you what. You get Rusty running nice and you can drop the no-talent part."

They exchanged a fist bump and Liam promised to call her with an estimate before noon. Despite the heavy issues weighing on her mind, Darcy made the mile walk from the garage to Perfect Pastries with a note of positivity. Hanging out with her old college buddy, even briefly, improved her mood and reminiscing about Eddie while she did so couldn't be beat.

After ordering a ham and cheese bagel and an Irish Breakfast tea, Darcy grabbed a spot on the sidewalk in front of the bakery. If today was like the day before, once she got to work, she wouldn't step outdoors until she locked up for the night. Enjoying the fresh air while she dealt with the mail would be good for her.

While she waited for the bagel to cool, she sorted the stack of documents into three groups. The first group consisted of junk mail, which she wrapped in a rubber band for recycling. The second one was made up of bills and a few payments the store had received. She'd deposit the checks on her way to the store. The bills could wait until Friday, her usual day for doing that task. The final group was small, but the most intriguing. The envelopes gave no indication who they were from.

She wasn't sure whether to be scared or excited.

A warm breeze pushed strands of hair from Darcy's eyes as she studied the eight-by-twelve manila envelope that was on the top of the stack. Her name was written in bold circular scrawl. Any doubt about who wrote her name was eliminated by the green ink used to write it.

A few years back, Darcy and Eddie had developed a code for written, in-store communication. The system had come about after a theft in which the perpetrator had given a letter to the staff indicating certain merchandise was to be "donated" to a charitable cause. The document was a fake and Eddie's signature had been forged. Ever since, he used green ink for all his in-store notes and memos. Darcy used purple. They'd never had a problem with theft due to forgery again.

Now, Darcy was equal parts excited and frightened. What had Eddie left for her?

With trembling fingers, she opened the envelope and pulled out a stack of papers. They were official-looking legal documents. She tilted her head to the side as she read the post-it note stuck to the top page.

When she was finished, she sat back in her chair. The news was stunning. "Can't be. Eddie would have told me."

She looked around to make sure nobody was filming her, a la Candid Camera, then read the note a second time.

Congrats on 5 years of sobriety! In honor of your hard work, you're now the President of Marysburg Music, Inc. Here's to a great future, kiddo.

A shadow came across the table as Darcy was studying the documents. She looked up to find Todd Meadows blocking the sun. The realtor was dressed impeccably in a tailored gray suit. The tie and pocket square were made of matching material that featured a paisley print in a variety of shades of red. A quick glance down confirmed his black oxfords, probably made in Italy, were polished to practically a mirror-like quality.

"Darcy." Todd extended a hand. His slender fingers were characteristic of the man's long, thin frame. "I wanted to express my condolences about Eddie's passing. I'm sorry for your loss."

She took his hand in hers. It was warm and smooth. Like shaking hands with Satan himself.

"May I join you?" He gestured to the open seat across the table from Darcy.

"Please do." She smiled, despite the warning bells going off in her head.

Todd was known around town as an astute businessman and generous philanthropist. With his hands in both real estate and construction, he was one of Marysburg's power brokers. And liked to make sure everyone knew it.

Darcy trusted him about as far as she could throw one of the cymbals from her drum kit. Twenty feet on a good day.

Todd started the conversation with some small talk, then cut to the chase. "I'm sure this is a terribly difficult time for you, but have you given any thought to the future of the record store?"

"I've actually given it a lot of thought. It wasn't just a store to him. It was his dream. A place for music lovers of all types to celebrate their common interests. It was the center of a community. He built that. I want to keep it going."

"You're keeping the store open?" Todd raised an eyebrow.

"I am. It's Eddie's legacy, something bigger than one person. I can't let that die."

He leaned back in his chair as he crossed his arms. The defensive posture was an obvious tell. Darcy's response wasn't what he wanted to hear. That begged a question.

Why not?

Was he involved with Eddie's murder somehow? She closed her eyes for a moment. Now she was seeing murder around every corner. Surrendering to paranoia wouldn't help. Especially if she was serious about figuring out who killed Eddie.

Todd straightened his tie. His fingers reminded Darcy of an eagle's talons. "That's admirable of you. At the risk of sounding insensitive, are you certain you're up to the task? You're assuming that's what he would have wanted, that is."

"I am." She showed him the document naming her president of the company. "I'm no fat cat lawyer, but I'm pretty sure this gives me the green light to keep the wheels rolling."

"Hmm." He flipped through the pages, rubbing his chin the entire time, as if he was trying to conjure some kind of magic to blow a hole in them. "Everything does appear to be in order."

"What are you trying to say?" Darcy sat up in her chair as her system dumped adrenaline into her veins. In mere seconds, she'd moved into fight mode. "Of course, it's in order. Eddie and me built that store from the ground up. There's no better person than me to take the lead."

"I'm not saying anything. Merely looking at this from the perspective of an impartial third party. The face of the company takes his own life and suddenly you have decision-making authority."

"But." She pointed at the date stamp on the top page. "This was filed last week. While I was hundreds of miles away in the Caribbean. And Eddie was still very much alive."

"Yes, he was." He handed the papers back to Darcy. "My point being this. Whether you like it or not, people are going to ask if you're capable of running the store. It happened when my father passed the reins of the agency over to me. I know from first-hand experience the challenges in store for you."

Darcy munched on her bagel while she considered Todd's words. She didn't like being around the man, but she couldn't deny that he was speaking the truth. Especially given her checkered past.

"Then I'll have to prove them wrong, won't I?" She put the documents back in the envelope and glanced at her phone. "And on that note, I need to get to work."

"Like I said, Darcy. I've been there." He gave her one of his business cards. "If there's anything I can do to help, let me know."

"I will." The card was made of heavy stock and featured metallic lettering. Expensive. The man was successful. No doubt about that. Maybe, it wouldn't hurt to give his words some thought. "Thanks for the advice."

The walk to the record store gave Darcy a chance to mull over the conversation. It had left her confused. Everything she heard about Todd had painted a portrait of a slick, wheeler-dealer who always got what his clients wanted. That made him respected, if not universally liked, around town.

Offering free advice to someone he hardly knew seemed out of character. From what she knew of the guy, he was way too competitive for that. If he had an ulterior motive, though, she couldn't see it. Well, maybe she should get over her distrustfulness and talk to him. If wouldn't be the first time she'd been mistaken about something. The important thing was to recognize the mistake and learn from it.

If he turned out to be okay.

As she unlocked the door to the store, Darcy made a decision. She'd give Todd the benefit of the doubt. Maybe, with all his connections in town, he'd even be able to help the investigation.

After all, if Eddie hadn't given her the benefit of the doubt, she wouldn't be in position to take the handoff from him. There could be no harm in giving the realtor at least a little bit of trust.

WWED. What Would Eddie Do? Eddie would have given Todd a little bit of trust. Darcy would do the same.

A little later, Darcy was in Eddie's office, it would always be Eddie's office to her, busy with the white board the store used to list upcoming releases. Normally, the board hung from the wall behind the cash register. At the moment, she was using it for a different purpose.

"Updating that? You can leave that to me or Charlotte now." Hank put his hand on Darcy's shoulder and gave it a friendly squeeze. "You have enough on your plate, especially if today's anything like yesterday."

"Thanks, buddy. I'm using it for something different, though." She stepped away from the board and gestured for Hank to look at it, a la Vanna White on *Wheel of Fortune*.

Using a dry erase marker, she'd written a list of names in blue ink on the left-hand side of the board. To the right of the names, she'd created a grid in black ink. Each column had a capital letter for a heading—*M, M, O, A*.

"Rafe Majors and Claude Ewing." Hank cracked his knuckles. "Is there something about them I don't know?"

"Yes. Well, maybe." Darcy pointed at the board with a marker. "Rafe and Claude both had motive to want Eddie dead. That's what the first M stands for. The second M stands for means. Did they have the ability to do it? The

O is for opportunity. Did they have the chance to do it? The A is for alibi, you know, like the Sue Grafton book. Eddie loved Sue Grafton, Anyway, do they have an alibi for when Eddie was murdered?"

Hank stared at the board for a few seconds, shaking his head. "Then he broke into a grin. "You think Rafe or Claude took Eddie's life."

"*May* have." She told Hank about her conversations with both men the night before. "I'm calling this my suspect board. Got the idea from *Death in Paradise*. What do you think?"

"Mr. Majors seems to benefit from his stepdad's death. It's a bit of a stretch with Mr. Ewing, though. Sorry."

Darcy crossed her arms as she let out a long breath. "It's okay. You're right. But I just started. I'm sure there are more people who belong on this board."

"Maybe." Hank grabbed a crate of used albums to be priced and put on the sales floor. "What are you going to do with this, though? Take it to the police when you get it filled out?"

"No." A tingling sensation ran through Darcy. For the first time in years, she was a woman on a mission. For this mission, failure wasn't an option.

"Eddie was murdered. I'm sure of it. And I'm not going to wait for the police to come around and admit their mistake. I'm going to figure this out. Come hell or high water."

Chapter Seven

The store wasn't quite as busy as the previous day, so Darcy used a brief moment of downtime to update Hank and Charlotte with the latest news. She started with the good stuff.

"It turns out that Eddie made me president of the company. I've made the call. We're officially staying open."

Hank and Charlotte shared a glance before Charlotte burst into an ear-to-ear grin. "Best news ever. Will we be in trouble if we tell you we already knew about it?"

"Knew about what?" Darcy's gaze went back and forth between them.

"We mean," Hank put of a stack of records under his arm and headed for the *Country* section. "That Eddie asked us what we thought of the idea. We told him we're completely on board."

"Yeah. It's the perfect way to reward you for all the hard work you've put into this place. And for how far you've come on a personal level. You deserve it." Charlotte rang up a sale and put the merchandise, three Rolling Stones albums, in a brown paper bag and asked the customer to come again soon.

"Y'all think I'm going the right thing?" Darcy winced at the uncertain tone of her words. If she was going to be the boss, she needed to improve her decisiveness.

"Not a doubt in the world." Hank slotted an Amanda Shires record into its proper place. "And since you're the boss, Char and I could both use a raise."

"I'll take it under advisement. That's what a boss would say, isn't it?"

Darcy joined in as Charlotte and Hank laughed. It felt good to share in the levity. The past few days had been full of negativity. The joke was a welcome change of pace.

"You said there's bad news, too." Charlotte took a rag from underneath the sales counter and began dusting the items on the shelf of DVDs. "Might as well lay it on us."

"The bad news is that I have no idea how to conduct a murder investigation."

"I don't know about that. The list you made is a rather good start." Hank dropped the final record in his stack, Kenny Chesney's latest release, into place.

A quartet of young men entered the store. Given that they all were wearing Ball State baseball caps and had backpacks slung over their shoulders, it was a solid bet they were students at the university. Darcy exchanged knowing looks and nods with Hank and Charlotte.

The record store had a checkered history with BSU students. Over the years, the vast majority had proven themselves to be enthusiastic music lovers, and many became regular customers. Others seemed to think they didn't need to pay for merchandise, and that they were too smart to get caught. The folks in that group couldn't have been more wrong.

After struggling for months with how to cut down on shoplifting, Eddie and Darcy had considered banning all backpacks. They realized that wasn't customer-friendly, so instead, they decided that all backpack-laden customers got the eagle-eye treatment. Over time, the potential shoplifters got the message. The number of thefts went down, and nobody got unfairly hassled.

With the flawless coordination that came from years of working together, Darcy's team determined the young men were not a problem. In fact, by the time the group left, each of them had made a purchase.

Darcy wasn't crazy about their musical choices. She wasn't a fan of slickly produced, chart-topping pop. It wasn't her position to judge, though. It was her position to make the music available. And it pleased her that Izzy had been so adamant when she insisted the store carry artists like Dua Lipa and Ryan Tedder. They'd been reliable sellers.

Once the young customers headed out the door with their purchases in hand, Darcy headed for the back of the store.

"I've got a ton of paperwork to go over. I'll be in Eddie's office if anyone needs me." She was sure it would always be *Eddie's Office* and she was happy with it that way.

A little bit later, there was a knock on the door. Charlotte leaned in. "Got a minute? I wanted to run something by you."

Darcy got up from the visitor's chair. Eventually, she'd need to move behind the desk, but today wasn't the day. Instead, she took a seat on the corner of the desktop and waved Charlotte into the vacant chair.

"Got it all warmed up for you." She plucked a pair of drumsticks off a file cabinet and began performing a riff on her thigh. "What's up?"

"I was thinking about our conversation earlier. You know, about investigating Eddie's murder." When Darcy nodded, Charlotte let out a long breath. "I think you ought to add Jasmine Longoria to your board."

Darcy raised her eyebrows. The woman in question was the owner of a fancy-schmancy art gallery in town. She'd visited the place once. For about ten minutes. After asking about the price of an oil painting of a jazz trio she wanted to get for Eddie, she'd made a hasty dash for the door. The price Ms. Longoria had quoted her had been exorbitant.

The price Jasmine had quoted was more than Darcy made in a year. She found a different piece at a music festival that was within her budget. Eddie had loved the painting and hung it in the office right behind the desk.

Darcy looked at the piece. After a moment, she blinked away tears that were forming. Tears wouldn't help her find Eddie's killer. Actions would.

Jasmine's gallery was on the other end of the business district and catered to a different clientele. At first blush, Charlotte's idea didn't make sense.

"Why would she have it in for Eddie?"

"Jasmine's a client of the accounting firm I used to work for. One of my co-workers spent time on the lease agreement for her gallery."

"And?" Sometimes Charlotte drove Darcy crazy with her lengthy build-ups to her stories.

"The location wasn't the one she wanted. This place, where we're speaking right now, was for sale at the time Jasmine was looking to open her gallery.

She wanted to be here."

Vague memories, like echoes of a song being played in the distance, coalesced in Darcy's mind. She'd been in rehab during the time Eddie purchased the building that became home for Marysburg Music.

The memories came into focus. "But Eddie beat her to it. He made a cash offer, which the seller took."

"Yep. Jasmine didn't have the capital for a cash purchase. She offered more money but needed time to finalize financing. Instead of waiting, the seller still took Eddie's offer. There are stories she got so mad, steam literally came out of her ears when her old accountant broke the news to her. The next day, she switched to my firm."

"Wow. This is a good spot, but a reaction like that seems pretty over the top."

"Think about it." Charlotte leaned forward in her chair. "This is a corner spot on the town's main drag. There's free parking in the back and a lot of other stores that help drive foot traffic. This location's like the Holy Grail of Marysburg small business. Eddie got it and Jasmine didn't."

"So, you're saying Jasmine killed Eddie out of revenge?"

"Only in part. She gets part of her revenge by murdering him. She might have figured that with him out of the picture, the store would close. Then—"

"She could swoop in and get the building she wanted in the first place." Darcy went to the board and added Jasmine to the list. She stopped halfway through writing the woman's last name. "But the store's going to stay open. That doesn't leave much in the motivation column."

"You're forgetting something, my friend." Charlotte tapped the stack of legal documents on the desk. "I'll bet you a soda pop she didn't know about your promotion. Eddie told me and Hank to keep it a secret so he could surprise you. The three of us and his attorney were the only people who knew about it."

"That you know of." Darcy backtracked when Charlotte's shoulders dropped. "Sorry, just playing Devil's Advocate. You're right, there would have been no reason for Jasmine to know about that."

She turned her attention back to the board, adding information to the proper columns. A little thrill ran through her. It was a sensation reminiscent of the one she got the moment before heading onstage to perform at a concert. Part anticipation, part fear, she always took the sensation as a good sign.

It meant she cared. That she wanted to give the fans a night they wouldn't forget, and then some. It was a feeling that had been absent from her life for too many years.

It was a sense of purpose.

Along with that sense of purpose came a question. "Any idea how long the lease Jasmine signed was?"

"Good question." Charlotte typed out something on her phone. "I'll ask my friends at the firm. I should be able to find out who owns her building, too. If you want, we could contact the property manager, act like we're interested in leasing some space, and get the scoop."

Darcy gave the woman a high five. "You rock. That is totally deserving of a raise."

Charlotte's eyes went wide. "Seriously?"

"Oh, um, maybe not. Got a little excited, so sorry about that. Would it be okay if I pick up the tab on lunch for you and Hank, instead?"

"Sure." She headed for the door. When her hand was on the doorknob, she turned to face Darcy. "For now, at least."

The next few hours ticked by as Darcy worked her way through the paperwork, taking a break only long enough to fetch carryout lunch from Selena's. Over the past two years, Eddie had slowly turned more and more of the store's day-to-day operations over to her. It was kind of like how the 80s pop group *Scandal* changed its name to *Scandal featuring Patty Smyth*, and then completely dropped the *Scandal* part as Patty became the face of the band.

Back then, when Darcy had whined that all she wanted to do was manage the inventory and turn people on to good music, Eddie had laughed.

"Someday, this will be all yours. It's my mission to make sure you're ready when that day comes." Then he'd chuckle and turn his attention back to teaching her how to use the payroll system or where to order merchandise and supplies from.

Now that the day had arrived, Darcy didn't want the store. She wanted Eddie back. Her vision blurred as teardrops landed on the electric bill. She gave in to her emotions and buried her hands in her face as she sobbed.

It was all so unfair.

The man deserved better. He was one of the most giving people she knew. He'd spent his life sharing his prodigious musical talent with others. And now, when he'd reached the age that his main responsibility should have been to enjoy his days doing what he wanted to do when he wanted to do it, his life had been taken from him.

Detective-Sergeant Rosengarten couldn't have been more wrong.

Eddie hadn't died by his own hand. He'd died at someone else's. Whether it was Rafe or Todd or Jasmine or someone else entirely, didn't matter. What mattered was that Darcy was going to use her newfound purpose in life to figure out who took her friend's life.

And make sure that person faced the music.

Chapter Eight

Business, while still brisk, hadn't been as busy as the previous couple of days. Darcy had been able to send Hank and Charlotte home at five and the kids at closing time. By the time she got home, though, two straight fourteen-hour days had taken their toll.

She was spent, both physically and emotionally.

Her thoughts were still racing like the cars at the Indy 500, though, so after giving Ringo his dinner, she went to the spare bedroom and took a seat behind her drum kit. It wasn't an extravagant setup. The punk ethic frowned on excess, after all. Her kit was modeled after the one used by Janet Weiss, who played drums for Sleater-Kinney, among other bands. There was a bass, two toms, and a snare drum. A hi-hat, two crash cymbals, and a ride cymbal completed the set.

It was straightforward, elegant, and above all, powerful.

She queued up punk band Bikini Kill on her phone, put in her earbuds, and got busy pounding the skins like she was performing in front of a theater filled to the rafters with rocking fans instead of a bored cat.

About halfway through the *Reject All American* album, her elbow started to ache. That was the signal to call it quits. Despite physical therapy and years of rest, the elbow was unable to withstand more than thirty minutes of Darcy Gaughan-style drumming.

At one point, she'd toyed with the idea of relearning to play, with less focus on power and more on technique. In the end, she abandoned the idea. Her fierce drumming style had helped put Pixie Dust on the map. One critic had called them an all-female counterpart to Green Day. She didn't want to abandon the fierceness that brought about positive comments like that. If that meant she only played short stints, and rarely in public, so be it.

That professional drummer part of life was in the past, along with the jet black hair coloring and eyeliner. She had her memories. She could look at some of them and smile. Like she did when she gazed at the two gold records and one platinum record hanging on a wall in her living room. Others made her cringe, like the time she punched out a fan who grabbed at her after a show. It turned out all the guy had wanted was a selfie, but the way he'd come at her, from behind, had scared the snot out of her.

Those experiences from back then were as much a part of her as Ringo was part of her now.

And that was okay.

She was in a new stage of her life. If she'd learned anything over the years, she knew the best thing was to take her cue from the Steve Winwood tune and roll with it.

Clouds had moved in while she played, covering the evening sky like a gray, woolen blanket. In April, it wasn't a bad thing. The clouds kept the warmth from the day in. Which was going to come in handy, since she needed to make another trip to Rafe's house.

Earlier in the day, Darcy had gotten word the coroner had released Eddie's body to a local funeral home. She wanted to know if there were funeral details yet. She wouldn't put it past Rafe to opt for the cheapest route possible and forego any memorial service.

That wasn't going to happen if Darcy had anything to say about it.

"Back in a bit, buddy. You're in charge." She gave Ringo's gnarled ear a scratch. "Remember, no one gets in without proper ID."

The cat stared at her from his spot in Darcy's recliner, once again failing to find humor in her line about him playing bouncer. He stretched out his long front legs and extended his claws into the chair's thick slipcover. It was the second one she'd purchased since Ringo had declared the chair his domain. She didn't mind him taking control of it. She only wished he'd use his claws on any of the three scratching posts in the house instead of on the nicest piece of furniture.

Oh well. The slipcover was only a thing. If getting a new one every year or so made Ringo happy, it was a small price to pay.

A breeze from the north cooled Darcy's skin as she strolled to Rafe's house. The conditions weren't gloomy, like out of a horror movie. They were calming, like out of the music video of a popular love song. She liked the placid vibe. It was a nice change from the nonstop craziness of the past few days.

The soft grass beneath her feet muffled her steps. It made it easier for her to concentrate on a question at the forefront of her mind.

Were there any other suspects she needed to investigate?

Each of her current suspects gained from Eddie's demise. Some more than others. Rafe got the house and whatever else was left to him in the will. Claude got peace and quiet now that a noisy neighbor was gone. Jasmine got the location she coveted for her gallery.

They all had motive for murder in varying degrees. While Rafe had the most to gain, he also had the most to lose, too. He'd been riding the Eddie gravy train for years. Unless there was something Darcy didn't know about, he hadn't been planning on jumping off of it any time soon.

As for Claude? Darcy had read stories of neighbors engaging in disputes ranging from property lines to annoying pets. Shoot, there was even a senator from Kentucky who got in a fight with his neighbor. But murdering someone because they had a few loud parties that lasted a little too late into the night? That was a stretch, even to Darcy, who'd seen some extreme behavior during her years with Pixie Dust. And exhibited plenty of it herself.

That left Jasmine. Outside of concert posters, Darcy didn't know much about the world of visual arts. What she did know was that people who could afford the kind of art Jasmine dealt in were rich. Rich people liked getting their way. Since Jasmine was part of that world, she might not be much different from her customers. It was possible she hadn't forgiven Eddie for taking something she wanted.

A man, swooping in and snatching something desirable from a woman, simply because he could. Where had Darcy heard that story before? Too many places to count.

What if losing out on her location of choice had harmed her in some way financially? If she had money problems she thought could be only solved through relocation, she might have gotten desperate enough to take things into her own hands.

Yep. Darcy would have to take a closer look at Ms. Longoria the art dealer.

The musings ended when she arrived at Eddie's house. The curtains were once again drawn and all the lights appeared to be off, but that didn't deter her. She knew enough hard-core gamers who preferred darkness while they played so they could see the screen better.

Rafe was among that crowd. She'd bet one of her gold records on it.

She scaled the steps with a confident stride. Rafe didn't scare her. Annoyed the heck out of her? Yes. But made her feel unsafe? No way.

When three sharp knocks on the screen door got no response, she tried the doorbell. After another few minutes with no sign of the man, Darcy drummed her fingers against her thigh. She debated knocking again but decided against it. Maybe he really wasn't home. Score one for the slacker stepson.

"You can't avoid me forever, dude," she said and headed back down the steps, thinking about how the Slacker Stepsons would be a decent name for a punk band.

And almost ran into Heather Ewing.

The woman had a bouquet in her hands. Even in the twilight, her watery eyes were impossible to miss.

"Oh, hi, Darcy. It's good to see you." She looked down at the flowers. It was an arrangement of multi-colored daisies, Eddie's favorite. "I was bringing these to Rafe."

"Looks like he's not home."

"Probably just as well." With care, Heather placed the bouquet at the foot of the door and gave the flowers a gentle pat. "I can't believe Eddie's gone. He was such a kind soul. I'll miss him so much."

Darcy had seen Heather in the store on a regular basis, easily twice a month if not more often. She and Eddie had always been on friendly terms.

"Were you close?" She sat on the top step and motioned for Heather to join her.

"We lived next door to each other for ages. He was a good friend and the best neighbor you could ask for. Always kept his house and yard so tidy. I have lupus and remember a few times when I wasn't feeling well and Claude was at the station, Eddie mowed the lawn for us. No questions asked. Never asked for anything in return. And his parties." She fanned herself with her hand. "They were so much fun."

Darcy raised an eyebrow. Heather's take on Eddie was quite the change from the one her husband had expressed. It seemed like a great opportunity for some sleuthing.

"I was chatting with Claude the other day. He didn't sound like much of a fan."

"Oh, that's good old Claude being Claude." She flicked her hand like she was flicking away a bug. "I love my husband, but he can be a Debbie Downer at times. He's an early bird and always grumbled about the parties keeping him awake, especially if he had to be at work the next morning."

"And you thought different."

"Oh, yeah." Heather tucked a strand of her silver hair behind an ear. "I used to be one of the last to leave. I'd help Eddie clean up before going home. After a while, I left that for the younger crowd. Can't stay up like I used to. The mind is willing, but the body is weak."

Darcy chuckled. "He did hate to see those things come to an end. I remember one time when I was living here, it was about two a.m. I hid his trombone when he went to the bathroom thinking for sure he'd see that as a sign it was time to send everyone home."

"And?"

"He got out a spare and went right back to playing. When I saw him the next day, he gave me an A for effort. Then he told me the hall closet was a way too obvious choice for a hiding place. He suggested I should be more creative in the future."

"Sounds like him." Heather pulled her jacket tighter around her. Despite the cloud cover, it was getting chilly. "He had such a knack for making sure you felt better after you spent time with him."

Making sure you felt better. That was Eddie in a nutshell.

"He taught me so much about music, too." The older woman sighed. "Especially, jazz. I would have never become a fan of Freddie Hubbard or Wayne Shorter if not for Eddie. He was always so patient with me when I'd tell him I wanted something different but didn't know exactly what."

"I had a great time watching him with customers who wanted something new. His eyes would light up and he'd practically float around the store. At times, his voice even went up a note or two." Darcy shook her head. "I'm going to miss that."

Heather sucked in a ragged breath. "And the police are saying it was suicide? I don't believe it. It doesn't make any sense."

"It sure doesn't. Which is why I think the cops are wrong. Do you know anybody who would have wanted to harm Eddie or held a grudge against him?"

"No. But second-guessing the cops? Is that wise? I mean, they're the ones with the training and expertise, and, well, with your past?"

Some people might have taken offense at Heather's comment. Darcy didn't. She'd earned the doubt. There was no escaping from years of poor decision making. There was the opportunity to make up for it, though.

"You're a hundred percent right. They are the experts. I refuse to believe that Eddie would take his own life. Not for a second."

Heather nodded. Darcy noted something in the woman's posture, the way she sat with her spine ramrod straight that indicated agreement, if not encouragement.

"I guess it comes down to this. Eddie did so much for me. He always went the extra mile. I don't see the detective on the case doing the same thing and it makes me mad. I owe him. It's the least I can do."

They sat in silence for a few moments until Heather's phone buzzed. She got to her feet as she looked at it.

"That's Claude. He's on his way home from hanging out with his firefighter buddies. I should get going. I appreciate what you're trying to do, Darcy. I really do. Eddie was a good friend. I'll to miss him."

She gave Darcy's arm a gentle squeeze and headed off into the night.

Darcy remained seated while she pondered the conversation. Eddie had treated countless customers the exact same way he treated Heather. Like she was the most important person in the world. He listened to them, learned their interests, offered them suggestions, and encouraged them to try new artists.

Living next door to the man, how could they have not become friends? Even if his parties did run a little late. Nobody was perfect, after all.

The chat made Darcy's resolve to keep up the good fight even stronger. As she bounded down the steps, she pointed toward the sky.

"I miss you, too, Eddie. And I'm going to do something about it."

If Darcy had been paying attention to her surroundings, she might have noticed that one of the nearby shadows was darker than the others. And had a human form. Unfortunately for her, she didn't.

Chapter Nine

One of the perks of working at a record store was the hours. For a night owl like Darcy, the fact that the store didn't open until ten, eleven on Sundays, was a huge plus. During her days with Pixie Dust, she'd gotten quite comfortable with the unorthodox hours that came with living life on the road two hundred days per year.

When the band didn't even take the stage until nine, that meant their shows didn't end until eleven or later. By the time the stage was struck, the equipment was loaded onto the truck, and it was time to hit the road to the next destination, it was often after one in the morning.

That didn't mean it was time to go to sleep, though.

For Darcy, even in the days before her alcohol abuse, between a post-show shower and meal, it took a while to come down from a performance. In the later stages of her addiction, she wasn't able to fall asleep much before four or five.

And often, she needed a bottle to help her drift off.

It was a vicious cycle. Play, eat, drink, sleep. Then do it all again in one city or town with a name she couldn't remember. Over and over again. The lifestyle of a touring band was far from glamorous. And it took a toll that, in the end, Darcy couldn't pay.

It wasn't all bad, though. One of the upsides to the lifestyle was that it conditioned her for a stay-up-late and sleep-in mode. It was a pattern that, with only a few adjustments, had worked pretty darn well for life at the record store.

When she started working for Eddie, she reported to work at eleven and spent her shift ringing up sales and helping customers. When her shift ended, she went home to Eddie's house, made dinner, and kicked back with a sparkling water. They'd spend their evenings talking about music, watching shows and films about music, and every now and then, playing music. Rafe didn't care for her presence in the house, but Eddie had made it clear Darcy was welcome to stay as long as she needed.

It was during those jam sessions that Darcy learned about things like restraint, control, and patience. It was also when she learned to play the cajón. With Pixie Dust, it had been all about energy and ferocity. With Eddie, and the cajón, she learned things neither her college program nor her punk band could teach her, like the willingness to try different things.

She also learned how invaluable it was for someone to have your back through good times and bad. Her parents and her sister gave what support they could, but they lived near Chicago and could only do so much when they were a three-hour drive away.

One thing she never figured out, though, was how Eddie managed to sleep as late as she did, yet always got up hours earlier, and functioned as flawlessly as a band that had been together for years. Every now and then, she'd whine about how unfair it was that he was up with the dawn and smiling after nothing more than a single cup of coffee while she needed practically a gallon of tea before she could function.

He always laughed and said he was blessed for being born without the need for much sleep. For as long as he could remember, five hours was all he needed. Having a job he loved made it easy to get up in the morning. Though in recent years, he had admitted to becoming fond of an afternoon nap on his days off.

Eddie's life as an early bird made it easy for Darcy to remain a night owl. Now, that needed to change. It was going to be on her, and her alone, to be at the store early enough to handle business that needed to be completed before opening the doors.

And to visit potential murder suspects.

On this morning, Darcy drug herself out of bed at six, much to Ringo's surprise. And annoyance. After breakfast, she spent a couple of hours at the store putting price tags on new records to replenish the inventory on the sales floor. Once that task was complete, she went to visit Jasmine Longoria.

Upon arriving at the gallery, she took a few minutes to marvel at the gorgeous lettering in the storefront window. *JL Art and Design* was painted on the glass in gold. Burgundy trim made the gold pop. It came close to ostentatious but stopped short of stepping over that line. Instead, it evoked the owner herself, classy with a flair for the dramatic.

Jasmine was seated at a glass table looking at a computer tablet when Darcy entered the gallery. A subtle, electronic *gong* tone prompted the woman to look up from her screen.

"Darcy Gaughan, this is a surprise." She stood and flipped her luxurious, long black hair over her shoulder. Her brown skin practically glowed as she approached, but her perfect smile didn't reach her brown eyes.

"I don't recall you visiting the gallery before." She swept her arm to the side to draw Darcy's attention to the artwork. A model from *The Price is Right* couldn't have done it better. "How can I help you?"

"I," Darcy's gaze scanned the room, "haven't been here in a long time. Thought today was a good day to change that."

Jasmine gave her a long head-to-toe look, apparently deciding whether Darcy was worth her time. After a moment, she nodded. "Are you interested in something for you? Or for a friend or family member, perhaps?"

Not skilled at small talk, Darcy took a deep breath and went straight to the point. "It's about Eddie Maxwell."

"I heard what happened. The poor man. Is it true he took his own life?" Jasmine guided Darcy to the table, where they took a seat.

"That's what the police say." It was time to get some answers. "I heard that you were interested in the record store's location back in the day."

"I was. It's a prime piece of retail space. In retrospect, overpriced. I think I've done all right here, though. Wouldn't you agree?"

"You've got a lot of nice stuff, that's for sure." The response was a calculated one. Darcy wanted to get a rise out of Jasmine. Maybe the woman would say something in the heat of the moment if she thought Darcy was insulting her merchandise.

"My dear, people don't come her for 'nice stuff.' They come here for the finest art in the Midwest. Now, if you really are interested in something, I'm happy to help you. If not, I really am rather busy."

"No, I'm interested." She went to an oil painting that featured concentric swirls of pastel colors. It reminded her of vacation. "I like this. How much?"

Jasmine rolled her eyes. "Why are you really here?"

"Looking for inspiration." Darcy pointed to a vase on the other side of the gallery. "That would look good in my kitchen. What do you want for it?"

"I understand your feelings for Mr. Maxwell. We all do, after all, we all know what he did for you. It doesn't change the fact he died by his own hand, though. And that vase is worth more than that fishing shack you call a home."

"Touché." Darcy returned to the chair across from Jasmine. "The problem is, I know for a fact that Eddie didn't kill himself. I also know he got the record store location over you. What I don't know is whether or not you've carried a grudge heavy enough to want him dead. And maybe get your hands on that property once and for all."

Jasmine stared at Darcy, her coal-black eyes unblinking. Eventually, the art dealer's ruby red lips curled up at the ends. Then she let out a laugh. It was short and clipped, like she'd been practicing it for ages.

"You poor soul. Let me offer you some advice. Before you go blundering about, accusing people of a crime, especially one as serious as murder, get your facts straight."

"Meaning?"

"I'll admit it. I was disappointed when I lost out on that location. It's not easy being a woman-owned business. I need every edge I can get."

"I heard you changed accounting firms over it. Doesn't sound like disappointment to me. That sounds like anger." Darcy imagined being in the sword fight from *The Princess Bride*. Thrust and parry, interspersed with witty repartee.

Jasmine's smile disappeared. Her eyes hardened. This was a woman who did not like to be bested.

"Believe what you will. That was a long time ago. It doesn't matter now. I got the last laugh by landing here. Once again, that part about getting your facts in order? I have it on good authority that Todd Meadows in the process of buying up the parcels on that block. He's going to knock everything to the ground, including your dreary, little record store, and build high-end condos to attract the university crowd. What do you think of that?"

Jasmine leaned forward, like a panther readying itself to pounce on unsuspecting prey. Darcy wouldn't fall victim, though.

"I know all about Todd's attempts to buy the property. I'll let you in on my own little secret. Eddie gave the store to me before he died. It's not going anywhere." She got to her feet. "And I don't want that vase, after all. It's eye-catching, but after spending some time with it, it seems a little phony. Kind of like certain people I know."

Darcy marched out of the gallery without so much as a glance over her shoulder. She'd gotten the last word in. Not that it really mattered, but it still felt good to get over on someone who was a big fish in town, even if she'd stretched the truth in order to do it. More importantly, she got what she really wanted.

Information.

Jasmine *had* wanted the record store property and wasn't happy when she didn't get it. Her gallery's current location seemed to be doing okay, though. Did that mean Marysburg's finest art dealer should be taken off Darcy's list of suspects?

No.

Darcy flipped up her jacket's hood to ward off the late morning chill. She'd learned in her last weeks with Pixie Dust how appearances were often deceiving. Her manager and bandmates had all acted like they wanted to stick by her until her injury healed. Then, in the blink of an eye, she was out of the band. Dumped along the roadside like an old cassette tape that had been crushed under someone's boot heel.

Somehow, Darcy needed to find out the state of Jasmine's finances. Just because the woman dressed like she'd stepped off a fashion runway in New York and dealt in the finer things in life didn't mean she had plenty of cash in her bank account.

While she waited for a car to pass at an intersection, Darcy nodded. Money, or the desire for more of it, could drive people to make some crazy decisions. Jasmine was smart. She had to be to remain in business as long as she had. But what if she had put a dollar figure on how much money she'd failed to make by not being in her preferred location?

Clearly, Jasmine had to keep up appearances. It wouldn't do for a high-end art dealer to dine on ramen noodles and wear off-the-rack clothing from a discount retailer. It wouldn't work for the woman's image. Frugality wasn't a part of Jasmine's vocabulary.

Darcy knew first-hand the benefits of living frugally. Despite her past troubles with alcohol, she'd been smart enough to save some money while still in the band. Between that, Eddie's guidance, and the low-key lifestyle she'd adopted, she was debt-free with a solid retirement account balance. There was no pressure on her to obtain things she couldn't afford. The trappings of wealth, like massive wardrobes and glittery jewelry, weren't her style.

Besides, she'd seen the lengths to which people went to keep up the appearance of success and wealth. There were folks she knew from all walks of life who were in debt up to their eyeballs, yet still drove luxury import cars and lived in exclusive, gated communities.

The other tidbit of note was Jasmine's mention of Todd. It piqued Darcy's interest that the man himself hadn't mentioned his interest in the store property. Then again, Eddie hadn't said anything, either. She made a note in her phone to ask the folks at the store if they knew anything.

She blew out a long, cleansing breath in relief that she'd been quick enough on the uptake to bluff her way through the conversation. Eddie had recently made her CEO of the store. He wouldn't do that while selling the building, would he?

* * *

Darcy was at the cash register, putting price tags on a stack of new CDs that had come in, when Charlotte arrived.

"Morning, Supreme Leader." She stuffed her jacket on a shelf under the sales counter. Then she hugged Darcy.

Darcy wasn't prepared for the friendly gesture. She stiffened for a moment before leaning into it.

"Um, I'm happy to see you, Char, but a simple 'hi' is plenty."

She took the records that Darcy had priced and moved to the sales floor. "I know. But if I've learned anything these past few days, it's not to take things for granted. Everyone here means a lot to me, and I decided it's time to start showing it."

A college-aged man with brown, curly hair came in and asked where he could find Dream Theater albums.

"Good to see you again, Ace. We've got a few new items on vinyl." Darcy led him to the far wall, where the Rock L.P.s were located. "We also have a few things on CD in the middle aisle."

When she was finished helping the customer, she joined Charlotte, who was slotting new Bob Marley albums into place. Some albums never went out of style. Fleetwood Mac's *Rumors,* Miles Davis' *Kind of Blue,* and the King of Reggae's *Legend* were always in demand.

"That's a good lesson idea. I'll try to do the same...as long as you never call me Supreme Leader again."

Charlotte laughed. "Deal. How about Cosmic Queen?"

"That has potential."

Darcy's attention went to the front of the store when the doorbell chimed. Her smile morphed into a frown when the person in the doorway removed her hat. It was Detective-Sergeant Rosengarten.

"I'd like a word, Darcy." The cop marched toward the office. Apparently, it was a word that needed to be exchanged in private.

"What can I do for you, Detective-Sergeant?" Darcy gestured toward the visitor's chair as she eased into Eddie's chair. It felt weird, but not wrong. That was a good sign.

"It's about Mr. Maxwell. The coroner report stated that traces of plastic were found in the stab wound. Does that mean anything to you?"

"Eddie's letter opener wasn't plastic. It was stainless steel."

"And yet, the one we found at the crime scene was plastic. We're running tests to confirm that the traces the coroner found match the weapon that was on the scene. It appears the letter opener wasn't quite what Mr. Maxwell led people to believe."

"That can't be. I mean..." Darcy gripped the arms of her chair. Arguing with Kaitlin would be pointless. The officer had her mind made up. "I appreciate you telling me this in person, but wouldn't a phone call have done the job?"

"This is additional evidence that his death was self-inflicted. It's information I thought should be relayed person-to-person. I wanted to give you the courtesy of informing you myself. It's time for you to move on."

"If you say so."

On the surface, the assessment made sense. A plastic weapon was found at the scene of the crime. Traces of the plastic were found in the wound. One plus one equals two. Case closed.

Below the surface, it didn't. Because the Detective-Sergeant's assessment didn't address a key issue. Where was the real letter opener? Darcy would deal with that issue as soon the cop was out the door. In the meantime, it couldn't hurt to play nice. "Thank you for taking the time to tell me this in person."

"That's what we're here for. Protect and serve." Kaitlin gave Darcy a little nod when she got to her feet. "I'll see myself out."

The second she was alone, Darcy removed a blanket covering the whiteboard and got busy writing down the new information. The real letter opener was stainless steel. She knew that like she knew Gina Schock was way underrated as a drummer simply because she was a woman.

Kaitlin had made a mistake. Simply because of Darcy's checkered past, the cop couldn't or wouldn't take her comments seriously.

"Boom." Darcy stepped back from the board and did a quick drum fill on her thighs.

It didn't matter what the cops thought. Darcy now had the first track of the album in place. Whoever murdered Eddie must have used a replica of his letter opener and made off the real one. For the moment, she couldn't imagine why someone would go to that trouble. That was a matter to be dealt with later, though.

For the past three days, Darcy had been going on faith that someone else had taken Eddie's life. Faith could only take someone so far, though. Now, she had something tangible to go along with that belief.

Eddie's murderer had a limited number of days of freedom. Because now, Darcy had a trail she could follow.

Chapter Ten

One of the things Darcy learned early on in her drumming career was that a steady beat was the key to a band's success. It was the launching pad for the bass, guitar, and other instruments a band may have.

She adored the scene early in the movie *That Thing You Do* when the drummer quickens the pace of the title song while the band was playing a show. The other members were forced to match the drummer's faster pace. That move changed the song from a nondescript ballad to a fun dance song that sent The Wonders to the top of the charts.

Fast, slow, or somewhere in between, the most important factor for the beat was the discipline to maintain control throughout a song. As a drummer, Darcy couldn't go off half-cocked and change the time signature mid-song or play a solo whenever she wanted. She had to stick to her role. That was the only way those around her could play theirs.

Now, she needed to do the same thing. Be steady. Keep herself under control.

That meant following up on the notes on the board in an orderly fashion. Otherwise, she ran the risk of going in a handful of directions all at once.

At the moment, though, she had a business to run. She returned to the sales floor.

"Things good, Char?"

Her friend was at the cash register, finishing up a sale to Ace, the customer who'd asked about Dream Theater. There were no other customers in the store. Evidently, now that the uproar over Eddie's death had died down, so had the public's interest in the store.

"Yep." She turned her attention to the customer. "I agree with you that the band isn't the same since Mike Portnoy left. The new drummer, Mike Mangini, is pretty good, though. My boss thinks highly of him."

"Why's that?" Ace turned his attention to Darcy and raised an eyebrow.

"I met him when he was teaching at Berklee and got to sit in on a jam session with him." She went to a color photo hanging on the wall. Her hair was shorter in the picture, coming to an end at the jawline instead of at the shoulder, and parted down the middle. A total Joan Jett vibe. "That's us."

First, his eyes went wide. Then his jaw dropped when he got closer to the picture and recognized Darcy.

She shrugged. "I used to play. When you've given those records a good listen, come back. We'll turn you on to some great prog-rock, jazz, whatever you want."

"I'll do that." He left the store starry-eyed. Evidently, he hadn't been prepared to meet someone in Marysburg, Indiana who hung out with famous musicians.

When they were alone, Charlotte gave Darcy a high five. "Nice going. Five bucks says he'll be back this weekend."

"Let's hope so." She looked around. "The past couple of days weren't sustainable. Still, I was hoping…"

"It's not even noon and it's the day before payday. We'll be fine. Especially if you keep showing off your rock star cred. I've never seen you do that before."

"Never had to. This was Eddie's store. People came to see him. He could talk people into a sale better than anyone else." She shoved her fists into her jeans pockets. "I'm going to try to emulate that. We'll need all the help we can get. Know what I mean?"

"I do. And you'll be great."

Darcy's cheeks got hot at the compliment. It warmed her heart, too. Eddie had harped on her for years that she needed to learn to take a compliment. She had a long way to go on that end, but she was making progress. Now was a perfect time to show it.

"Thank you. We all will." She rubbed her hands together. "I've got some artwork for Record Store Day to review. Give me a shout if you need anything."

With an unfamiliar sensation in her belly, Darcy ambled back into the office. It took a moment to recognize the feeling. It was self-esteem. Something she'd often lacked in recent years. Now that it was back, she let the feeling spread throughout her. It felt good. And affirmed that she was doing the right thing.

She dove into the designs like Ringo dove into the vanilla ice cream she gave him as a treat. Eddie had shown his belief in her by turning the store over to her. She'd show everyone that vision had been well placed.

The store's bank account still looked fine by the time she ordered the selected artwork, processed payroll, and paid the bills. She gave herself a high five in celebration.

With those immediate needs taken care of, she turned her attention to Jasmine's claim about Todd. Eddie kept meticulous records. He scanned all paper documents and backed everything up to the cloud. If Mr. Meadows had made a pitch for the building, it would be a quick and easy search for confirmation.

A minute later, she hit gold. "Thanks, Eddie. I promise to follow your example. Cross my heart." She clicked on a folder labeled *Meadows - Realtor*.

The folder didn't contain a lot. Only three documents, all in *pdf* format. The time stamps on them were from within the last ten months. Darcy started with the oldest one.

"What game are you playing, Mr. Real Estate Tycoon," she asked while waiting for the document to open.

It was a letter from Todd's office. Short and to the point, it informed Eddie that a client had expressed interest in purchasing the store property. The letter writer wanted to know if he could pay Eddie a visit to discuss "this once in a lifetime opportunity."

Darcy wanted to gag. "Once in a lifetime, I'll bet."

She pulled up Eddie's calendar and went to the date of the letter. If he agreed to a meeting, there'd be a calendar entry for it. There was no doubt in her mind that Eddie had turned down the invitation, but she wanted to make sure. Cutting corners could come back to bite her later. The investigation couldn't have that. A couple of minutes later, she had her answer. Eddie didn't meet with anyone from Meadows Realty or anything that seemed similar in the two weeks that followed the letter.

The second piece of correspondence was seven months old. It came from the man himself. In it, Todd described his plan of building a complex of condos and apartments on the block where the record store stood. There were assurances all impacted businesses would be given assistance to find new locations. The letter concluded with flowery language extolling the increase in property tax revenue the community would receive from the development and how that would benefit everyone in Marysburg, including Eddie.

She clicked on a hyperlink that took her to a site containing renderings of the completed project. It was impressive, indeed. Residential units of various sizes occupied floors two through four. The first floor provided space for a grocery store, a handful of small storefronts, and a parking garage. It was sleek, modern, and attractive. Even Darcy had to admit it was an appealing project.

Another calendar search indicated Eddie met with Todd ten days after the date of the letter.

"Wish I could have been a fly on the wall when Eddie told him 'Thanks, but no thanks.'"

The third letter was only a month old. It carried a menacing tone. Todd was indirectly telling Eddie the development project would not be stopped. By the time of its writing, owners of all the other relevant properties had agreed to sell. Without the record store property, the project wouldn't move forward, though. Its position on the street corner made the development a make-or-break proposition.

If Eddie didn't agree to sell within the next ten days, the letter threatened that "legal procedures" would be taken.

As far as Darcy could tell, Eddie and Todd didn't meet to discuss the third letter. For a second, she debated calling Rafe to see if he knew anything about Todd's overtures and Eddie's responses.

"Girl, that's opening a big ol' can of worms. Rafe'd sell Eddie out faster than you could say 'drum solo.'" Instead, she added notes about Todd to the whiteboard. This far along in the project, the man must have sunk a lot of cash into it. A question was how much. Enough to drive one to commit murder? She'd have to pay him a visit to find out.

Charlotte was dusting a collectible one-sixth scale Prince figurine when Darcy returned to the sales floor. Prince Rogers Nelson, the legend behind *Purple Rain* and so much other amazing music was one of Darcy's favorite artists. Eddie, too. They'd spend hours dissecting the man's compositions, delighting in the layer upon layer of musical magic that went into every one of the songs.

"Be careful with The Purple One. Don't want to anger the music gods by damaging him."

"Giving him a nice shine. Nothing more. Someone called and said they saw it online and want to come by to take a closer look." Charlotte ran a cleaning wipe over the signature white guitar that accompanied the figure and took a step back to inspect her handiwork.

"Did they ask about the price?" The item came had been valued at a thousand dollars. Despite Darcy's entreaties, Eddie had never divulged how much he paid for it.

"Nope. Only whether or not it came with something to transport it in." She gave Darcy a thumbs up. "I said we had the original packaging. Figured when they get here, I'd show them the whole ensemble. Should make for an easy sale."

"Good work." She gave Charlotte a high five. "Earning that raise already. It'll be in tomorrow's check by the way."

The woman blinked a few times, then brushed a few strands of her cobalt blue hair from her eyes.

"Thanks. I thought, I mean, I didn't think you were really serious."

"I'm gonna be leaning on you all a lot. You deserve something for putting up with me."

To avoid making a scene by getting all mushy, Darcy changed the subject.

She recounted her conversation with Kaitlin.

"If that's true, then that means someone made a copy of the letter opener, stabbed Eddie with the copy, and took off with the original." Charlotte frowned. "Eddie always said it was a one of a kind. It would be tough to sell."

"My thoughts, exactly." Darcy leaned against the cabinet where music-related books were shelved. "Unless the murderer doesn't know how unique it is."

"Or, they do and have a way to sell it under the radar? Like a black-market kind of thing."

"Regardless of how the murderer got rid—"

"Or will get rid."

"True. Right now, it doesn't matter to me what they did or will do with the real letter opener." Darcy drummed her fingers against a wooden cabinet shelf. "What matters is that Eddie's murder must have been planned. That raises a question. Where did the killer get the replica made?"

Their conversation stopped when a young lady entered the store and headed for the *World Music* section. When they asked her if she needed any help, she told Darcy and Charlotte she was just looking.

"I might be able to help you on that." Charlotte kept her voice low. "The Hobbit's got a 3-D printer at his game store. Go talk to him."

Darcy grimaced. "Ugh, that guy creeps me out. Do I really have to?"

"No. But you'll never know what he knows if you don't ask. Go right now, before you talk yourself out of it. I've got things covered here." Charlotte nudged her toward the door with a friendly hip bump, then wandered over to a middle-aged couple who had recently entered the store.

Darcy, wracked with indecision, remained rooted to the floor for a moment. For five years, she'd been content to let others take the limelight. Usually, it was Eddie. Now that he was gone, she had no choice but to step into it. And not only in terms of running the store.

This was one of those moments she'd been working toward from the first step she too into the rehab center. Eddie had helped set her along that path. It was time to show the world she was ready.

"I'll be back, Char." She grabbed her jacket. "With info. And lunch."

* * *

It was only a five-minute walk to her destination, so Darcy didn't have time to formulate much of a plan. Or any plan, actually. As the Hobbit's store came into view, she slowed her steps.

"Okay, Darc. Let's keep this friendly. Try to get info about the printer and get out. Don't overplay your hand this early in the show."

She was greeted with the smell of cardboard, essential oils, and Italian spices as she entered the store. A short, beefy man with a mane of shaggy ginger hair and an unruly beard was perched on a stool behind the sales register. He was munching on a slice of pizza and reading a paperback copy of "Shadow and Bone." Even though the temperature outside was in the low fifties, he was dressed as though it was the summer, sporting a black Dungeons and Dragons T-shirt and tan cargo shorts.

It was Sean O'Sullivan, the Hobbit himself.

He gave Darcy a quick glance, then slipped a greasy napkin between the pages to mark his place.

"Darcy Gaughan, this is a nice surprise. What brings you to The Magic Box?" He got down from his stool and ran his hands down his shirt, as if he was attempting to rub out any wrinkles. In a standing position, he was almost as wide as he was tall. He might be five feet, five inches on a good day.

Between the squat build, unruly hair, and unsurpassed knowledge of all things fantasy, his nickname was an apt one.

"Thinking about expanding my horizons." She took a close look at a pack of cards wrapped in garish shades of purple, orange, and yellow. The word "Magic" dominated the image.

There were different packs for all sorts of games. Darcy's mind boggled at the variety. More jaw-dropping were countless boxes of board games with names like *Catan* and *Ticket to Ride*. As she perused the merchandise, it occurred to her that there wasn't a game of Monopoly in sight. Growing up, she'd spent untold nights playing Monopoly with her family.

At times like this, she felt *so* old.

"Looking for anything in particular?" He'd come up right alongside her and hadn't made a sound in his movements. For a roly-poly person, he had an uncanny ability to move with the stealth of a panther.

"Not really. Looking for something to pass the time between my *Riverdale* Comics."

She was a regular at the Hobbit's comics store, The Comic Castle, next door. As an adult, board games didn't have a lot of appeal to her, though. It had been ages since she'd last set foot in The Magic Box.

She scanned the store as she stopped by a shelf of rulebooks. The printer was nowhere in sight. Toward the back, there was a doorway with a curtain drawn, though. People of all ages got together in that room to play hours and hours of card and board games. Word had it that the Hobbit made as much money charging people for game time as he made selling his merchandise.

The printer had to be behind the curtain.

Letting her gaze fall on instruction manuals, tiny game figurines, and all other manner of role-playing-game materials, she made her way toward the back. Once there, she pushed the curtain aside and strolled through the doorway.

"There's nothing much in the gaming area besides tables and chairs." The Hobbit tapped her elbow in an effort to guide her toward the sales floor. Darcy couldn't escape the feeling he was trying to keep her eyes in front of the merchandise.

Or keep her from seeing something important.

As she turned, Darcy spotted the machine on a table in a corner of the room. She'd done a bit of research on the walk from the record store. Thank the Rock Gods for the Internet.

"Oh, cool. What's that?" She marched right up to the cube-shaped device. It reminded Darcy of a squarish microwave oven. There was a door on the front made of clear plastic. Sections of the top and left sides were also clear, so one could watch the printing magic in action. On the inside, the printing plastic emerged from a chamber that housed a nozzle suspended from the top of the chamber by two horizontal rods running from side to side. The rods reminded her of an old dot matrix printer that carried the printing mechanism from left to right and back again.

"That's Drogo, my 3-D printer." He ran a hand across the top of the cube. "I make all kinds of things that I sell up front. Game dice, custom figurines that customers can paint. Stuff like that."

"Very cool." Darcy let out a low whistle. It was an impressive piece of technology. She was far from being a computer illiterate, but the thought of creating something solid from a long, thin string of plastic and some computer code baffled her.

"How's it work?"

"Like this." The Hobbit's eyes lit up as he rubbed his hands together. In that moment, he was like a friendly teddy bear. "I use a program on my computer to design an object. When I'm finished, I send the instructions to the printer and..."

He tossed a blue object to her. It was cylindrical in shape, with a wide, round base at one end and an ornate crown and cross on the other end. It weighed next to nothing, despite its two-inch height.

"Impressive king you've got here. Are there more?" She tossed the chess piece back to him. The conversation was going right where she wanted.

"That's the first one. I'm making a set for a friend. In blue and red instead of the traditional black and white. He's coming by later and if he likes it, I'll move forward with the rest of the pieces."

"That must take a lot of your time."

"Not as much as you'd think. The designing doesn't take long. The printer can take a while, though. This piece took two hours. I can do other things while it's printing, though."

"That is too cool. Can you print something with more than one color? Like if someone wanted a Mickey Mouse head where his face is white and his eyes and ears are black."

"As a matter of fact, yes." He opened a box next to the printer. It contained spools of plastic in every color of the rainbow. "Printing a multi-color object can be tricky. I'm not very good at it. My goal is to have it mastered by the fall so I can print items like that and have them on sale in time for Christmas."

"Pretty slick. So, you take custom orders, then? Like, say if I wanted a 3-D version of the record store's logo, could I hire you to do it?"

"Sure." He took a step closer. It was too close. The man had no qualms about invading Darcy's personal space. "I'd be happy to do something unique to you, I mean, for you."

Ugh. Maybe he was a nice guy, but after that comment, she wanted to go straight home and take a shower for three days to get the slime off her. There were bigger issues at play, though, so she held her ground and kept her feeling of disgust bottled up inside.

"I'll talk to everyone at the store and if we can come up with a design we all like, I'll let you know." She made her way toward the doorway. "How long have you been doing this printing work? I mean, I thought this was for super high-end research projects. I didn't know people like us use them."

He held the curtain open for her as she passed into the front room. At least this time he was being considerate instead of acting like a total creeper.

"I got my first printer about a couple of years ago. It was okay but was kind of slow and I could only print one color at a time. I got the one back there six weeks ago."

Darcy came to a stop in front of the cash register. *Six weeks ago*. The timing worked out. If the Hobbit printed the letter opener used to murder Eddie, the questions came in fast and furious. Did he print it for a customer who went on to commit the crime, or did he do it for his own use?

If it was for his own use, the next question was why.

"Anything else I can do for you, Darcy?" He put his hand on her shoulder. It roused her from her ruminations.

"No, thanks." She grabbed a deck of playing cards and put them on the counter. "I think I'll start with these and play some solitaire. That way I can work my way up to your fancier merch."

She paid for the cards with a promise to get back in touch with the Hobbit soon. She didn't tell him whether it was to make a purchase or to accuse him of murder.

Chapter Eleven

On her way back to the record store, Darcy popped into Selena's to order some chicken fajitas with chips and guac to go. She sipped on a lemonade and chatted with Thea while the cook prepared the order.

"I heard you all had customers lined up all the way out the door. That's good, right?" Thea took a beer mug out of a dishwasher under the bar and wiped it dry with a towel.

"Yeah. Even though the circumstances were totally the worst, a lot of times it had a real festive vibe that Eddie loved. The constant sales helped my head, too."

"How so?"

"You know how it is when it gets packed in here, right? You're so busy taking orders and pouring drinks you don't have time to think about anything else."

Thea nodded. "Oh, yeah. I call it being in the zone. Time flies."

"Totally. And that made it easy to focus on work instead of dwelling on what happened to Eddie." Her throat closed up, stopping her from saying more.

"I'm so sorry." She gave Darcy's hand a reassuring squeeze. "And I'm proud of you for taking a stand. Between you and me, I'd dropkick Kaitlin between the goalposts if I had the chance. Just because she doesn't like you shouldn't mean she can blow you off."

Normally, Thea didn't have much bad to say about anyone. The woman was a proponent of the mantra if you can't say something nice, don't say anything at all. Her comment caught Darcy off guard.

"I had no idea you felt that way. Did she take you down on the rugby pitch or something?"

Thea snorted. "As if. That string bean couldn't tackle a scarecrow in the middle of a bean field. Nah, my complaint is that she's lazy. She'd rather spend the day looking for a job in a bigger city than do the everyday work here."

"Like looking for Eddie's murderer?"

"She wanted an easy win, and she took it when it fell in her lap. I'm not saying she's a bad person. It's like she's got tunnel vision. Always thinks she's got all the answers." Thea took Darcy's order from the cook and put it into a plastic bag. "Speaking of which, I've heard you're looking for some answers of your own."

"You could call it that." She told Thea about the results of her asking around so far. "The thing with the letter opener doesn't make any sense to me. What do you think?"

"That you keep at it. This investigation is giving you a mission beyond getting from one day to the next. That's good. And I'll tell you this." Thea tapped her index finger on the bar. "Eddie and the Hobbit weren't exactly the best of friends. It was a fight over money to fund business district development needs."

"Really? Thanks for the tip. Between a fight over cash and owning the printer, that gives the Hobbit both a motive and the means to go after Eddie. Sounds like I've got work to do."

A bit later, Darcy cleared away the remnants of the lunch she and Charlotte had reveled in. She wiped her mouth with a satisfied sigh. Selena's fare always hit the spot. And it tasted even better in trying times like this.

Comfort food at its best.

With their bellies full and a handful of customers taken care of, Darcy gave Charlotte a full report of what she'd learned during her quest.

"What do you make of it?" Darcy organized a stack of Marysburg Music stickers so they were all facing the same way. "Clearly, I've been living in a bubble of cluelessness around here."

"Don't be too hard on yourself. You've been focusing on yourself, as it should be. I think I know what Thea was talking about, though."

Darcy got a roll of receipt paper and a pen. She didn't want to forget anything. "Fire away."

"Here's what I know. Eddie was a member of the business district beautification committee. My old boss was part of the same group. What they wanted to do was create a fund that would pay for things like sidewalk cleaning, installing planter beds and benches, and hiring artists to paint wall murals."

"I remember Eddie talking about that. Seems like a no-brainer to me."

"Same here." She paused to ring up a customer who was purchasing a CD of Thundercat's latest album. "Anyway, the idea was that all businesses in the district would contribute. A sliding scale for the suggested contribution amounts was put together. The bigger the business, the larger the contribution. Non-profits were exempt."

"Right." Darcy put a new roll of receipt paper in the register. "Eddie asked me what I thought we should do with the funds. I told him a mural on the side of the building would be cool." She smiled. "He laughed when I suggested a musical mosaic."

"But you got your wish."

Eighteen months ago, a Ball State Art School student had painted a mural of legendary musicians throughout the ages, from Mozart to Wes Montgomery to Ariana Grande. It was on the east exterior wall. The one that ran along the driveway and row of parking spaces separating Marysburg Music from a bank. In times of stress, Darcy was fond of going outside and gazing at the mural until she felt better.

"One of the best uses of that fund, in my mind." Darcy made a note in her phone to contact the artist and ask if she could add Eddie to the mural.

"I totes agree with you, but not everyone was on board." Charlotte raised her eyebrows. "The Hobbit was opposed to the idea from the start."

"But it's been a great thing." Darcy rattled off a handful of the improvements the fund had provided in a single breath. "What's his problem?"

"He didn't want to have to pay for it. He claimed that if businesses wanted to beautify their own immediate surroundings, they should pay for it themselves. He complained that it amounted to corporate welfare and didn't trust the organizers when they promised that all parts of the business district would benefit."

"Okay, I'm sorry." Darcy massaged her forehead in an attempt to ward off a headache that was trying to burrow behind her eyes. "That's stupid. Why would anyone be opposed to a beautification initiative? Marysburg needs all the help we can get to compete."

"Preaching to the choir, sister."

It was true. Marysburg had to fight tooth and nail to maintain its identity as a community separate from Muncie that had its own vibrant business district. Like countless communities across the Midwest, every day was a struggle for local entrepreneurs competing with the convenience that came from e-commerce giants and big box stores. The influx of shoppers and customers from the Ball State campus helped the situation, but a noticeable chunk of those dollars went away during the holiday and summer breaks when many students went home.

It wasn't out of the realm of possibility that some sort of disaster could shut the university down. Both Marysburg and Muncie would be in a world of hurt if those twenty-five thousand or so people went away at the snap of a finger. It was the kind of thought that Eddie admitted kept him up at night.

It was the kind of worry that Darcy was now saddled with.

"At the risk of sounding like I'm beating a dead horse, why would the Hobbit be so shortsighted? He owns two stores, for the love of Nirvana."

Charlotte shrugged. "Money. How do you think he can afford two shops?"

"Never really thought about it. He doesn't have any competition and he's got a loyal customer base. Especially for the comics store. I see the same people in there all the time."

"You're right. But it's also because of his location. He's been there for years. The rent's cheap thanks to the lease he signed ages ago. Plus, he's a few blocks off the main drag, so he doesn't get the traffic like we do."

It was like a light bulb flared to life above Darcy's head. She smiled.

"Now I get it. His expenses are low and he wants to keep it that way."

"Exactly. The beautification push was like a gentrification test case. Once that got passed, the door could be opened for development in ways this town hasn't seen in years."

Darcy drummed her fingers on the glass countertop. Over the last eighteen months, Eddie had given her a thorough education in the world of running a small business. At the time, she thought her mentor was simply wanting to ease up on his workload. She'd had no idea what his endgame had actually been.

Regardless of the man's reasons for them, his teachings hadn't been ignored. And Darcy was relieved she'd given them her fullest attention. She understood how many small businesses had profit margins thinner than a drum skin. An increase in expenses without a way to counter them with additional revenue could cripple a business.

Even put it out of business.

"The Hobbit saw the beautification push as a threat to his bottom line," Darcy said.

"Exactly. Short-sighted, I know. But then, nobody's ever accused him of being a financial wizard, only a gaming one. He does have an amazing knowledge of everything about *Game of Thrones*, though." Charlotte took a couple of CDs a customer had left on the sales counter and returned them to their proper location on the sales floor.

"Good for him. GoT is my jam. I only wish it wasn't so graphic with the violence. Anyway, now that we're talking about it, I remember Eddie mentioned a list of beautification projects he wanted the city to do." She told Charlotte about the gas station on the edge of the business district that had been closed almost a decade. "If they knocked that down and replaced it with something nice, and that fit in with the existing buildings, do you think the Hobbit would be opposed to that?"

"Totally. The more gentrified the area becomes, the more attractive the older, less expensive buildings become to purchase and renovate. Then the existing tenants are forced to pay more for rent or move out."

"Good golly, Miss Molly." A shiver went down Darcy's spine as a scenario played out in her head. "Is there anything in the Marysburg business world you don't know about?"

Charlotte laughed. "Working at the accounting firm, I never turned down work when one of the partners sent it my way. I thought that was the way to get ahead. Instead, I ended up getting burned out. I did keep my eyes and ears open, though. Learned a lot about the Marysburg business community that way."

"In that case, I'm glad you're on my side." Darcy gave Charlotte a fist bump. "You are, right?"

"Indeed, I am." She pointed a finger at Darcy. "Provided you don't cross me. In my head, I like to think I'd make a pretty fearsome enemy."

"Message received. I'll be in the back if you need me."

Darcy headed for the office deep in thought. The whiteboard needed updating.

What if the Hobbit thought Eddie's revitalization efforts put his businesses at risk? Maybe he confronted Eddie, they argued, and he stabbed him with the fake letter opener. Then he positioned the opener so it looked like Eddie took his own life and made off with the real one. With his experience in collectibles, especially the way cool superhero merch he had at the comics store, he could probably sell it with ease.

Diabolical.

A while later, there was a knock on the door.

"Hey, Boss. What is up?" Peter grinned. When they first met, the young man had been in braces. He'd been out of them for a few months and flashed his million-dollar smile every chance he got.

"Adding new inventory into the system." She pointed to a plastic milk crate on the desk that was holding two dozen records. "Want to put those out for me?"

"Yah, mon." He reached for the milk crate, but Darcy put a hand over it.

"Hold on." I've got something for you." She handed him a package wrapped in a brown paper bag. It was square and flat.

He pulled out a record and let out a little whoop. "No way! Toots and the Maytals. Thanks."

"A little thank you for your hard work the past few days."

Peter's grandmother had emigrated from Jamaica and the island still held a great influence over the family. From brightly colored clothing to spicy food to reggae-infused music, the Douglas family celebrated its Caribbean roots with pride. It was the young man's dream to visit the island when he wasn't under the watchful gaze of a parent. Until then, he was content with immersing himself in Jamaican music and borrowing turns of phrase from his grandma.

"This is too cool. Can I put it on the turntable out front?"

"Sure, but not too loud. And no dancing on the chairs. We don't need a repeat of that fiasco."

A few months ago, he'd gotten a little too wrapped up in a Peter Tosh record and got up on a chair to dance. The chair slipped out from under him, and he landed on his backside with a scary *thwap*. Luckily for all, especially Peter, he escaped with a bruised tailbone and scraped elbows. A sign now hung above the store's entrance that said *Chair Dancing Prohibited*.

"My feet will stay on the floor." He saluted and skipped out of the room.

Darcy laughed. Giving Peter the album was a little thing. Yet, his reaction filled her with warmth. Acts of kindness made the world such a better place. Eddie had done them often. She made a vow to do the same.

She couldn't wait to see Izzy. There was a gift waiting for her, too.

Her phone's ringtone interrupted her thoughts. The number was Liam's. Normally, he communicated via text. Curious about why he was calling, she pressed accept.

"I thought I'd call and check in on the jeep. Any problems?"

"Nope. Purrs like Ringo after he's had his favorite dinner. Do you always call customers after a repair job?"

"For bigger jobs like yours, yes. We started doing it first of the year. Trying to be really customer-service-focused. What do you think?"

"Actually, I kind of like it. I detest those e-mail surveys I get. When you don't give someplace nine or ten stars, they want you to write an essay why not. I ain't got time for that."

He laughed. It was a rich, rolling baritone that was full of mirth.

"That's exactly what I told our general manager. Only two customers were unhappy with the work when I called them. One even started yelling. Thanks to the calls, we were able to take care of their problems and now they're satisfied. Can't do that with a survey."

"Well, I promise you that if Rusty starts giving me problems, I'll call you. And I won't yell." There was a pause on the line. After a few seconds, it got awkward. "I'm at work, so is there anything else?"

"Yeah, I was also wondering how you're doing." He paused again. "You know, with everything going on."

A lump formed in Darcy's throat. Liam had been an unwavering source of goodness in her life. He was like one of those guards with the big, black hats in England guarding the queen. Silent, content to be in the background, but always nearby.

It wasn't in her nature to be open about her feelings with others. It made her feel way too vulnerable. But it was also something she was trying to improve upon. It couldn't hurt to be honest with him.

"Could be better. I mean, I lost my boss and my hero. Eddie meant more to me than I'll ever be able to put into words." She let out a jagged breath. "I'm trying to keep my act together for everyone here at the shop, but when I stop to think, even for a second, it starts to really hurt. I mean, if not for him, I probably wouldn't be here."

"I'm sorry. I really am." He left it at that.

She appreciated the simple sincerity. All too often, people tried too hard to tell her how sorry they were. Sorry for elbow injury. Sorry for her being kicked out of the band. Sorry for her struggle with alcohol.

They all talked *way* too much when expressing their feelings. The excess words never helped. Simplicity, brevity, like what Liam had expressed, did help.

"Thanks. It's a constant struggle, but I'm taking it one minute, one hour, one day, at a time."

"I've got an idea." His voice took on a tone that seemed like the sun had broken through a thick blanket of clouds. "Let me grab some cuts from the market and I'll make dinner on your grill. We can hang out and shoot the bull. I'll get something for Ringo, too."

She wanted to say no. It had been her default answer to invitations like this for so long. Saying no was easier, less complicated. Then she looked at her phone. It was a little after five. She'd been on the go non-stop since Monday. Some time to kick back couldn't hurt.

"You handle the grill. I'll handle the sides." They agreed to meet in an hour, then Darcy ended the call.

For the first time in days, the muscles between her shoulder blades didn't feel like they were tied up in steel knots.

A little while later, Darcy and Liam were lounging on the concrete patio in her back yard. She nibbled on a carrot stick while he fed Ringo tiny bites of grilled chicken. The sun was setting behind a smattering of puffy clouds, turning the sky from an azure blue into a brilliant shade of orange. A light breeze came from the south, bringing warmth that promised a lovely Spring evening.

For the moment, all was right with the world.

Darcy took a sip of water from a plastic cup. It was splashed with the logo of the local chain, HotBox Pizza. At last count, she owned two dozen of the cups. They held twenty ounces of her favorite drink, lasted forever, and were dishwasher safe for the glorious occasion when she would own one of those appliances. Who needed fine glassware when you could have HotBox cups? Not Darcy.

"If you keep feeding him chicken, he's gonna get fat. And he might try to follow you home."

Liam chuckled. "As if. I was going to give him some sirloin, but you ate all of that. I couldn't let him go hungry."

"Hey, I'm a hard-working woman. I need the calories."

"Wish I could say the same." He patted his belly as Ringo devoured another morsel. "How *are* you doing? Really? And don't give me any fake 'I'm going okay' B.S."

Darcy ran her fingers through her hair as she groaned. When she needed to confide in someone, Eddie had been the person she turned to. Could she allow Liam to step into that role now? They'd been friends since freshman year in college. She trusted him. He'd kept his distance when she was at her worst but had never severed contact. Once she started on the road toward sobriety, he'd been there to lend a hand whenever she needed it.

And he'd managed to keep Rusty running. In the early days, often at his own expense. When a tire went flat or a headlight went out, he'd taken care of it. No questions asked. Now, here he was again, at the ready to give her a hand up when she needed it.

"I'm doing pretty bad. My boss was murdered but the police are convinced it was suicide. I've got four people who are depending on me to keep the store open. And I have a cat who's going to want to eat nothing but gourmet chicken from now on."

As if on cue, Ringo pawed at Liam's leg and let out a pitiful-sounding *meow*.

"I gotta hand it to you, Darc. That's a full plate." Liam dropped a tiny chunk of chicken in front of Ringo. "Have you had a chance to think about a game plan?"

"Yep. I'm going to figure out who murdered Eddie. After that, everything else will fall into place." She got to her feet. "Want to help?"

Without a moment's hesitation, Liam stood up. "What do you need?"

She rubbed her hands together. Then she cracked a half-smile. It wasn't one of happiness. It was one of determination.

People were lining up by her side. It gave her another strange feeling. One of belonging. All along, amazing folks like Liam and Charlotte and Hank and Renee had been by her side. She simply hadn't recognized their willingness to stand by her. With each passing day, it was becoming more obvious that she should have taken their outstretched hands much earlier.

If these good folks believed in her, then it was high time for Darcy to start believing in herself.

"You know a lot of people. Find out everything you can about Todd Meadows, Jasmine Longoria, and the Hobbit, especially their business interests."

"Do you think one of them did it?"

"I'm not sure. I do know one thing, though. I won't let whoever murdered Eddie get away with that. You can take that to the bank."

Chapter Twelve

Darcy was roused from a deep sleep the next morning by Ringo pawing at her nose.

"Come on, man." She batted his paw away. "If you want more chicken, go find Liam."

The cat responded by bumping his head against her hand. It was one of the ways he let her know it was time for a head scratch. She obliged. After a minute or so, he gave her hand a tiny bite to let her know he'd had enough and leapt from the bed.

The wind-up clock on her nightstand read 6:50. In the past, Darcy would have fed Ringo and gone back to bed for a couple of hours. In the past, Darcy wasn't in charge at the record store, though.

"Eddie always said the early bird gets the worm. Guess it's time to find out." With a grumble, she threw back the covers and followed her cat to get breakfast. The alarm was set to go off at seven, anyway.

A few minutes later, with a mug of English Breakfast tea in her hand, Darcy stepped outside. The first golden rays of daylight were peeking over the horizon. As the sun began to rise, birds started singing. It was as if the local wildlife knew it was going to be a glorious day and didn't want to miss it.

She held her mug close to her nose before taking a drink. The aroma of the potent brew tickled her nostrils. The steam helped clear out her sinuses. When she took a sip, she let the tea rest on her tongue before swallowing. It was a full, rich flavor that, in the past, she rarely had taken the time to appreciate.

"I need to change that. Guess there's something to be said for getting up early, after all."

With a chuckle, she ambled down toward the water. The leisurely flow of Mary's Creek was soothing and almost hypnotic. She took a seat on a plastic chair she'd bolted to the deck and became still.

This spot was her Listening Point. It was where she went to block out all the noise from the world and commune with nature. Her version of meditation. She didn't do it often enough, but when she did, she always ended the moments of solitude feeling better.

Little did she know how much she was going to need that peace of mind she'd just obtained.

She pulled into a parking spot behind the record store at nine o'clock. With an hour to go before opening, her goal was to use a solid portion of the time updating the store's social media accounts. Normally, she scheduled posts every Monday. It was one of many tasks that had been put off. If she was going to walk the boss walk, she needed to get back on schedule.

She was whistling a Grace Potter tune as she strolled toward the front of the building. The melody died on her lips once she turned the corner.

Rafe Majors was standing by the entrance, scrolling through his phone.

The only time he ever showed up at Marysburg Music was to ask his stepdad for something. Usually money. His presence couldn't be good. Still, there was no reason to be antagonistic. He might have helpful information about Eddie. Maybe that was why he was here.

"Morning, Rafe." She gave him a nod as she unlocked the door. "What brings you by this fine morning?"

The man took a pull on a vaping pipe. He blew out a cloud of water vapor before answering. It had a cloying, sweet smell. Like bubblegum. He grinned in a way that made her skin crawl.

"Two things. The old man's memorial service is tomorrow."

"Thank you." She'd seen the announcement online the day before. It was no surprise he hadn't informed her earlier, despite his promise to.

"Also, this is his will." He pulled a folded group of papers out of his coat. "We need to talk."

So much for my social media posts. She turned the alarm off and waved for him to follow her to the office.

"I'll cut to the chase," he said as they got seated in the office. "He left the record store to me. I'm the owner now."

A wave of nausea powerful enough to make Darcy want to barf coursed through her. It was like handing the keys to the castle to a pirate. It couldn't be. Eddie wouldn't be so cruel.

"You mind if I take a look?" She pointed at the papers in Rafe's hand. "I'm sure everything's in order, but it's like Eddie used to say, 'Trust, but verify.'"

Rafe furrowed his eyebrows in apparent confusion. The fool evidently hadn't been paying attention when his U.S. History class covered the nineteen-eighties.

"Read it and weep." He flipped the document at her. It spun like a frisbee until it landed on the desktop in front of Darcy.

With deliberate slowness, she smoothed out the pages. It was to give herself a few seconds to focus on maintaining composure as much as to annoy Rafe.

There wasn't time to read the document from front to back in detail, so she scanned it until her gaze landed on the relevant sections. They were as disheartening as they were to the point.

Eddie's house and the building housing the store went to Rafe. A fund was to be established at the high school to support students participating in the music program. The rest of Eddie's possessions went to his other stepson, Wesley, except for one thing.

The collectible Beatles album went to Darcy.

She blinked away tears that wanted to burst forth. She wouldn't give Rafe the satisfaction of seeing how badly hurt she was, though.

Without much enthusiasm, she flipped through the rest of the document. Rafe's chuckles as she neared the final page drove away the sadness. It was replaced with her resolve to catch Eddie's murderer. None of this would be happening if someone hadn't taken his life.

As she stared at the final page, something started niggling at her. Then she saw it.

The date.

She went to the front page of the will and took her time reading it. If she was right, everything else could wait.

Eventually, she smiled. Yep, the language was clear enough once she took the time to really read it. Rafe wasn't going to be happy. That was for sure. First things first, though.

"It's recent." She tapped her index finger on the top page. "You sure it's legit?"

He blinked and leaned back in the chair. Her verbal slap in the face had done its job. He didn't seem angry. More like surprised. Evidently, it was a thought that had never occurred to Rafe.

"Yeah. I got it from the old man's lawyer earlier today." He ran his thumb and index finger around his mouth. "What are you trying to say?"

"The timing's interesting." She pulled the document naming her the president of the company from a file folder. "In fact, it was the day after he filed this with the Secretary of State's office."

With a furrowed brow, he studied the filing. After a while, he handed it back to Darcy.

"What's that supposed to mean?" He crossed his arms and even attempted to puff his chest out. He failed.

"It means that the building may go to you, but I own the business." She looked at the clock on the wall. It was a handmade vinyl record cut into the shape of the Rolling Stones famous lips and tongue logo. "I've got a store open. Since you'll own the building, you've got a stake in the store's success. I could use your help. Let's get to work."

Without giving him a chance to object, she gave him a stack of used CDs. "These need to be put out on the floor. They all go in the *Rock* section. Everything's organized alphabetically by band or artist's last name. These are all recent releases, so you can slot them in front of the artists' other discs."

A little while later, Darcy was tidying up the front of the store when Hank arrived. His jaw practically hit the textured concrete floor when he saw Rafe.

"What's he doing here?" Hank kept his voice low but couldn't mask his incredulity.

"Came by to tell me he's the new owner of the building. I told him since he was here, we could use the help. I'm going to make him part of the team."

"You are?" Rafe and Hank said at the same time.

"Why not? Rafe, you need a job. I need the help." Darcy went to the back room and emerged a few minutes later with a stack of red Marysburg Music T-shirts. She placed them on top of the remaining CDs that were in the man's hands. "When you're finished with the music, you can put the shirts out. They go in the cubbyholes across the aisle from the register. Hank, why don't you get the front end ready for opening."

"What are you going to do," Rafe asked. He sounded like a whiny six-year-old.

"I have Chief Executive Officer duties to attend to." She exchanged a glance with Hank and returned to the office.

With a little spring in her step. She had her social media posting to return to.

The store had an advertising budget. It was only a few thousand dollars, though. Most went to Record Store Day and to help sponsor the Marysburg Summer Festival. In all honesty, thanks to Eddie's larger-than-life personality, the store never had to do a lot of promotion. People adored the man, so he was able to let word of mouth do the lion's share of the advertising work.

A few years ago, though, he asked Darcy to set up social media accounts for the store. She'd been happy to do so but was curious to know why. His answer had been enigmatic back then.

"Time moves on and things change. We should be prepared to change, too," he'd told her with a wry smile.

Now, as those words bubbled up in her memory, she realized they were, more than anything, prophetic.

"Holy smokes. He was preparing me. He was planning for me to be in the big chair all along." She barked out a laugh so loud, Hank opened the door to check on her.

"Everything okay, Darce? I was afraid you stubbed your toe or something."

"It's all good. Had one of those moments when you realize something important. You know, an epistle."

He gave her a blank stare for a moment, then shook his head. "I think you mean epiphany, dear."

"Epiphany, right. Thanks, Hank." She turned her focus to the computer monitor, chuckling as she did so. Word choice had never been a strong suit. She jotted down a note to get a dictionary. Eddie had always proofread her posts. She didn't have that luxury anymore. That was okay. Things were going to work out. She was going to make sure of it.

A few hours later, Darcy was perusing a list of upcoming new releases, debating what to order, when raised voices from the sales floor caught her attention.

"Is there a problem?" She marched toward the sales counter, the heavy *thunk* of her combat boots echoing around the store. Normally, a situation that involved tempers flaring involved a return or exchange that was leaving a customer dissatisfied.

She came to a stop and looked around. There were no customers, but Rafe and Hank were hovering over the cash register with fire in their eyes.

"Yes, there's a problem. Rafe keeps trying to take money from the register. I've told him three times that's inappropriate," Hank said.

Darcy stepped between the men. The register was closed. Either Rafe hadn't been able to open it or Hank had closed it on him.

"Rafe, is this true?" She used her voice as if she was a teacher addressing an elementary-aged student. Chronologically, she was younger than Rafe. Maturity-wise, she was decades older.

"What of it?" He crossed his arms and stuck out his lower lip. It took all of Darcy's self-control to refrain from laughing at the six-foot-tall child-man.

"The old man didn't care. Besides, I've been working my tail off all morning. I'm starving and need some lunch."

"Well, I'm sorry, but Eddie's not here anymore." She took a deep breath. "Like it or not, I'm in charge now. And I say all cash needs to be accounted for."

"What am I supposed to do, then? I don't have any money right now."

Hank's hand moved toward his hip pocket. Darcy placed her hand on his elbow. When their gaze met, she shook her head. It wasn't much, but it was enough to get the message across. This was her issue. She'd deal with it.

"Come with me." She made her way to the office. The heavy sound of Rafe's footfalls behind her confirmed she had the situation under control. At least for the moment.

When she reached the office, she stepped aside to let him enter first and closed the door behind her. Then she started rummaging through her purse, which was really a small, triangular-shaped backpack.

"Here." She held out a twenty-dollar bill. "Take it and go get yourself some lunch. Wouldn't want you to starve to death in my store."

"Your store?" He practically spat out the words but still snatched the money out of Darcy's hand.

"Yes, my store." She placed her hands on the desk and leaned toward him. "Whether you like it or not, my store. I don't have the money to help you out like your stepdad did, so that's a one-time offer. I'll make a deal with you. If you come back after lunch and finish a full day's work, I'll write you a check for your time on Sunday. Then, on Monday, when the bank's open, you can cash it. Deal?"

He shoved the bill into his pocket. "How much an hour?"

"Twelve." Eddie paid the hourly staff fifteen an hour. Darcy wasn't ready to pay Rafe that much. She wanted to make a good-faith gesture, though.

"I'll think about it." He got up to leave. "Soon enough, I'll have all the money I need."

"Don't hold your breath. It'll be months before Eddie's estate is settled." She shifted her gaze to the computer monitor. "Now, if you'll excuse me, I have a record store to run."

Rafe attempted to slam the door on his way out, but only managed to get his jacket caught on the handle. Darcy had allowed herself one under-her-breath chuckle while he struggled to get loose, but no more. One of the many lessons she'd learned in recent years was that everyone had problems they were dealing with. Simply because people couldn't see them, didn't mean they weren't there.

She didn't like Rafe. She didn't trust him, either. That didn't change the fact that the man's stepfather was gone. Sure, Rafe had his part-time job. But Eddie was the one who made sure he had a roof over his head, food in his belly, and clean clothes on his back.

That safety net was gone. The sudden change had to be weighing heavily on the man. God knew Darcy was struggling enough. She wouldn't condemn Rafe.

She would look into him, though.

The way he'd waltzed into the office and flashed the will reminded her of the swagger she and her bandmates had after they signed their first record deal. Cocky, bordering on arrogant.

She'd knocked him down a peg when she pointed out that he didn't own the business. She'd knocked him down another when she informed him any proceeds from the will would be paid out down the road.

In the moment, it had felt oh, so good. The moment was over, though. Rafe would be back at some point. She'd need to be ready.

As she refocused on writing social media blurbs, her mind kept returning to the man. It made as much sense for him to murder Eddie as it would be for her to kick a hole in her bass drum because she didn't like the way it sounded.

And yet, Rafe wasn't good at taking the long view. On anything. If he had money in his pocket, he spent it. What if Eddie had finally told Rafe enough was enough? It wasn't impossible to imagine the younger man flying off in a rage and committing the horrific act. Especially if he thought he was in line for a sizeable inheritance.

Darcy stopped typing to ponder a question. Did Rafe have a way to get into the store after hours?

She'd need to confirm with Charlotte whether Eddie had asked her to lock the door on her way out. With the person coming in later, it was possible Eddie wanted the door left unlocked. That would be out of character, but not out of the realm of possibility. If he had asked her to lock it, she'd need to do an inventory of store keys.

"Got a minute, Hank," she asked as she re-entered the sales floor.

He put up his index finger. He was in the middle of ringing up a sale. When he slid the purchase, two albums into a brown paper bag, she approached the counter.

"What's up?"

"You've got your key to the building, right?" Darcy showed him her key.

"Yep." He pulled a set of keys out of his pocket. "Here it is. Thinking of changing the locks?"

"I dunno. Maybe. First, I'm trying to make sure all of the keys are accounted for. Eddie kept a list. There are five of them. One is in a safety deposit box at the bank. The keys you, me, and Char have, makes four. Do you know where Eddie's key might be?"

"No. I assumed it was on him the night of...," he shrugged, "you know."

"On his keyring, yeah. But we don't know that for sure, do we? What if the murderer somehow used his key to get in the store that night?"

The older man drummed his fingers on the counter. "With the surveillance cam turned off at the time of the, you know, I suppose it's possible. But surely Eddie would have noticed if his key to the building was missing, don't you think? And who's to say it was Eddie's key? For all we know, it could have been yours, mine, or Char's."

Darcy scratched her forehead. "Very true. If the murderer got in the store that way, they must have made a copy at some point beforehand and returned it without him knowing."

"Who would want to do that, though? More to the point, who'd be willing to risk getting caught doing that?"

She smiled. "I know the exact person. And he left here a little bit ago with twenty bucks that I gave him out of the goodness of my heart."

Chapter Thirteen

The following morning, Darcy was up before her alarm went off. As she swung her legs off the bed, Ringo was nowhere to be found. Normally, she had to roust him out of bed. Today, the only evidence of his presence during the night was a slight, roundish indentation in the comforter by the foot of the bed.

She found him in the living room, sitting atop her threadbare futon that functioned most of the time as a couch. He was gazing out the window, keeping an eye on the birds flitting around the yard.

"Couldn't sleep either, huh?"

He turned his head to her and blinked once. Then went back to his surveillance. His tail swishing from side to side every now and then was his only other movement.

Sometimes, Darcy wished she could bottle the serenity her cat exuded. It would come in handy, especially today. Eddie's memorial service was in five hours.

"How about some breakfast, buddy? I got something special for you at the store last night." She went to the kitchen, letting out a laugh when a light *thunk* came from the living room. Ringo might enjoy watching the birds, but he enjoyed eating a whole lot more.

With a little flourish, she peeled back the foil covering of gourmet chicken chunks. Ringo responded with a loud *mrrow* and pawed her leg until she placed the food on the floor next to his water. She'd barely let go when he attacked the bowl with the gusto of an energetic kitten, not a laidback, old tomcat.

While Ringo gobbled down his breakfast, Darcy made herself a cup of tea. Its citrusy aroma was a definite mood booster. She hummed a soul tune by Bill Withers while she spread strawberry cream cheese on a wheat bagel.

Before she sat down to dine, she took a pen and notepad from a drawer. It was going to be a full day, and an emotional one, so she wanted to make sure she didn't forget any of the tasks she needed to complete.

The first thing after breakfast was to figure out what to wear at the memorial service. The store didn't have a dress code, so her wardrobe mostly consisted of jeans and casual shirts. Three glittery tops from her Pixie Dust days that she couldn't bear to part with were hanging in the back of the closet. She'd put on fifteen pounds since she got sober, now tipping the scale at one hundred, thirty, so those items weren't an option.

"What do you think of this, dude?" She pulled a long-sleeved, cotton top off a hanger. It was sky blue, which was a plus. Eddie liked sky blue.

The cat jumped onto the bed and gave the shirt a sniff. He rubbed his head on one sleeve, then curled up to take a nap. Evidently, he approved.

"Outstanding. I'll wear it with my tan chinos. Thanks, dude."

A little bit later, after an extra-long shower so she could give her hair a thorough conditioner treatment, she adjusted the shirt's collar as she took a final look at herself in the mirror. The reflection made her smile. Her hair, which reached her shoulders when not in a ponytail, had a pleasant sheen to it. Her skin was still tanned from her trip. Her brown eyes had a little sparkle to them.

She looked healthy. The weight she'd put on meant she wasn't skin and bones any longer. Sure, she was thin, but the term that came to mind now was wiry. It was a good thing. Something Eddie would be proud of. And that thought was the one she'd hang onto to get through the service.

But first, she had to get through a few hours of having the store open.

She arrived with mixed emotions. She'd given the team the day off to attend the service or mourn him in their own way but didn't think she could afford to keep the store closed all day. Among the most recent social media posts she'd scheduled were ones alerting the public that the store would only be open from ten to noon, in observance of Eddie's passing.

CHAPTER THIRTEEN

Saturdays were Marysburg Music's busiest days. There were times during the dead of winter when the snow and ice reduced the number of customers during the workweek to fewer than Darcy could count on one hand. Saturdays weren't like that, though. Regardless of the weather, on that day of the week, a steady stream of traffic kept the team, and the cash register, busy.

Opening for two hours wouldn't come close to recouping the losses that would come from being closed the rest of the day. It would help a little, though. As she unlocked the front door and turned off the alarm, she stood a little taller.

She was thinking like the boss.

The record store needed to survive. Her team needed to remain employed. Those two facts needed to remain Darcy's main focus. She'd continue the search for Eddie's murderer. She wouldn't let her hunt for justice jeopardize the store, though. Catching Eddie's killer but letting Marysburg Music go under in the process would be a pyrrhic victory.

Not good enough.

Good enough would be ensuring the person who took her mentor's life ended up behind bars *and* guaranteeing Marysburg Music remained a vital part of the community for years to come.

Was it a tall order? Sure. Could she do it? There was only one way to find out. Just like there'd been only one way to get sober. Taking things one day at a time.

It turned out letting folks know the store was closing at noon was a good thing. From the minute Darcy turned on the *Open* sign at ten o'clock until she turned it back off at a quarter after twelve, she rang up sale after sale. A heartwarming number of customers were old friends of Eddie in town for the memorial service.

One man, with salt-and-pepper hair, round glasses, and a goatee bought her entire selection of fifteen Bob Marley albums. When he placed the stack of vinyl on the counter, she raised an eyebrow.

"Professor Maxwell was my music teacher back in the day. He also introduced me to reggae and other music from all over the world."

"That's really cool." Darcy placed the records in a canvas Marysburg Music bag the gentleman had included in the purchase. "What do you do now?"

"I own a nightclub in New Orleans. Live music seven nights a week." He handed Darcy a business card. "If you're ever in the Big Easy, come by. We can raise a glass to Big Ed."

"I'd like that." Darcy tacked the business card on the corkboard behind her. It would remind her how far and wide Eddie's influence had extended.

New Orleans with its one-of-a-kind music scene was one of the places on Darcy's bucket list. She'd been there twice with Pixie Dust but had barely looked around while walking between the tour bus and the venue. That didn't count.

With a nod, she promised herself she'd make the trek to New Orleans, have a drink to salute Eddie, and enjoy a few nights of New Orleans-infused jazz and funk. As for the drink? She'd have it without alcohol.

Living life itself was intoxicating enough.

The memorial service was held at the Marysburg Center for the Arts. Situated in the middle of the town's main street, two blocks from the record store, the art deco-styled building got its start in the thirties as a movie theater. With a large foyer that featured silver framed posters of upcoming films and a massive concession stand, the theater had provided a large serving of Hollywood-style glitz to the small community.

As the years went by, and multiplexes superseded the grand old cinemas, the Marysburg fell out of favor. For most of the eighties, it stood silent, abandoned by the changing entertainment preferences of the Central Indiana citizenry. In 1989, it began a brief run as a concert hall. Difficulty in attracting touring acts led to the lights being turned off again in 1996.

It was reborn at the turn of the twenty-first century as a multipurpose performing arts center and had thrived in that role ever since. A community theater group, a dance troupe, and a youth orchestra called the Marysburg its home.

Eddie had played a big role in raising the funds to rehabilitate the Marysburg so it could re-open. After that, he'd been instrumental in establishing an endowment to keep it financially secure. A lot of folks saw it as Eddie's crowning achievement. Darcy couldn't argue with that and thought whoever made the call to hold the service there deserved a tip of the hat.

Amid a buzzing crowd, she quietly slipped into a seat Charlotte had saved for her. It was near the back, but Darcy didn't mind. What mattered to her was that, as she shrugged out of a jacket, her entire team—Hank, Charlotte, Izzy, Peter—was there. Each of them greeted her with a smile.

"Team Marysburg Music, all present and accounted for, Boss," Peter said as he gave her a fist bump.

"I was getting worried you weren't going to make it," Charlotte said. "Hasn't been easy keeping this seat open for you."

"Got here as soon as I could. It was hopping at the store. Had to shoo a couple of customers out the door." She pointed to a group of apparent dignitaries who were being seated way up in the second row. "Those people were the last ones to leave."

Hank opened his mouth, but Izzy shushed him and pointed toward the stage. A man in a dark gray suit and red tie had approached the podium. It was Christopher DeYoung, the Dean of the Ball State School of Music. He'd been a good friend of Eddie and was a frequent visitor to the store.

Charlotte leaned against Darcy. "Glad to see they're doing this right."

Darcy leaned back. "The least they would do."

The service began with a video montage of Eddie through the years. The photos were followed by performances of musical pieces he'd written, then loving tributes from students, friends, and colleagues. There was as much laughter as there were tears. Eddie would have liked that.

No mention was made of the way his life ended. That was good, too. The service was a chance to celebrate his years on the planet, not mourn his passing.

By the time Eddie's elder stepson, Wesley, closed the service with a heartfelt reading of Dylan Thomas' "Do Not Go Gentle Into that Good Night," Darcy had gone through a dozen tissues. Eldred Maxwell had lived a grand life. The service had done that life justice.

On their way out of the theater, a young man sporting a Ball State Music

School pin handed her a piece of paper.

"What's that?" Hank looked at the paper over her shoulder.

"An invitation to a concert presented by the students and faculty of the Ball State Trombone Studio. It's over on campus. In an hour." She handed it to Hank.

"We should go. You don't have to get back to the shop, do you?"

"No. I have some things I have to do around the house, though. It's been a crazy week. know what I mean, jellybean?"

"I do." He hugged her. "And I shall enjoy the show for the both of us. If you need anything or anyone, I'm only a text message away."

She gave him a hug in return. The reminder to contact him wasn't a throwaway offer. He knew today was an especially tough day for her. The kind of day where being alone with only her thoughts to keep herself company wasn't a good thing.

"I'll be okay. Promise. See you at work tomorrow morning."

She made her goodbyes to the rest of the group, then asked Izzy to walk with her to her jeep. "I've got something I've been meaning to give you."

Once there, Darcy withdrew a pink greeting card-sized envelope from under the passenger seat.

"What is it?" Izzy's blue eyes were wide with curiosity.

"A little token of appreciation for all you've done for the store. Go ahead. Open it."

The young woman let out a little gasp when she read Darcy's note. "Private lessons? For real?"

Darcy shrugged. "I know how important private lessons are at this stage of your musical career. This teacher's a friend of mine from my college days. You're covered for a weekly lesson until school starts in August. Think of this as a little thank you for all your hard work this week."

Izzy shook her head. "Wow. The band director at school's been telling everyone if we want to make it into wind ensemble, we need to think about private lessons. I was going to use my paycheck to pay for them."

"Well, now you can put that money to good use in other areas. Maybe even save it for lessons down the road."

Darcy was aware of the young woman's financial situation at home. Izzy's mom was a nurse at the local hospital. Her dad took off when she was nine and her little sister was six. The three of them were happy together but sometimes money got tight. And pursuing an interest in music could get expensive for a high school student.

Izzy was a hard worker and an all-around good kid who had some talent. Darcy wanted her to have the same opportunities in music that she'd enjoyed at that age. If spending a few hundred dollars of her own money helped Izzy improve to the point where she could get admitted to a college to study music, then it was money well-spent. It was an investment in the girl's future.

The girl bounced up and down on her toes. "I can't wait to tell my mom. She'll be stoked."

"Yeah, about that. If you could keep this between you, your mom, and your instructor, I'd appreciate it." The gift was much more generous than the one she'd given Peter, so she didn't want word to get out. The young man didn't have the financial pressures Izzy did, though. Still, Darcy didn't want anyone to think she was playing favorites.

"No problem. I'm going to call the instructor as soon as I get home. Thanks."

Izzy dashed off, practically at a sprint. As she rounded a corner and left Darcy's field of vision, the sun peeked out from behind a cloud. It warmed Darcy's face, even as another tear escaped and ran down her cheek. It was like Eddie was sending her a message. Things were going to be okay.

"Darn right they will be, Eddie. And that's a fact."

* * *

A few hours later, Darcy wiped a bead of sweat from her brow and plopped down on a chair in the kitchen. She took a long swig of lime-flavored water, then let out a long belch.

Ringo, who'd been getting himself a drink, pinned an ear back in response to the offending sound.

"Sorry, dude. I know it's not very ladylike. Then again, you should know me and the term 'ladylike' rarely cross paths."

While the cat returned to his drink, Darcy leaned back in her chair and let her heart rate return to normal. She'd finished hauling boxes of ceramic tile and bags of grout into the bathroom. The rest of the day was going to be spent replacing the old Linoleum floor with six-inch, black and white tile to create a checkerboard look. The walls were going to be covered in the same tile. They'd be white, with a horizontal row of black and white in checkerboard style at shoulder height.

It was going to be a long, sweat-filled project. She'd also really have to focus on what she was doing to make sure she did it right. In other words, it was the perfect task to keep her mind on things other than Eddie's murder.

She'd read five different blog posts to learn how to do the project. It would be a challenge. It was the kind of challenge she enjoyed, though.

She'd done most of the rehabilitation work around the house and took pride in doing it herself instead of hiring someone to do it for her. Sure, it saved money. But there was something gratifying, deep down in her soul, she got from taking something worn out or broken and fixing it.

Other people like Eddie and her family had worked hard to put the broken pieces of her life and career back together. She wasn't big on self-analysis but rehabbing her little home by herself was a demonstration that, after being healed, she could heal something else.

It was a good workout, too. Physical exercise and mental health often went hand in hand, after all. Like the old saying went, she'd come a long way, baby.

By the time she hauled the pile of worn, cracked Linoleum flooring out the back door, Darcy's back was sweat-soaked. Her biceps had a dull ache from all the scraping she'd done during the removal process. She chuckled at the notion that her parents would have called the sensation a good ache. One that came from the result of hard work or vigorous exercise.

"Y'all weren't wrong." She dropped her dusty load into a trash barrel. "But I wouldn't mind if it had been easier."

After an hour cleaning and ensuring the floor base was level, she spent the rest of the day installing the tile. At first, she hummed the melodies of the pieces that had been performed at the memorial service. After a while, though, as she got into a steady rhythm of spacing, then setting the tiles, her mind drifted to thoughts of Rafe.

The day before, the man hadn't returned to the store after lunch. No big surprise, there. Darcy had worked him pretty hard before he made his escape. She was confident he didn't work that hard at the library.

His work ethic, or lack thereof, wasn't her biggest concern, though. The man had zero self-control when it came to money. If he had a dollar in his pocket and it was ten below zero in the middle of a snowstorm, he'd find a reason to go out and spent it that minute.

Now, he was being given the deeds to both a house and a commercial building. While Eddie had paid cash for the building, the LLC he formed as a holding company had taken out a mortgage to pay for updated LED lighting and a new HVAC system.

Darcy had helped Eddie with the books enough to know the store made a monthly rent payment to the LLC to cover certain expenses. She knew nothing more about the LLC. Nor did she know who was responsible for paying the building's utility, mortgage, and other bills.

As she cut a piece of tile so it fit against the sink to her satisfaction, she came to a startling realization.

Even if Marysburg Music continued to pay all of its expenses, if Rafe didn't keep up on his end of the bills, the store could still close. It was hard to sell music products when the lights were off and there was no heat.

"Dang it!" The upsetting scenario had distracted her. In turn, she'd cracked the tile. There were a few extras, but not many. "Pay attention, girl. You can only solve one problem at a time."

While that may have been correct with the bathroom project, it wasn't as simple in the bigger picture. She wanted to find Eddie's murderer. She needed to keep the record store open.

Without any idea how long it would take to solve the case, the first couldn't be done without the second. If the store closed, that meant she'd be without income. She needed income to support herself while she looked for clues.

Some people might call the dilemma a conundrum that couldn't be solved.

After she cut the replacement tile to perfection, she made a fist pump. It slipped into place like a puzzle piece. She sat back on her haunches and wiped her hands with a rag. Only a few more tiles to go, then she could do the floor grouting.

"So much for one thing at a time, Ringo." She tossed the rag into the hall. It landed at her cat's front paws. "Forget the haters. I'll do both."

The cat gave her a tiny nod and sauntered away. It was as if he was agreeing with her.

While having her buddy's approval was great, he couldn't help her with one whopper of an issue. If she was going to do both, she was going to have to do it quickly, before Rafe had a chance to mismanage the building into foreclosure.

Chapter Fourteen

The following evening, Darcy eased into a chair with a groan. She dug a ginger ale out of a cooler, then propped her feet up on it. It had been a long, arduous day at work. And she was sore from the tile work the day before. She'd earned this time on the deck and was going to enjoy a cold drink while she watched the water flow by.

She'd been up way too late finishing the job. One of the things she couldn't stand was leaving a job unfinished. Even if it meant staying up until three to get it done. And then getting up at seven when the alarm went off.

She let out a long yawn as she stretched her arms above her head. Two water enthusiasts on kayaks raised their paddles. It was impossible to tell if they were greeting her or mocking her raised arms. To be on the safe side, she made a small wave with one hand.

"God, Ringo, sometimes being sociable is so anxiety-inducing." She tossed a piece of sliced ham to him.

He gobbled up the morsel, then licked his paw. When he was finished cleaning up after his snack, he curled up in a ball by the cooler and closed his eyes.

"I like the way you think, buddy. Less work. More sleep."

Once the kayakers were around the bend, Darcy's sense of quiet serenity returned. It had been an extreme seven days. She shook her head to think at this time seven days ago, she'd just returned from the best vacation ever.

Now, her mentor was gone. She was in charge of her own business. And a murderer was on the loose.

"That, friends, is one whale of a week." She raised her ginger ale to nobody in particular and slugged the last of it down.

A small rock landed on the deck a few feet from her. She turned to see where it had come from.

"Hey, Darc." Liam tipped his Ball State baseball cap to her. "Sorry about the rock. Didn't want to startle you."

"No big. We've got a nice view tonight. Care to join us?"

"Absolutely. I brought snacks."

She took a bag of pretzels and a container of Nutella out of the canvas tote Liam handed to her. "Nice! To what do I owe the honor?"

"I figured after your week from hell, a Snack from the Gods would come in handy." He took a can of sweet tea from the bag as he got settled in a chair next to her.

Darcy laughed as she opened the Nutella container. The hazelnut spread had a heavenly aroma that took her right back to her college days. Growing up, Nutella hadn't been on her radar. Liam introduced it to her one night while studying for an exam. She more than made up for the lost time in the ensuing months.

"How'd you know?" She opened the bag and commenced dipping pretzels straight into the spread.

"That was always your go-to snack when you were stressed out. Like, preparing for an ensemble performance level of stressed out." He helped himself to a small handful of pretzels. "I figured it might come in handy about now."

She chewed on a pretzel covered in the chocolaty spread while she pondered her friend's words. Of course, she'd been under a ton of stress the past week. Everyone at the record store had.

In the past, there'd been tough weeks before, too. Preparing for Record Store Day and Small Business Saturday always left her short on sleep and high on anxiety.

This time, it was different. Liam had seen it. And now that he'd brought it up, she could see it, too. The team at the store, and Jenna for that matter, had probably seen it, too.

So, Liam had arrived and offered his shoulder to lean on. Without insulting her by making a big deal it.

"Thanks." She offered him the Nutella.

His eye went wide at the gesture. He'd known her to value her Nutella stash like a musician valued their first Grammy award.

"Heard the service was nice. Some folks at the garage were talking about it today."

"You know, it was." She gave Ringo's gnarled ear a scratch. "Eddie would have liked it. It was sweet but didn't get so overly sentimental that people wanted to go cry in their beers. God, he was so full of life. One of those people who you think is going to live forever because they can't be bothered with something as trivial as death."

They talked about Eddie for a while. Liam let Darcy do most of the talking. Most of the conversation involved anecdotes about a deed Eddie had done for someone. Like the time a trombone student's horn had been stolen. The next day, a replacement trombone had appeared on her doorstep. Or the time a colleague had lost his partner to cancer. In days, Eddie had collected enough to pay for the funeral expenses.

There were countless more. He always tried to do them anonymously. After a while, though, everyone knew it was Eldred Maxwell who'd done the good dead.

"Did you ever see him lose his temper," Liam asked. "Nothing ever seemed to get under the guy's skin."

"Not very often, but when he was mad, you knew it. Instead of yelling, he'd get real quiet and stare at you for a long time with his arms crossed. The second you'd start to sweat, he'd tell you in a low voice what you'd done wrong and how much you'd disappointed him."

"Oh, man." Liam grimaced. "My grandma was that way. The worst thing ever was when she used the D-word."

"I know, right?"

They sat in a comfortable silence for a while, Ringo content at Darcy's feet. The cat sat up for a moment when a blue jay's call was so loud, he apparently thought it was within striking distance.

Not that he'd ever caught a bird. Mice were another matter. Within a few weeks of taking him in, Darcy's mousetraps were gathering dust. Ringo wasn't as quick as he had been but was still clever and agile enough to keep his crown as the best mouser in the neighborhood.

As the sun began to dip behind the row of trees on the other side of the river, Ringo wandered toward the house.

"No point in sticking around without a sunny spot to lounge in, huh?" Liam tossed a pretzel into his mouth.

"He does love being warm. He'll probably be curled up on my bed when I go back inside."

"It's good you two have each other." He rubbed his chin. "Especially now."

"You're not wrong." She let out a long sigh. "I may have cried myself to sleep with him in my arms a night or two last week."

"One or two? No more?" Liam raised an eyebrow. It was his way of letting Darcy know he wasn't buying what she was selling.

"Okay, every night." She pointed toward the house with her thumb. "Except last night. I think I was asleep the second I hit the bed."

"See? That wasn't so hard, was it? I want to help in any way I can. I can't if you won't be straight with me, okay?"

When she nodded, he raised his drink to her.

"Now, then. Any idea who took Eddie's life?"

"Kind of." She told him about the suspect board in her office. "I've got plenty of suspects, but not many leads. And thank you for believing me that he didn't commit suicide."

"I didn't know him as well as you did, obviously. I knew him well enough that he wouldn't do that. It seemed like he was in a good mental place, know what I mean?"

"I do. I mean, I get that people can hide their true feelings under a shiny veneer. But with as much time as I spent with him, I never saw even the tiniest cracks. Besides, it doesn't make sense that he'd turn the store over to me and then do away with himself. He loved the place. He had big plans. And we have Record Store Day in a few weeks. That day was like Christmas to him."

"And the cops?"

She shook her head. "Kaitlin's satisfied with the suicide determination. Doesn't matter what I think. I'm pretty sure she's holding my past against me."

Liam leaned forward, with his elbows on his knees. "That's b.s. Just because you went through a bad patch years ago doesn't mean the cops should discount what you tell them now. Want me to go talk to her? You know, like as a witness with new information?"

"Nah. I appreciate it. She'd probably decide you were trying to help me and ignore whatever you tell her."

"What about going over her head?"

Darcy picked up a twig Ringo had been batting at. She held it like a drumstick as she tapped her knee with it. The offer was tempting, but…

"I don't want to do that. What if it turns out that she's right? I mean, I think she's wrong. I know she is. But Eddie was a big wheel in town. If the police chief wasn't satisfied, he would have done something by now. No. I need to prove her wrong."

"Then tell me about your suspects."

"Todd needs the store property for his condo project. Without it, the project doesn't go forward and who knows how much he's invested into it already. Rafe's the building's owner now. I don't doubt for a second that he'd sell and roll in all his new cash."

"So, they'd both benefit. Todd's a smooth operator. I see him being more of a poisoner than a stabber. Cleaner that way. For him, at least." He went to the edge of the deck and stared out at the river for a few moments. "Who else?"

"Jasmine. The thing is, what's she get from killing him, besides revenge?"

"The building, if she could talk Rafe into selling to her instead of Todd. That way, she'd get the location she always wanted and screws Todd over in the process. They don't like each other, from what I've heard."

"Why's that?" Darcy joined him at the platform's edge. Having someone to talk the case through was proving helpful.

"They had a fling a while back. That was in between his wives. Story goes that Jasmine didn't appreciate getting thrown over for the young, pretty woman he's married to now."

Todd's second wife was about half the realtor's age. Darcy had chatted with her a few times in the record store. She was friendly and seemed smart, but Darcy couldn't ignore strains of Kanye West's tune "Gold Digger" running through her head whenever she thought of the young Mrs. Meadows.

"Well, nothing like the fury of a woman scorned. Not to mention, Rafe still comes out ahead in that scenario. The only one who doesn't seem to have a connection to Rafe is The Hobbit."

"What's your take on Mr. O'Sullivan?" Liam rubbed at an oil-stained knuckle with his thumb. "And be nice. We're on the same softball team. He's a heckuva catcher."

"I didn't know playing on a rec league team automatically made someone innocent of a crime." The snippy comment was out before Darcy had a chance to pull it back in. "Sorry. That was mean."

"No worries. You've got a lot going on right now. All I'm saying is that he's always been a nice enough guy around me. Sure, he's a little weird, but who isn't? And if he is a murderer, I'd rather know sooner rather than later so I don't have to scramble to find a replacement behind the plate."

He gave her a long blank stare, then cocked his head to the side and shrugged. It was his classic move designed to make Darcy laugh. It worked.

"Glad to see you have your priorities in order."

"Most important position on a softball team." He batted away a gnat. "With that issue out of the way, what *is* your take on him?"

"I know it's a long shot, but I can't help wondering if he got sick of Eddie's revitalization efforts. Hank thinks it's plausible. Then, when I went to his store, I got to see his Three-D printer. It's a cool piece of machinery. Eddie's stab wound had traces of plastic in it. What if the Hobbit printed the murder weapon on his machine?"

"I thought you said they found Eddie's letter opener under the desk, and it had his fingerprints on it."

"I did. That's why Kaitlin says it's suicide. The only way she can explain the plastic fragments in the wound is that they came off the letter opener when Eddie was stabbed."

"Okay." He scratched his forehead. "If that's what happened, where's the real one?"

She shook her head. "I don't know."

"Now, let me get this right. You're suggesting the murderer stabbed Eddie with an exact replica of his letter opener, left the replica at the crime scene, and took the original to make it look like a suicide."

"And stole the Beatles record." She kicked a pebble into the water. "Which was the one thing Eddie left me in his will."

"That stinks on ice. Setting the record theft aside for a second, though, don't you think it was an awful lot of trouble for someone to make an exact duplicate of the letter opener? Why not use the real one?"

"Because the original is valuable. The King himself gave it to Eddie. And the Hobbit, who deals in that kind of stuff, would know that. Have you been in his comic store recently? He's got tons of collectibles. I guarantee you that he'd know how to move it without getting caught."

"Okay, okay." Liam put up his hands in surrender. "I'm not disagreeing with you. I'm only trying to help you think things through. I don't want you to find yourself making an allegation you can't back up. Now, anybody else?

"Claude Ewing, the next-door neighbor."

"I know him. He's one of my regular customers. Keeps his truck and his wife's crossover spotless. What's his deal?"

"He didn't like Eddie's parties. Said they kept him up at night." She shoved her hands into the back pockets of her jeans. "I'll admit, it's not much of a motive, especially because his wife and Eddie were friends."

"Yeah, neighbors can be a hassle sometimes. Has anyone ever complained about your drumming?"

"Nope. Which is one of the reasons I like this place. That, and the solitude so I can meditate in the mornings. I can be loud when I want and not bother anyone, or I can be quiet and not be bothered by anyone. The best of both worlds."

"Nice." He gave her a fist bump." Anybody else on your suspect list?"

"Nope. It's already long enough. Hopefully, the killer's on it." She picked up her cooler. "On a lighter note, want to see how the project turned out? I think you'll be impressed."

He gestured with his hand for Darcy to go first. "I always am. After you."

With a little spring in her step, Darcy led Liam into the house. She was grateful that he'd come by. His company was always welcome, but this time, he'd really helped her think about her suspects. Now she had a better view of who stood to gain the most from Eddie's demise.

A lot of people stood to benefit from her mentor's absence. In the end, Rafe seemed to gain the most in the short term. Todd likely would benefit most over the long haul. The question was whether they committed the heinous act by themselves, worked together on it, or if one was the unwitting beneficiary of the other's despicable act.

Chapter Fifteen

Darcy Gaughan hadn't lived a stereotypical life. No marriage to a loving spouse with two kids and a house with a two-car garage in the burbs. Instead, she'd already reached the pinnacle of one career, saw it come crashing down around her, come face to face with a chronic disease, almost lost her life to it, but triumphed over it.

And she was still only in her early thirties. That was a lot of ups and downs for someone so young.

She was also unconventional in one other way. She didn't hate Mondays.

In fact, she didn't mind them at all. Throughout high school and college, on days when Darcy wasn't in school, she was working. Her first job was scooping ice cream at her local Baskin Robbins. She got fired when her manager caught her "playing the drums" on a few cartons of ice cream with scoops for sticks. Then, she got gigs teaching percussion to elementary and middle schoolers. Once Pixie Dust came together, weekends were spent playing gigs.

The idea of having a weekend off was as foreign to Darcy as trying to converse with someone from Jupiter. Even in recent years working at the record store, her days off were usually Wednesdays and Thursdays.

For her, Monday was simply the start of a new week. But that idea of starting anew is what made it special. New music would be arriving at the store. New customers might visit, which made for opportunities to turn them on to new artists. And it was a chance to catch up on her co-workers' weekend activities.

Darcy wasn't particularly looking forward to the start of this work week, though. While getting ready to leave for work, she asked Ringo to wish her luck.

"Supposed to meet Rafe Majors at the store today. I can use any cat mojo you're willing to share."

The cat responded by sneezing.

"Thanks for the support." As she pulled the door closed behind, she told herself Ringo wanted to wish her well. The less than supportive reaction was probably a reaction to Spring allergens. Sure, she'd go with that.

Despite the threat of seasonal allergies, Darcy enjoyed a glorious drive to work with the top down. The sun spread a warm glow over everything in sight. Without a cloud to be seen, she sang along with reggae legend Jimmy Cliff. Despite the impending meeting, it was indeed a bright, sunshiny day.

And she wouldn't let Rafe ruin that.

She stopped by Jenna's place for a cup of tea and a croissant before making her way to the record store.

"Hey, girl." Jenna waved at her with a free hand as she wiped down an unoccupied table. "Take a seat. All tidied up and ready for you."

"I bet you say that to all your customers." Darcy winked as she sat.

"Only those who come in right after I've cleaned a table. Consider yourself special."

"In your amazing establishment, I always do." They chatted for a bit, then Darcy gave Jenna her order.

When she was alone, she jotted down notes of what she wanted to say to Rafe. Trying to convince the man of the value of keeping the building, and consequently, the record store open, while at the same time determining if he had murdered his stepfather was going to take some tact.

Something that wasn't Darcy's strong suit.

Jenna placed Darcy's order on the table, then took a seat across from her. She gave Darcy a long look.

"You holding up okay? This past week must have been the worst."

"Is there a word for worse than worst? That would be my last seven days." Darcy steeped the tea bag in the steaming water. "I'm hanging in there. Too busy to sit around and brood. That's what would get me in trouble."

"Well, I'm sorry it's been so tough, but," Jenna smiled wide, "I'm also really proud of you. People in here talk. They're impressed with you keeping the store open."

"Didn't think I was up to the task, I'd imagine." She dipped her croissant in the tea, then took a bite. The buttery pastry melted in her mouth. The chai flavor from the tea gave it a pleasant kick.

"Can't lie, there's been some of that. Most people seem genuinely impressed that you didn't close for at least a while."

"I've got four people on my team that need their jobs. I couldn't leave them in out in the cold like that."

Jenna pointed at her. "And that, my friend, is why you're the talk of the town. You stepped up, made some tough decisions, and put your people ahead of yourself. I always knew you had it in you. Now others are seeing it, too."

A lump formed in Darcy's throat. It was humbling to hear people were talking about her in positive terms. She took a sip of her tea, using the moment to compose herself. When one hadn't been on the receiving end of compliments in a long time, receiving such a big one was a little overwhelming.

"Keep doing what you're doing." Jenna gave Darcy's hand a reassuring squeeze. "Both at the store and with the other thing, you know." She tilted her head to the side. "I believe in you."

Before Darcy could thank her, Jenna got up to take care of another customer. Wow. People in this town actually believed in her. And not only Liam, Jenna, and her team. Other people did, too.

Another odd sensation began to stir inside Darcy.

It was something she hadn't felt in a long, long time. It had been so long, she couldn't quite give the sensation a name. She knew what it wasn't. It wasn't the self-loathing she'd carried with her for years. In fact, it was the polar opposite of it.

Self-confidence, perhaps? Or a little more on point, self-respect. With some pride mixed in.

Whatever the term was, she didn't care. It felt good. As she sipped her tea and munched on her croissant, she basked in the sensation.

Other people believed in Darcy Gaughan. Apparently, it was time for Darcy to start doing something, after oh so many years of failing to do so.

It was time for her to start believing in herself again.

The first person on the receiving end of that belief was Jenna. Darcy tapped her on the shoulder. When the woman turned around, Darcy hugged her. It was a sign of her old self displayed in public. Her new self had been doing it a lot lately. And it felt good.

Hopefully, that was a sign of her continuing growth.

"I don't tell you this enough, Jenna. Thanks for having my back. I love you." She stuffed a twenty-dollar bill in Jenna's apron and scooted out the door, wiping away a tear along the way.

Darcy Gaughan, after years slogging her way back from the wilderness, could finally say that the return trip was complete.

* * *

A little while later, she was on the phone, firming up details with a band scheduled to perform on Record Store Day, when Rafe entered the store. The man was wearing an expensive tracksuit and a pair of basketball shoes. The white leather of the new kicks gleamed in the store's light.

For someone who only worked part-time and whose primary source of income was gone, the outfit seemed outrageously extravagant. She'd have bet her lunch money that the tracksuit wasn't part of a new fitness regime, either.

It pleased her that she'd decided to wear a polo shirt. It gave her a more professional look. Even if it was only a tiny bit more professional, she'd take any appearance of authority she could get. Still, it wouldn't serve any purpose to be snarky with Rafe about his wardrobe.

"Nice outfit, dude. Is it new?" Darcy gave him what she hoped was her sweetest smile. Hopefully, it didn't make her look constipated.

"Got it yesterday." He ran his fingers down a sleeve until they reached the wrist, where they settled upon the logo of a leaping cat. "You have to go to

Indianapolis to get something this fine."

She withheld a sudden urge to barf. The man was hopeless. And that was before she factored in his status as a murder suspect.

"Well, it looks good on you." It didn't, though. It emphasized how rotund and unathletic he actually was. Darcy was hardly a fashion trend-setter. Still, thanks to her years in the spotlight, she knew the difference between a good fashion choice and a bad one.

"Give me a minute, and I'll cut you a check for your work on Friday. You worked three and a half hours, I think."

"Yeah, about that." He placed both palms on the sales counter, smudging it with his handprints. Darcy had cleaned the glass surface only minutes earlier. "I don't want a check. I want cash."

"Oh. Um, well." The request caught Darcy off guard.

Her mind raced to come up with a reason he might have for the request. Was he worried Darcy would report it to the IRS, like he was an independent contractor and he'd have to pay taxes on it? Did he think the store didn't have enough money in its account to cover the payment? It had to be the latter.

"It won't bounce. We're on solid financial footing."

Rafe shook his head. "Says you. We can go to the bank machine, and you can pay me that way."

"Oh, come on, dude." She rolled her eyes as she ran her fingers through her hair. "You can't be serious."

"As a heart attack." He crossed his arms. "The old man trusted you and look where that got him."

"What's that supposed to mean? I was on an airplane when Eddie was murdered."

"Maybe so. Doesn't mean you didn't want him dead. And now, you're in charge. You see, I'm not like the old man. I see the world as it is, not how he wanted it to be. You," he pointed his index finger at her, "can't be trusted."

Darcy held her tongue, but the rest of her started to tremble. The man's comments were infuriating. She wanted to slap some sense into him. Like, literally slap him across the face.

Then, she remembered Jenna's encouraging words. She took a deep breath, and the anger dwindled away, like a song on an album that ended by slowly fades out.

"And why do you say that? Are you aware of something neither I nor the rest of the world is?" She gave Rafe a smile. He was *not* going to get the best of her. Not now. Not any time in the future.

"It's human nature." He shrugged. "Once a lush, always a lush. Without the old man around to keep you on the straight and narrow, it's only a matter of time until you get back on the bottle."

"Okay, I'm a murderer and a drunk. Anything else you want to accuse me of before I pay you? Want to include thief?" She pointed behind toward a blank spot on the wall. "You know, so you can hold me responsible for the collectible Beatles album being stolen, too?"

"Dunno. Maybe you did."

She stared at him, utterly dumbfounded. Rafe had always been a slacker, but he'd never been mean. At least, not to her face. Maybe, with Eddie gone, she was getting a look at the real Rafe Majors, not the one kept in line by his stepdad.

"As you know, Eddie left the album to me in his will. It makes no sense for me to steal something that he was going to give to me." She closed her eyes and counted to five. "This is stupid. We're not getting anywhere with this conversation. Excuse me. I have work to do."

The moment Charlotte arrived for her shift, Darcy and Rafe were out the door. They walked to the bank in silence. On the way, she sent up a thank you to whichever celestial being was listening for giving her the strength to deal with Rafe without losing her cool. The man was aggravating to no end.

But was he a murderer?

Their conversation had made it clear beyond any doubt Rafe wasn't mourning Eddie's loss. It was possible he'd nicked Eddie's key to the building at some point. He might know the alarm code, too.

Darcy didn't have evidence to support any of that, though. All she had was conjecture. She needed something substantial to go on. Something that would prove how wrong about her Rafe was. And how right about her everyone else had become.

"Hey, do you have that set of Eddie's keys I gave you?"

"Why?"

"I think a key to the store was on the ring. I figured I'd take it off your hands. Lighten the load, so to speak."

He dangled the keyring in front of her. There was the fob for Eddie's car, a house key, a small padlock key, and the store key. *Bingo.*

"Awesome." She reached for the keys but stopped halfway. "Are these all there were on it when I gave them to you?"

"Yeah. You want the store key, take it."

With a word of thanks, she slipped it off the ring. The key might have been in Rafe's possession now, but did he have it the night of the murder? It was another question without an answer.

They came to a stop by the bank's front entrance. At this point, the best path forward with Rafe was to get him his money so he'd be on his way.

She made a show of going through her backpack before they went inside. The reason for the delay had nothing to do with the bag's contents. Across the street, Todd and the Hobbit were having a discussion. Between the finger-pointing and the arm-waving, it was a heated one.

The wind was to her back, so she couldn't hear what they were saying. That was a bummer. Rafe may have been her prime suspect, but the sight of two other suspects arguing was attention-grabbing.

"Are we gonna go inside or not?" Rafe tapped his toe on the concrete sidewalk.

"Sorry. Let's go." She opened the door and gestured for him to enter.

Once their business was finished, Darcy wished Rafe a good day and started back toward the record store. Before he could get away, she stopped him.

"Before we went inside, did you happen to see Todd and the Hobbit across the street?"

"Yeah, I did." He chuckled. "They were really going at it."

For the first time all day, Rafe smiled. It made him look ten years younger. Almost handsome, too. It was probably just because he had cash in his pocket. Didn't matter. Here was her opening.

"Would love to have been a fly on that wall."

"Sean's probably trying to talk Todd out of buying his building. I think that guy's on a mission to buy up the whole downtown area."

That was news to Darcy. Then again, pretty much everything outside the record store was. She was going to have to start paying attention to local business issues.

"Why do you say that?"

"He came by the house yesterday. He told me as much when he made an offer to buy the old man's building."

Darcy's blood ran cold. Rafe would be a lousy landlord, but Todd would bring Marysburg Music to the end of its existence at its current location. One of the main reasons the store had survived was because it paid rent way below market rate. A different location meant full market rent.

Something Darcy couldn't afford.

"News travels fast." A knot formed in her belly as she worked up the courage to ask the question that was the key to her future.

"Did you accept?"

"Nah. I'm not stupid. I know why he wants the building. I told him to come back when he wanted to make a real offer."

Despite the tension that had built up inside her, Darcy let out a laugh.

"What's so funny?" Rafe crossed his arms and scowled.

"Sorry, I had a vision of you putting Todd in his place. I'd bet my lunch money he doesn't get turned down, especially that way, very often. Actually, not sorry."

"Yeah, he wasn't happy. Then he tried to tell me that since I wasn't the legal owner yet, all he wanted me to do was sign a letter of intent to sell. That we could renegotiate a final sales price after the old man's estate is settled."

"Sounds kind of sketchy to me." She had Rafe talking in a way that wasn't hateful. That was a first. While he may still be Eddie's murderer, she wasn't going to pass on a chance to pump him for information on another suspect.

"No lie. He said he can't go ahead with his condo project without me signing the letter. Then, he started in with a bunch of construction mumbo jumbo. That's when I told him to get lost."

"Do you think you'll end up selling to him? You know, down the road?"

"Don't know. Maybe. If the price is right. Gotta look out for number one, right?" He glanced at his watch. It was a garish timepiece, covered in jewels and almost the size of a hamburger bun. "Gotta roll. Catch you later."

"Before you go, did Eddie ever give you the store's alarm code? Insurance wants me to change it. I wanted to check with you before I did, in case you have it and I need to make sure you get the new one."

Rafe shook his head. "One time, he asked me if I wanted it. I said no. Figured it was a way of roping me into working there."

"Okay. I'll go ahead with changing the code, then. Thanks."

Darcy said goodbye and returned to the record store. She took her time so she could give Rafe's words her undivided attention. One conclusion came to the surface more quickly than any others.

Her race against time had now doubled in importance. The building's long-term ownership was yet to be determined. Somehow, she needed to figure out a way to keep it from falling into Todd's hands long enough to convince Rafe she could make him a better offer.

Solving Eddie's murder might go a long way toward putting her in a position to make that offer.

Especially if it turned out that Todd was the murderer.

Chapter Sixteen

"Things go okay with Rafe?" Charlotte asked when Darcy returned to the store. "You were gone a while."

"Could have been worse, I guess." She recounted her conversation with the man. "The fact that he gave me Eddie's key and said he doesn't know the alarm code doesn't mean anything, really."

"At least the keys are all accounted for now. That's a good thing."

"Truth. If nothing else, now I know that Todd's not going to get the building right away. Rafe's going to make him pay. And dearly."

"That's good, too. Isn't it? I mean, the last thing we want is Todd getting the building. He'd kick us out, right?"

"No doubt." Darcy drummed her fingers on her thigh. "I can't help think that's only delaying the inevitable, though. Still, it buys us time. Record Store Day's less than two weeks away. That's what we focus on."

"You got it, Boss." Charlotte stood up ramrod straight and clicked the heels of her cowboy boots together.

Darcy pointed at a new whiteboard leaning against the wall by the sales register. "How about you update the upcoming releases list. And then arrange a spot near the front here for RSD specials."

"Ooh, I'll start a countdown on the new releases board, too. Get people excited."

"Girl, I like how you think." She gave Charlotte a fist bump. "I'll be in back if you need me."

In need of some solitude so she could think, Darcy closed the office door behind her. A To-Do list she'd compiled at the cabin before leaving for work glared at her from the desktop. Meanwhile, the whiteboard, currently hidden from view by a blanket, loomed in silence. It seemed to mock her. Letting her know that the case wasn't going to solve itself while it was covered up.

There were calls to make, orders to place, stock to check in. There was also a murder to solve. She cracked her knuckles.

"Hang tight, Eddie. Gotta take care of business first." She chuckled at the reference to the classic Bachman Turner Overdrive song. Eddie loved putting it on at the end of the workday to infuse energy into the team as they set about their closing tasks. Even if she'd been on her feet for hours on end, Darcy always found herself dancing to the song as she swept the floor and did other chores.

Those were precious memories. She'd do everything in her power to make sure Marysburg Music continued to be a place where good memories were made.

The task at the top of the To-Do list was entering new stock into the inventory system. First, the system prompted her to choose what category the item fit into—record album, CD, Apparel, turntable, miscellaneous. Then it asked for the quantity of the item. There was also a field to indicate whether it was new or used merchandise.

The final step was entering the price. Eddie priced used merch based on a formula he'd devised that considered a piece's condition, anticipated customer demand, and the amount the store had paid for it. All new merch was sold at suggested retail. Darcy couldn't afford to cut prices on select items simply to drive traffic into the store like online and big-box retailers. The store made up for that the old-fashioned way.

Unsurpassed customer service.

That included doing a lot of special ordering. If someone wanted a new copy of Jason Mraz's *Look for the Good* deluxe edition on vinyl, Marysburg Music would get it. A U2 T-shirt featuring the cover art from the *War* album? No problem.

Once Darcy finished all the data entry, she printed price tags, put the items in plastic milk crates, and took it all to Charlotte.

"New merch, my darling." She set the crates on the floor behind the sales counter. "There are some special orders in there. I've taped the customer's contact info to each item. If you'd let them know their order's in, that would be amazing."

"You got it." Charlotte pointed toward the jazz section. "Someone's here to speak to you."

It was Heather Ewing.

A jolt of electricity coursed through Darcy. Heather was a regular customer, but Eddie had always taken care of her. If she was here, maybe that meant she wanted to patronize the store, not merely the store's former owner. That was an exciting thought.

One of Darcy's fears had been that the store would suffer a noticeable drop-off in customer traffic with Eddie gone. People loved to come and hang out with him. Most of the time, they left with a purchase under their arm.

Darcy couldn't replicate that. But she could try.

"Great to see you, Heather. Can I help you find something? Maybe some Diana Krall or an album from the Marsalis brothers?" Darcy had observed Eddie and Heather often enough to know the woman was a jazz fan.

"Actually, I'm looking for something different. A change of pace, as it were. Can you recommend any saxophonists?"

"I know the perfect artist." Darcy grinned as she flipped through a group of albums. When she found what she was looking for, she displayed it like she was on a game show.

"This is Mindy Abair. She plays the sax across all kinds of genres. Jazz, blues, rock—she can do it all. I saw her at a festival in Louisville a few years ago. She is absolutely electric."

"Alrighty, then." Heather laughed and took the album from Darcy. "You sold me. If you show this much passion with all of your customers, you'll have people lining up to get in the door."

Darcy's cheeks got warm. She looked at the floor, still unaccustomed to receiving a compliment from someone outside of her tiny circle of friends and co-workers. After a moment, she looked Heather in the eye. The women were about the same height, but the physical similarities ended there. Heather had silky, black hair and a brown complexion hinting at her Peruvian heritage. She also seemed to have about thirty pounds on Darcy, given the woman's curvy figure.

"Thank you. That means a lot coming from you. I mean, I know how you relied on Eddie for recommendations. Thanks for giving me a chance."

"My pleasure." She placed a hand on Darcy's arm and drew in close. "And since I've got you, do you have a couple of minutes? There's something I'd like to talk to you about."

"Sure, how about in the back."

Darcy told Charlotte they were going to be in the office and got a thumbs up in return. When Heather was seated, Darcy closed the door and perched herself on a corner of the desk. It didn't seem right, taking Eddie's seat in front of one of his best customers.

"So." She rubbed her hands together. "What can I do for you?"

"It's about Eddie." Heather licked her lips. "I heard you're conducting your own investigation."

When Darcy nodded, the woman let out a long breath and sat back.

"Thank goodness. Eddie wasn't just a next-door neighbor. He was a friend. I swear to you that there is no way he would have taken his own life. I want to help you any way I can."

Darcy raised her eyebrows. It was unusual to have someone believe in her enough to offer to help.

"Since you offered." She settled into Eddie's chair. Now wasn't the time to be hung up on ceremonial gestures. Not with a killer on the loose. She kept the suspect board covered, though. It wouldn't do for Heather to be influenced by her work so far.

"Who held a grudge against Eddie, or disliked him enough to be considered an enemy?"

Heather ran her index finger along her chin while she considered the question. It was encouraging that she was taking time to think instead of throwing out names without a second thought.

"I know Todd Meadows wants this building, so that would be one. I suppose his stepson would be another."

"Why Rafe?" Darcy flipped to a blank notebook page.

"Every now and then, I'd overhear the two of them arguing. It was the typical things. Eddie wanted Rafe to get a full-time job, cut the grass, help out around the house more. Basically, grow up."

"Okay. But that sounds like normal stepfather-stepson stuff."

"Things changed over the last year or so. They argued more often, more loudly. Eddie would threaten to cut Rafe off and kick him out if he didn't get his act together. I'd hear things crashing, like glassware breaking after being thrown across a room."

Darcy's pen flew across the page. Pretty much everyone in Marysburg knew that Eddie hadn't been happy with Rafe's lack of interest in anything other than video games. He'd tried every trick in the book from a positive reinforcement perspective. It simply wasn't in his nature to yell at someone or employ negative reinforcement.

Yet, he'd gotten angry enough to make a pretty drastic threat. Kicking someone out was a last resort-type of move.

And Rafe's response? Was it something that fell into the last resort category, too?

"When's the last time you saw Eddie?"

"Sunday morning." Heather nodded after a short hesitation, as if confirming her recollection was correct. "I was coming home from church. He was on his way to work. We waved to each other."

"And what about Rafe?" This was Darcy's first chance to nail down where her suspects were the day of the murder.

"I'm not sure. No, wait. It was Saturday afternoon. He and I went to get the mail at the same time." She puckered up her lips like she'd bitten into a lemon. "I said hi, but he just looked at me for a second, nodded, then walked right back into the house with the mail under his arm. He's got no manners at all."

Darcy tried to stifle a laugh. And failed. Her recent encounters with Rafe proved Heather's observation was spot on.

"What about Sunday evening? You sure you didn't see him any time then?"

"No." The woman shook her head. "I was at my sister's house. We were binge-watching *All Creatures Great and Small*, the original version. I didn't get home until ten or so."

"What about Claude? Do you think he might have seen something? Even the smallest thing might be important."

"He spent the afternoon working in the yard. It was around five when I left. He said he was going to meet some of his friends and watch basketball. I was asleep when he got home."

"Did he mention what he was going to watch?"

"The Lakers or Heat or something like that. I'm not much of a basketball fan. I know for someone born and bred in Indiana, that's heresy."

They shared a laugh. Folks from Indiana sure had a reputation for being passionate about the game.

"I know the feeling. I like the X Games sports, especially skateboarding. Beyond that, I'm not much of a sports fan."

"Now that the weather's improving, will you be getting out on your board?"

"Hope so. What I'd love to do is get back to using it for my work commute. We'll have to see how things go, though."

Darcy had gotten into skateboarding in college. It was an inexpensive mode of transportation and a lot of fun. Then, when the band was on tour, getting out for a ride on her board had been a healthy alternative to drinking. It was tough to get out on her board in Boston or Pittsburgh during the winter months, though. Which turned out to be a big contributing factor to Darcy's problems with alcohol.

On the other hand, skateboarding around Marysburg had helped her get in shape during her post-rehab days. It was a fun and inexpensive way to get around town. There was no way she'd be giving that up.

"A lot's unsettled for you now, I'd imagine."

"It is. But Eddie was a great teacher. We've got a good thing going here. I'll keep it going as long as we're allowed."

Heather furrowed her eyebrows. "Why do you say that?"

"While I can do everything I can to keep the store going, there's not a lot I can do about the building. If Rafe keeps it, things probably won't end well. If he sells it, things definitely won't end well."

"Well, I agree with you that Rafe would be an awful landlord. That won't be for a few months, though. Maybe you can come to some kind of agreement with him between now and then."

"Let's hope. Todd's got some deep pockets. I can't compete with him." She paused. "Unless it turns out that he's the one who killed Eddie."

"Well, he is the ultimate type-A personality, and ruthless when he wants something. But to actually stab someone? Heaven forbid he get one of his custom-tailored suits dirty."

That was the second time someone hinted at Todd conspiring to murder Eddie.

Darcy had a thought. On the surface, it sounded crazy, but Heather didn't seem to be in any rush to get going. Charlotte could handle the sales floor.

Let the discussion of suspects continue, then.

"Do you think Todd and Rafe got together on this? Todd needs the building. He knows Rafe and Eddie haven't been getting along recently. He tells Rafe that if he'll...take Eddie out of the picture...he'll buy the building and Rafe can live off the proceeds. That way, they both get what they want."

Heather shook her head. "I don't think so. One, Rafe said he didn't know he was inheriting the building until he saw the will. If that's true, it wouldn't make any sense for Todd to hatch a plan with him."

"That's fair." Darcy drew a line through that scenario. "But, what if Rafe already knew and was lying?"

"Then, it's possible." Heather shifted in her chair and leaned her forearms against the desk. Her diamond engagement ring shown like a star in the night. "Todd's a perfectionist, though. If he was going to hire someone to do something drastic like murder, he'd get a pro. I wouldn't trust Rafe with something like that. Would you?"

Darcy pointed at her and laughed. "Not in a million years. I guess that means if they did it, they did it on their own."

"Are you considering anyone else?" When Darcy didn't answer right away, Heather got to her feet. "I want to help. Maybe, there are things I know but don't realize it. You can trust me. Promise."

Wow. Someone asking Darcy to trust them would take some getting used to. The notion made her heart swell.

"Okay, then." She pulled the blanket away from the whiteboard, letting out a chuckle when Heather gasped. "We've talked about Rafe and Todd. What can you tell me about the Sean O'Sullivan and Jasmine Longoria?"

Heather picked at a corner of one of her fingernails while she paced back and forth in front of the desk. There was only about ten feet of space, so she made a half dozen turns before speaking. When she got to the end of the office where the extra merch was held in reserve, she stooped over and picked something up.

"Is this yours?" She had a small glass sphere, ruby red in color, in her hand.

"Nope. I bet it fell off an art project one of the high schoolers was doing. If we're not busy, Eddie let them do homework back here. I'll ask them about it. And speaking of art."

"Right. I don't know Jasmine. I like things you can get from the craft fair. I've heard she's a lovely woman but can be a tough negotiator when people want to haggle with her."

"Tough enough to hold a grudge? Like, for years? Eddie got this location over her, after all."

"I don't know about that. Maybe. Jasmine strikes me as a methodical person. Plus, she's an art dealer. She probably knows people who could sell Eddie's letter opener under the radar. It could be worth a small fortune if the right collector's found. Still, it's not like she went out of business where she is."

"I didn't think of mentioning Eddie's opener when I paid her a visit." Darcy jotted down a note and circled it. She was going to have another conversation with Marysburg's preeminent art dealer.

"She would have denied it." Heather began picking at another fingernail. If she wasn't careful, she'd start removing the purple nail polish. "What does she get out of murdering him, though? Revenge and the money from the sale of a collectible? That doesn't seem like much."

"What if she still has a thing for Todd? Maybe she did it as a favor to him?"

Heather broke out in a wide smile. "And in return, he agreed to give her a sweetheart deal on one of the retail locations in his condo development?

We've all heard about people doing crazy things for love."

"Ooh. That is some devious thinking right there. I didn't know you could be so underhanded." They exchanged a fist bump.

"I spent decades teaching high school. Over the years, I learned to spot students hatching some plot or another from a mile off."

"I'm glad you're on my side." Darcy added a few notations to the whiteboard.

"I won't lie to you. When Eddie decided to help you get sober, I thought it was a fool's errand. He was always such an optimist. I thought your relationship from Ball State was clouding his judgment. That all the investment he was making in you, both emotional and financial, would come back to bite him in the backside."

Darcy tossed the marker onto the desk but kept her face to the board. She didn't want Heather to see her hurt expression. No matter how hard she tried, she'd never be able to escape her past. She'd worked so hard to move on. Why wouldn't other people do the same?

"And now?" She had to choke the words out.

"And now." Heather out a hand on her shoulder. "It makes me happy to say how wrong I was. You've proven Eddie's faith in you was well placed. I'm sorry for not having faith in you back then. I totally believe in you now."

"In that case, let me get your take about something interesting I saw earlier today." She recounted Todd and the Hobbit's argument.

"Interesting." Heather tapped the whiteboard where the Hobbit's name was written. "I know Sean. He's a strange man, but a nice one, too. Claude likes to play role-playing board games. I've gotten him birthday and Christmas gifts at The Magic Box."

"How well do you know him? You said Todd was the type to get someone to do his dirty work. The murder weapon was a copy of the real letter opener. Something the Hobbit could have made on his 3-D printer. Do you think he could be Todd's guy?"

"Hmm. That's a more likely scenario than Todd working with Rafe. But could he even make something so intricate? And what's he get out of it?"

"I think he could." Darcy drew a circle around his name. "Probably too much of a stretch to suggest a sweetheart deal for a storefront location or a promise to keep his property taxes down, isn't it?"

"Afraid so. There'd have to be something else." Heather put up her index finger. "If they were working together. Do you have—"

A knock on the door brought the conversation to a halt.

"Sorry to bother you, Darcy. I need you up front. Izzy isn't here yet and a big crowd of high school students came through the door a second ago. I could use another set of eyes to make sure nothing walks out the door that shouldn't."

Darcy exchanged a quick look and a nod with Heather. Their chat would remain confidential. "Coming. Would you ring this album up for Ms. Ewing? Give her a fifty percent discount as a token of our appreciation for her continued support."

"You got it." Charlotte took the album and headed for the register before Heather got halfway into her objection.

As Darcy followed them out of the office, she couldn't ignore the niggling feeling that the interruption, though necessary, had come at the investigation's expense. One glance around the sales floor changed her mind.

A quick count confirmed fifteen people were in the store. After giving Heather her thanks, along with a request to resume their conversation later, Darcy turned her attention to the shoppers. Nobody was going to get away with any shoplifting on her watch.

Exactly like nobody was going to get away with Eddie's murder.

Chapter Seventeen

A little while later, Darcy was munching on a snack of carrots and hummus when a delivery person pushed a hand cart laden with boxes through the doorway.

"What's all that for?" Izzy asked as the woman in a brown uniform put the boxes by the sales counter and asked Darcy for a signature.

"That, my young friend, is our first shipment of special Record Store Day merch." She opened the top box with the aid of a pair of scissors. Her insides bubbled with the excitement of a little one on Christmas morning as she gazed upon the contents within.

"Check this out!" She held up a tan canvas tote with *Record Store Day* screen-printed on it in bright purple letters. "Last year, we sold out of these in two hours. I tripled the order this time. See, you've got plenty of room for your vinyl, CDs, and all kinds of other stuff in the main compartment. And the side pocket's great for small stuff, like your phone and ID, in case your pants don't have any pockets."

"Sweet. I love my yoga pants, but sometimes, I would kill for a pair with pockets."

Darcy tossed the bag to Izzy. "Now you're all set. Use it with pride."

With wide eyes, the young woman stared at it for a moment, then put a fist on her hip. "Can you afford to be giving this away?"

A lump formed in Darcy's throat. That the young woman standing by her cared enough to think of the store's well-being made her want to break down in tears. The happy kind. Izzy's mom had raised a sweet, compassionate daughter. The kind of daughter Darcy would be proud to call her own. And she was a musician, too. What a combo.

"Yes. It's in our budget. I appreciate you asking, though." Darcy fixed her gaze on the box containing the bags to keep the tears from welling over.

"Thanks. I didn't want to assume with," she waved her hand back and forth, "everything that's been going on."

"I appreciate that. The store is and will be fine. Don't worry. How about you take these to the office while I see what other fun stuff we got." Involving Hank and Char in her investigation was one thing. Subjecting the high school kids to it was another.

Growing up was tough enough. Darcy didn't want to add to any of the teens' day-to-day challenges by traumatizing them with info about her search for Eddie's murderer. She blew out a breath of relief that she'd covered the whiteboard so Izzy wouldn't see her investigation notes.

The remaining boxes contained other RSD goodies. From stickers to posters to limited edition vinyl albums and CDs, Marysburg Music went all in for the event. Despite the trying circumstances, the anticipation building inside Darcy couldn't be denied.

"What's it like to work on Record Store Day," Izzy asked upon her return. Eddie had hired her the previous May, after her predecessor in the position graduated from Ball State and moved to Indianapolis to work as a band director. The store had an unwavering commitment to helping music students. Darcy was going to keep it that way.

She greeted a pair of customers who entered the store before answering the question. The commitment to making customers welcome was going to stay, too.

"It's crazy. There's a ton of prep we'll do the week leading up to the day itself, including running a second cash register. And not only inside. We'll need to get the parking lot ready for our outdoor concerts and food vendors. People will start lining up early Saturday morning.

"Then it's pedal to the metal all day." She chuckled. "You know the song 'Bad Reputation'?"

Izzy's eyes lit up. "Yeah, it's from the first *Shrek* movie, right?"

Darcy's right eye started twitching. Eddie had taught Izzy a lot about jazz.

Punk rock? Clearly, not so much. That was going to change.

"True, but it was originally recorded by Joan Jett way back in 1979. Avril Lavigne did a decent cover. It was one of the first songs Pixie Dust played. Anyway, you know how that song goes about five billion miles an hour? That's what Record Store Day's like."

"Whoa." Izzy took a step back. "Are we going to be able to pull it off? I mean, that sounds like a lot and we're..."

"A little shorthanded?"

Charlotte came through the front entrance, sipping from the straw of a thirty-two-ounce plastic cup. She stopped short when she got a look at Izzy.

"You okay, girl? You look like you've seen a ghost."

"She's fine." Darcy gave the teenager an encouraging pat on the back. "I was just telling her about the glorious insanity that is Record Store Day."

"Oh no." Charlotte put an arm around Izzy. "Did she compare RSD to 'Bad Reputation'?"

"Yeah." Izzy ran her fingers through her long brown hair. "Guess I wasn't expecting it to sound so extreme."

"Because it's *not*." She gave Darcy a side-eyed stare that made her disapproval beyond doubt. "Yes. We'll be very busy, but it won't be that different from Small Business Saturday. If you want insane, try being an accountant during tax season. Ugh, I'm never doing that again. The Boss lives for RSD, so she can get a little overly dramatic about it."

"Hey." Darcy put her hands up in surrender. "It's the biggest day of the year for us. I'm trying to be honest. That's all."

"Ignore her. It's not that bad." Charlotte picked up a box of the newly arrived merch. "Come on. While we put this into inventory, I'll give you the real RSD lowdown."

"And if you know someone who's interested in making a few bucks, like a classmate, send them my way," Darcy said. We *will* need some extra help, regardless of Char's rose-colored glasses take."

With her team members in the back, the store had grown quiet. The lone customer remaining was at one of the store's two listening stations. Every week, the store made samples of five new releases and five random picks available for customers to listen to.

The stations had been one of Eddie's passion projects when the store opened. He'd gone on and on, talking about the hours he'd spent in listening booths during his youth, soaking in the latest jazz cuts from artists like Ella Fitzgerald and Chick Corea.

These days, customers listened to mp3 samples instead of actual vinyl. Based on the way this customer was tapping his toe and swaying ever so gently from side to side, Darcy was pretty sure he was reveling in the experience as much as Eddie had done back in the sixties.

She shook her head. Her friendship with Eddie had crossed generations, genders, and so many other things. They'd made an amazing team. He'd gotten virtually all the credit for the store's success, and rightfully so.

A couple of times a year, though, when they were kicking back in his office after a long day, he'd told her that Marysburg Music couldn't exist without her. Between her knowledge of musical genres Eddie didn't know, like punk rock and EDM, and her insistence on using technology whenever possible, she was Tammy Tyrell to his Marvin Gaye. They were partners, and together, they truly had made something greater than the sum of its parts.

"And we're gonna keep it that way, Eddie. Promise."

She left the young man to enjoy his listening and returned to her tidying up. It never ceased to amaze her how easily a record was placed back in a bin after someone had looked at it, yet nowhere near the record's proper location. Oh well, it gave her something to do until Charlotte and Izzy returned to the floor.

A bit later, the three of them were debating where to place the RSD canvas bags when a couple who looked to be about Izzy's age entered the store. She greeted them with enthusiasm.

"Hey, guys. Welcome to Marysburg Music. Can I help you find anything?"

The girl smiled and waved at Izzy. After a surly greeting that was little more than a grunt, the boy declined her offer. He followed his companion around as if he was being led to the gallows, hands shoved in the pockets of his jeans and feet shuffling across the floor.

Darcy looked at Charlotte and raised her eyebrows. Charlotte responded with a shrug. It was common for couples to browse the aisles of Marysburg Music. It wasn't out of the ordinary for one person to be way more interested in the store's offerings than the other. It was exceedingly rare for someone over the age of ten to be so outwardly hostile while there, though.

Since Izzy knew the couple, Darcy decided to hang back. She wanted to see how her young employee responded. She was impressed with Izzy's next move.

"If there's something you're looking for and you can't find it, let me know. I can check to see if we have it or if we can special order it."

"Just looking. Thanks, Iz," the girl said and gave her another smile.

After a few more minutes of browsing, the twosome headed for the exit.

The young man let out a huff. "See, I told you coming here was a waste of time. The only people who listen to records are dinosaurs and freaks. Better be looking for another job, Izzy. From what I hear, this one won't be around much longer."

Izzy covered her mouth with her hands. Her cheeks turned as bright red as Charlie Cardinal, the Ball State mascot, himself. Once they were gone, she turned toward Darcy.

"I am so, so sorry. I'm in a band with those kids. I told them to come by to check us out. I didn't mean—"

"No apologies necessary." Darcy put her arm around Izzy. "We've been called worse in this store. Since I'm the oldest, I guess that makes me the dinosaur. Are you the freak or is Char?"

"I was a total geek in high school, so that makes you, Miss Izzy, the freak." Charlotte joined the other women in a group hug. "And to be clear, since the cast of *Freaks and Geeks* included Linda Cardellini, John Francis Daley, Jason Segel, Seth Rogan, and Busy Philipps, I'd say we're in pretty good company."

"God, that was a great show." Darcy let out a wistful sigh. "I'd marry John Francis Daley in heartbeat."

"And I'd do the same with Busy Phillips," Charlotte said. "If she wasn't already married, that is. Wouldn't want to be accused of being a homewrecker."

Izzy laughed. "You two are such nerds. I think I can live with being the freak between you."

"What's that make Hank and Peter," Charlotte asked.

Darcy drummed her fingers on her thigh. "Well, if I'm a dinosaur, I guess that would have to make Hank something even older, maybe a wizard."

"And if I'm a freak then Peter's a total spaz." Izzy wiped a laughter-induced hear from the corner of her eye.

"I'll order the shirts. Great meeting." Darcy moved toward the sales counter. Izzy cleared her throat, which stopped Darcy in her tracks.

"Is that kid right, Darcy? I mean, about the record store not being around much longer?"

It was a fair question. Both in terms of the store's short-term survival with Eddie now gone, as well as the longer-term challenges of selling vinyl and CDs in an age dominated by streaming services.

"Let me put it this way. It's a challenge every day to run a small business. I honestly believe that businesses like ours—record stores, bookstores, independent restaurants—have our niche, though. We have to be smart and pay attention to new trends in music and the buying habits of our customers. Part of that's why Record Store Day and Small Business Saturday are so important. They're basically made for businesses like us. When we do our part to make those days true celebrations of music, it helps keep the party going all year round."

"We're really going to be okay?" The hopeful look in Izzy's eyes spoke volumes. She believed in Darcy. And trusted her.

"We are." Darcy placed a hand on the young lady's shoulder. "Both in the short term and in the long term."

"I know the perfect song for right now," Charlotte said. With a grin, she plugged her phone into the store's PA system. A moment later, *Le Freak* by the legendary band Chic filled the room with its disco beat and singalong lyrics. Darcy grabbed Izzy's hand and they started dancing to the hit song. A moment later, Charlotte joined in, laughing and clapping along.

Yes, things were going to be okay. And even better once Darcy made sure Eddie's murderer was behind bars.

Chapter Eighteen

When the clock struck six, Charlotte told Darcy to go home. "You've been here all day. Izzy and I can handle closing. Hang out on that deck I'm so jealous of. Spend time with your cat."

The mention of Ringo clinched it. She gave Charlotte and Izzy high fives and told them how much their support meant. It was becoming easier to tell herself when she went to bed that she was doing the right thing. That she was making good decisions, not solely easy ones.

That she was turning into a leader.

She stepped outside the store and took a moment to soak up some sun. On this April evening, the clouds were wispy, like cotton bolls that had been stretched to their limits. The sun's warming glow had driven the temperature into the low seventies. The conditions were rare for this time of year. Which made it all the more special.

Just like her little band of record store misfits.

She tapped on the front window's glass to get Izzy and Charlotte's attention, then waved goodbye to them. Instead of going around the back to climb into Rusty, she strolled in the direction of Selena's. Ringo would be fine without her for another hour while she enjoyed a green tea with Thea.

"What up Darcy-patra, Queen of the Vinyl?" Thea grinned. "Get it? Instead of Cleopatra, Queen of the Nile, Darcy-patra, Queen of the—"

"I get it. Very clever." Darcy laughed as she got seated on a barstool. It was a corny joke, the kind her dad would tell. It was a fun one, though. Besides, she was always ready for a good laugh to provide a remedy for whatever ailed her. "What's a girl got to do around here to get an iced green tea?"

"You need only ask, my Queen." Thea chuckled as she lumbered to the other end of the bar to fix the drink. When she returned, she asked if Darcy wanted a menu.

"I'm good." She raised her glass to Thea. "You know, I needed that laugh. Thanks."

"Happy to be of service." Thea leaned forward and placed her forearms on the bar's wooden surface. "You hanging in okay? The To-Do List helping?"

"Happy to say I am, and it is." She told Thea about the Record Store Day merch the store had received, along with the pep talk she gave Izzy.

"It sounds like being a boss suits you." Thea gave Darcy's shoulder a friendly jab.

"It's early days." Darcy took a drink. The cool liquid soothed her throat, which was parched from working too long without paying attention to her fluid intake.

"Sure, but you've got a ton on your plate, if you don't mind me saying so. Have you even had a day off since Eddie..."

"Was murdered? It's okay. You can say it. That's what happened." She took another drink, as much to quell the flame kindling in her belly as to quench her thirst. "We closed the store early on Saturday for Eddie's memorial service, so I only worked a couple of hours then."

"That's not exactly a day off. Are you taking care of yourself? Eating right? Getting enough sleep?"

"Believe it or not, I am. Been sleeping like a rock the past couple of nights. Even Ringo isn't waking me up in the middle of the night asking for one of his three A.M. snacks."

"That's good." Thea, doing a credible impersonation of a counselor, nodded. "How's your other thing going?"

"Making progress." Even though she was the only customer at the bar, Darcy kept her voice low. It wouldn't do to be overheard by accident. "Right now, things are pointing toward Rafe."

Thea scrunched up her nose. "Really? Is he ambitious enough to actually murder someone?"

"I don't know that he's ambitious enough. He seems greedy enough. Todd

Meadows has already made an offer to buy the building from him. He told me he's holding out for a better offer."

"Interesting. Since you brought him up, I'd take a closer look at Mr. Meadows. He's been working on that condo project for over two years now. He's spent a lot of money to get this far. Eddie was the one person stopping him from taking deposits from potential residents. Every day that project gets delayed costs Todd money. Just sayin'." Thea shrugged.

"Which reminds me." Darcy sat up straight. "Were you working a week ago, Sunday? The night Eddie was murdered?"

"Yeah, why?"

"You guys have sports on the big screen pretty much all the time, right?" Darcy pointed with her thumb to a seventy-two-inch flat-screen TV on a far wall. "Did you remember seeing Todd, or any of the other suspects that night?"

"We were busy, so give me a minute to think about it. Had the women's NCAA basketball championship on, and a NASCAR race that had been rain-delayed. I remember seeing Sean. He got pretty loud during the basketball game. I think he had money on it."

"Do you remember what time this was? It's really important."

"It wasn't long after the basketball game tipped off, so eight-ish? He was sitting at a table next to a group of retired firefighters that gets together here a lot. They were watching an NBA game on one of the other screens and telling him to quiet down."

"Do you remember who was in the group?"

"Gil Morgan, Claude Ewing, and four others. I don't remember who, exactly."

Darcy drummed her fingers against the edge of the bar. So, Claude was among the group. That tracked with what Heather had told her. It also meant they both had an alibi for at least part of the evening.

"What about Todd or Rafe?"

"I don't remember." Thea pointed toward the bar's entrance. "Todd's right over there. Why don't you go ask him yourself?"

"I'll do that." Darcy made her way toward the realtor at a casual pace. She didn't want onlookers to think she was over-anxious.

A moment before, he had gotten seated at a table with two other men in suits when Darcy arrived.

"Evening, Todd. I've been wanting to circle back with you. Got a minute?"

"Not really." He glanced at his fellow diners. "My colleagues and I are having a working dinner."

Darcy had learned a thing or two about dealing with reporters during her Pixie Dust days. The majority of the press she'd interacted with were decent folks who were trying to do their jobs. They were persistent, though, and knew how to respond when being rebuffed.

"I wanted to make sure you're okay." She turned her attention to the diners seated across from Todd. "I saw Mr. Meadows earlier today in a rather heated argument with one of our local business owners. It had me worried for his safety. The other man seemed awfully agitated."

"Please." Todd got to his feet. "I'm fine. Gentlemen, could you excuse us for a few minutes."

The moment they were in the bar area, Todd wheeled on Darcy. "What, exactly, do you think you saw?" He made air quotes with his fingers around the word saw.

"I was at the bank earlier. You and Sean O'Sullivan were really going at it. Things looked heated."

"It was a private matter. None of your business." He ran his fingers down the lapel of his suit jacket. A ruby-encrusted ring on his right pinkie finger gave the impression of blood on his hands. It was as if he was making the gesture to let Darcy know he was above being bothered by her, he'd failed.

"I don't know. Maybe it is. Rafe Majors told me you paid him a visit the other day. If he sells the building to you, that will make you my landlord. Maybe Sean likes that idea about as much as I do."

"I have no idea what you're talking about. If you'll excuse me—"

"Where were you between the hours of six and nine Sunday before last? The night Eddie was murdered?"

The abrupt change in direction caught him off guard. His brow furrowed as he straightened the knot of his tie.

"I don't know what you're implying, but I'd be careful of making wild accusations."

"Which is it? You don't know where you were that evening, or you won't tell me?" She took a step closer to him but kept her tone conversational. "You see, I know all about your condo plan. I've read the letters you sent him. With Eddie gone, it's only a matter of time until you convince Rafe to sell and the project can move forward. A lucky break for you since Eddie wasn't going to sell."

"You should be ashamed of yourself. I'm sorry Mr. Maxwell took his own life. It doesn't do you, or his memory, any good accusing people of murder, though."

Darcy put her hands up. She'd kept her cool the entire exchange. There was no doubt Thea was keeping an eye on things and would corroborate her version. Still, she wasn't ready to let him off the hook. Not quite yet.

"I hear you. Which is why if you've got nothing to hide, there's no reason not to tell me. For instance, I was on a plane, then driving here from Indy. Sean O'Sullivan, your verbal sparring partner, was here, watching a basketball game."

"Fine. If it'll get you to go away." He tugged at his collar. "I have a place on Prairie Creek Reservoir. I was there. Getting my boat ready for the season. Now, if you'll excuse me, we're done here."

He turned on his heel and was through the doorway before Darcy could have said "drum fill." Still, it had been a most informative chat.

"That went well." Thea rolled her eyes when Darcy turned toward her.

"Actually, it did. He wouldn't tell me what his argument with the Hobbit was about and doesn't have an alibi for the time of the murder. I'd call that a productive five minutes."

They exchanged a fist bump. "Look at you, girl. Kaitlin Rosengarten better watch out. Before long, you'll be taking her place."

"Slow your roll, there, Thea. I've got a record store to keep me busy." She glanced at her phone. "And a cat to feed. Gotta go."

Darcy leaned over the bar to give Thea a hug, then dropped a five-dollar bill on the bar for the drink. At times, it seemed like Thea was as good of a counselor as the one Darcy had seen for a few years after she got out of rehab.

And Thea was a lot more affordable.

Or maybe it was because Darcy was healthier, physically, emotionally, and mentally. She hadn't seen her counselor for over a year. Before that, the appointments had gone from every week to every month to only four times per year.

As she stepped back outside, she shook her head at a sudden revelation. She'd been getting better for a while now. And hadn't even noticed the progress she'd made.

With that empowering thought in mind, Darcy took a detour back to Rusty. She'd left Ringo with plenty of dry food and a clean litter box. He'd survive another short delay.

A few minutes later, she arrived at Jasmine's gallery.

"Ms. Gaughan. Two times in one week. How humbling." Sarcasm dripped from the woman's words.

"Thank you." This time Darcy would play nice. And ignore her counterpart's insincerity.

She went straight to a painting on the wall. It was an eight by ten, oil on canvas painting of the Marysburg Center for the Arts. The Ball State Fine Arts Department had commissioned a recent graduate to paint it. An anonymous donor had won it at an auction and gifted it to Jasmine's gallery to boost the artist's profile.

"I'd like to purchase this." Purchase sounded fancier than the word *buy*. If Darcy was going to start swimming with the big fish like Eddie had, it couldn't hurt to start acting like one.

Jasmine raised an eyebrow. When Darcy didn't move, she sauntered toward the painting, her five-inch heels clicking on the gallery's parquet floor.

"It's a special piece. Are you sure you..." She shrugged. It was an elegant way to deliver an insult.

"Can afford it? Absolutely. There's a space at the record store that will be the perfect fit for this. I want to start featuring local artists and artisans at the store. This is my first step."

"If you're certain." Jasmine tapped away at her tablet. Her manicured nails sounding like mini versions of the clicking of her heels. After a few moments, she turned the tablet toward Darcy. "Please review the purchase order, then sign at the bottom."

Darcy did as instructed, then returned the tablet with a wide smile.

"And what form of payment would you like to use? If you need it, we can arrange financing at a very reasonable rate." Jasmine returned the smile. It was cold and predatory, shark-like. This woman was better at dishing out microaggressions than the snooty sales ladies in the movie *Pretty Woman*.

"That won't be necessary." She handed the woman a credit card.

Once she got sober, Eddie helped get her finances in order. Other than the drinking, Darcy had maintained a frugal lifestyle. She'd split the rent on an L.A. apartment with the Pixie Dust's bass player. The Dodge Journey she'd bought in college had served her so well, she never gave a second thought to replacing it with something flashier. And, as the drummer in a punk band, where stickin' it to the man was a lifestyle, her wardrobe hadn't evolved from the jeans and T-shirts of her teen years.

By the time the endorsement contracts came to an end, Darcy would have banked enough money to be set for life if she hadn't drank so much of it away. To this day, she shook her head that the Darcy of back then didn't give a second thought to dropping three grand on a bottle of twelve-year-old bourbon. And then drinking it in one night.

Nevertheless, with Eddie's help, she came to find out that even though an alcoholic haze, she'd managed to make a handful of wise investment choices. She'd gotten on the Apple train because she loved using her iPod while practicing on the drums. A few other tech companies hadn't done as well but had made her some decent returns over the years.

Meanwhile, Eddie had put her on a strict, but sensible, budget. He'd initially balked when she floated the idea of buying the fishing cabin but relented when her parents put their support behind the idea to sell the Journey and use the proceeds to start a home improvement fund. Her battle with alcohol had strained Darcy's relationship with her mom and dad almost to the breaking point. The house was the first thing they'd agreed on in ages. If they shared her vision of fixing up the ramshackle structure while she fixed herself up, Eddie wasn't going to argue.

So, it was no surprise to Darcy that the sale, using her platinum credit card, was approved in seconds. She may have been imagining things, but she sensed a change in Jasmine's demeanor toward her at the sale's conclusion.

"Would you like me to wrap it for you?"

Visions of the sucking up scene from later in *Pretty Woman* flashed through Darcy's head. The hilarious actor Larry Miller's performance had been unforgettable. Darcy had to stifle a laugh at Jasmine's sudden shift from contempt to sucking up. That notion was followed by a desire to tell the team at the store about the change.

Darcy banished it. Jasmine was a businesswoman. She'd just made a four-thousand-dollar sale. Of course, she'd be in sucking up mode. Darcy did the same with customers who made purchases of much smaller dollar amounts.

It was customer service, pure and simple. And it was smart business.

"You know, I'll save you the trouble." Darcy took the painting off the wall. After giving it a long look, she grinned. It was a cool piece of artwork. "I do have one question, though."

"If you're wondering about getting it insured, call your agent first thing in the morning. That way you'll have the call on record. I can provide an appraisal if you need one, too."

Darcy's cheeks got hot. It hadn't occurred to her that she'd need to insure the piece. *Welcome to the world of expensive stuff, girl.* She'd make the call as soon as she got home. Otherwise, she'd be up half the night stressing about forgetting in the morning, even if she wrote herself a note. Sometimes, it took a while to overcome years of self-doubt.

"Thank you. I'll do that. I was wondering if you saw anything odd around here a week ago last Sunday. The night Eddie was murdered."

And like a spotlight flicking from on to off, Jasmine's attitude turned to ice cold. "Why?"

"Here's the thing. Eddie's time of death was somewhere between six and eight that evening. Your sign says you close at six on Sundays. I was wondering if you might have seen someone acting weird or someone who seemed out of place around closing time. I know the record store's a few blocks away, but I thought it couldn't hurt to ask."

"Since you're asking, does that mean that I'm no longer a suspect in your little investigation?" Jasmine crossed her arms as she began tapping her toe.

"I'm convinced the cops got it wrong. Detective-Sergeant Rosengarten won't listen to me, though." It was a decent non-answer to Jasmine's question.

"Can you blame her?"

Darcy took a breath. She would not take the bait. This was too important to screw up because she lost her cool.

"No. But, I'm not the person I was back then. Unfortunately, she isn't inclined to recognize that. And I'm afraid a murderer could go free because of my past sins. Eddie Maxwell deserves better than that, don't you think?"

Silence hung over the women for a few moments. Then, Jasmine clapped.

"I never figured you to be a speechmaker. That one wasn't bad." She returned to her perch behind her tiny sales counter. Whether it was to buy herself some time to cook up an answer to the question, or for some other reason, Darcy couldn't tell.

"This isn't about me. It never has been. It's about Eddie. What if it had been Sean O'Sullivan or Jenna Washburn? You'd want the truth, right? Eddie deserves the truth."

That was the God's honest truth. The man had done too much for Darcy, for the whole community, for his murder to be dismissed with a virtual flick of the wrist.

"Well, as much as I'd like to, I'm afraid I can't help you. I didn't see anything out of the ordinary. I was home, with a glass of wine and a book at half-past six."

Darcy didn't believe Jasmine's story for a second. Still, she sensed nothing more would be coming from the art dealer. At least for the time being.

"Couldn't hurt to ask. Thanks for your time. And for the painting. Come by the record store some time so you can see it on display." She turned to go.

"Maybe, I'll do that. Thank you for the invitation."

"My pleasure." She turned to go. "By the way. What was it?"

"I'm sorry?" Jasmine had a blank look on her face.

"The book you were reading that night. What was it? I'm always looking for new stuff to read."

"Oh, right." Jasmine pushed a few strands of her long, black hair back behind an ear. "It was a book about T.C. Steele. The Indiana painter. I'm a fan of his. I got the book at his museum in Bloomington. You never know when one might come on the market at a reasonable price."

"Gotcha. Thanks." Darcy made her exit. With her back to Jasmine, she was able to keep her smile to herself.

Gotcha, indeed. Darcy didn't know much about art. She did know about T.C. Steele. He was her mom's favorite. Among the things she knew was that T.C. Steele's museum wasn't in Bloomington, Indiana. It was in Brown County, the next county over.

Which begged the question. Why had Jasmine been wrong about something so basic for an Indiana art dealer, Was it an innocent slip-up? Or a mistake made in a panicky spur-of-the-moment move to hide something?

Chapter Nineteen

"And there you go, fella." Darcy placed a bowl of gourmet wet food in front of Ringo. "Sorry about being gone so much recently. Once we get through RSD, I'll take a day off. Promise."

The old tom stopped eating long enough to glance at her and lick his chops. Then he resumed his breakfast.

"Or you could come to work with me. You could be the store cat." She'd read a number of books in which cats were fixtures in bookstores and other mom-and-pop businesses. With the extra hours she was going to be putting in, maybe she could give it a go and see if it worked in real life as well as it worked in the pages of a book.

Ringo sat up and wiped his face with his paws. It was an entertaining process to watch in which he licked a paw, then rubbed it along one side of his face. After that, he did the other side with the other paw. The cat was missing part of one ear and walked with a limp that his vet thought was the result of a tussle with another cat or a raccoon. Yet, he could be as fastidious as those fancy felines on cat shows.

"Tell you what. Think about it and get back to me." She slurped down the last of the tea in her mug emblazoned with The Misfits logo. After giving Ringo a few scratches around his ears, she put the mug in the sink next to a collection of plates, bowls, and utensils. With the bathroom remodeled, installing a dishwasher was her next project.

A bit later, while she was getting dressed and debating between a Go-Go's T-shirt and a Sleater-Kinney one, her phone rang. It was Liam, so she picked up instead of letting it go to voice mail.

They exchanged pleasantries and then he told Darcy the reason for his call.

"The grapevine's been running hot the past few days. I've got some news."

"Okay, you have my anxiety through the roof. Spill it."

"It's about the Hobbit. A buddy who plays Magic there overheard him telling people that if you try to talk to them, they should walk away. You're trying to stir up trouble around town."

"Seriously? The guy knows this is a free country, right?"

"I'd imagine, but when it comes to O'Sullivan and business, the freedom he wants most is the freedom to spend money in his stores. I figured this has to be about Eddie, so I wanted to let you know."

"I wouldn't consider looking for a murderer to be stirring up trouble. It does make me wonder, though."

"About?"

"Whether or not I'm making him nervous. Eddie's letter opener is still missing." She got some scrap paper from a junk drawer and started scribbling down notes. "Whoever made the copy made a darn convincing one."

"That means they're good at what they do." The connection went quiet for a few moments as Liam seemed to be thinking. "I'd bet there are thousands of people with the skill to make a good copy."

"No doubt. But if you wanted to have something like this made, and you didn't want to leave a digital trail, you'd try to find someone you trusted, though. Or do it yourself. That would leave fewer tracks to cover. Right?"

"That would help. Sure."

"So, what if it turns out the murder weapon is beyond doubt, something the Hobbit made?"

"First, you'd have to prove he made it. Then you'd have to prove it was made with the intent of harming someone."

Darcy looked at a piece of artwork on her living room wall. It was a concert poster from the first show the Pixie Dust performed as a headliner. All three members of the band, as well as the crew, had signed it. She'd been so proud of the keepsake that she'd given it to her parents so it wouldn't get lost while she was on tour.

Years later, her younger sister Aisling had returned it to her, now in a gorgeous black frame, as a housewarming present. At that time, Darcy's relationship with her parents was still fraught, at best. The fact that they'd worked with Aisling to turn the poster into a true work of art hadn't been lost on her. Her parents still loved her.

They denied any involvement and insisted Aisling deserved all the credit, but Darcy knew better.

The same as she knew with all her heart that Sean O'Sullivan had created the weapon used to murder Eddie. She did a fist pump as an idea popped into her head. A way that she'd be able to prove it.

"Thanks for the heads up, Liam. I gotta get to work."

Hank was running a feather duster over the albums when Darcy arrived at the store.

"Morning, Darcy. Thought I'd come in a little early in case you need help with anything." He pointed at the display of the canvas Record Store Day bags. "Getting closer all the time."

"As a matter of fact, you can." She dashed to the office, returning moments later with a sheet of price tags, a crate of used vinyl records, and a half dozen boxes containing turntables. "Here are some things I want to put on sale for RSD. If you would tag them, then put them someplace secure, that would be amazing. We'll put them out the night before the big day."

"Your wish is my command." He swept his arm to the side and bowed from the waist. "Anything else?"

Darcy rolled her eyes, then let out a laugh. "You're too good to me. You know that?"

"I do, indeed. Now, go do your boss stuff while I make the store presentable. You know I love Charlotte and Izzy, but I wonder if either of them has ever been introduced to a dust rag."

"I'll let you ask that question." Until Darcy bought the cabin, she hadn't spent more than thirty minutes dusting anything that wasn't her drum kit. As one who wasn't in a position to criticize anyone's dusting skills, she beat a hasty retreat to the office.

Hank was tidy to the max. Which was great for the store. Except for the fact that nobody else on the team was capable of getting things as spotless as he wanted. Oh, well. It was a problem Darcy didn't mind having.

She had other things than the store's upkeep on her mind, though. As he opened the desk drawer, she took in a little breath. The tiny red orb was still there. Right next to a yellow one Darcy had come across in a corner of the office the other day. She'd forgotten to ask Izzy if they belonged to her. Which was fortunate because she already knew the answer.

They didn't belong to Izzy. Or Peter.

They belonged to Eddie's murderer. Or, to be more precise, they belonged on the murder weapon.

She dreaded the phone call she was about to make. It needed to be done, though. The conversation would bring her closer to figuring out who Eddie's murderer was, after all.

"Hi, Detective-Sergeant Rosengarten, it's Darcy Gaughan."

The sigh on the other end of the call was so loud, Hank could have heard it. "What can I do for you Darcy?"

"Well, I've found these little glass balls in the record store. I was wondering if they might have come off the weapon used in Eddie Maxwell's...death."

She wanted to say murder more than she wanted to have a drum battle with Dave Grohl, but discretion prevailed. If Kaitlin blew her off, her hunch was going to become way harder to prove.

"I was wondering if I could bring them by. If it turns out they did come from the letter opener, I thought y'all might want them."

"Hmm." A few clicks, like the sound of a computer mouse being operated, gave Darcy hope. At least the police officer was checking something. "I'm available for fifteen minutes at three this afternoon. Don't be late."

The line went dead. That was okay. The investigation was coming together like one of Pixie Dust's songs. They were recorded track by track. Each individual instrument track was then layered one on top of the other until the entire piece coalesced to the band's satisfaction.

The pieces of the investigation were coming together, too. It wouldn't be long until everything came together. She could feel it in her bones.

Darcy arrived at the Marysburg Municipal Building and Police Department at five minutes until three. Hank and Peter had things under control at the store. When she left, the two were debating who was a more important recording artist from a historical perspective, Miles Davis or Bob Marley.

The disagreement was civil, but neither side was interested in backing down. She was happy to have been spared officiating that discussion. Even if it meant meeting face to face with her nemesis.

Not much had changed at the station since Darcy's last visit, which had been almost three years now. The flat-roofed, single-story structure had been built in the eighties with one thing in mind—function. Poured concrete had been the architect's material of choice. Beige paint had flecked away in spots to reveal a slightly darker shade of beige underneath.

Large windows spanned the front of the building in an attempt to give it a non-threatening look. Some workers had taped items to the insides of the windows. No doubt artwork done by their school-age children or photos of friends and family. It was as if the building was trying to say, "Hey, look at how pleasant it is here. No need to be scared of what's inside. Trust us."

A breeze blew Darcy's hair in front of her eyes. It also prompted her to zip up her jacket. Or, it might have been the flood of bad memories in which she was hauled into this very building through the back entrance. The one without any of the welcoming windows the public passed by every day.

"You can do this, girl. This isn't about you. Or Kaitlin." She entered the building, took the first right, and held her head high while she told an officer at a counter why she was there.

After a seemingly endless wait that had Darcy sweating buckets from anxiety, Kaitlin finally emerged from behind a windowless door. The cop rolled her eyes as she took her time walking to the counter.

"Allie." She nodded her head ever so slightly.

"Detective-Sergeant Rosengarten. Thank you for taking the time to see me."

Darcy maintained eye contact until Kaitlin pressed a button underneath the counter. At an adjoining door, a tooth-rattling buzz was followed by the simple click of a lock releasing. She grabbed the door's lever before the lock could re-engage. Something told her that if she didn't get it right the first time, there would be no second time.

They walked through a doorway, down a hall, and into an office with walls painted a pale shade of green. Once inside the room, their footfalls were dampened by wall-to-wall carpet in a blue and gray checkerboard pattern. A small conference table was in the center of the room, with three chairs on either side.

"Take a seat." Kaitlin gestured to one side while moving to the other. The message was clear. Darcy was an opponent, not a collaborator. Especially because there was a mirror that spanned the wall behind the cop. There was probably an observer or two on the other side of the mirror, too, their gazes intent on Darcy's every movement.

When the women were seated, Kaitlin opened a manila file folder and glanced at a tiny stack of papers. In Darcy's view, if that was the case file, it was woefully insufficient.

There was also a paper bag on the table. Kaitlin removed the letter opener from it. The pointed end of the device was marred by a dark reddish-brown stain. Darcy's blood ran cold at the unsettling sight.

"You said you have some decorative pieces that you believe came off this, correct?" Kaitlin placed the opener on a clean piece of paper in front of her.

"Yes." Darcy pulled a small, plastic bag from her pocket. She placed it on the table. "Two glass beads. Take them out if you need to."

Kaitlin studied them through the plastic for a moment, then looked at the letter opener. After writing something down, she removed the beads from the bag and placed them on the sheet of paper, next to the letter opener. She used a pen to roll them around a few times. When she'd had enough of that, she went back to the opener, first taking a close-up look at one side, then the other.

"Well." She pointed at two tiny indentations in the jewel-encrusted handle. "It's possible one of those could go here, and another there."

"How about that? I was right." Darcy did a quick drum roll with her index fingers as adrenaline surged through her. Finally, she had the actual hard evidence that had been proving to be so elusive.

"Slow your roll, Darcy. Just because these beads *might* fit these indentations, it doesn't mean they *do*. And even if they do, there's no way to verify that they actually belong there."

Darcy's shoulders slumped. It was as if Kaitlin had dumped a bucket of frigid water from the White River all over her.

"What are you saying? That this was a big waste of time?"

"Let me put it this way. These beads were in your possession. Who's to say they're not yours. You say you found them. That doesn't necessarily mean that's true."

"Oh, come on. Heather Ewing found the yellow one yesterday. You can ask her yourself."

"All she can tell me is where she found it. She doesn't know anything more." She shook her head. "I'm sorry Darcy. Truly. I know Mr. Maxwell meant a lot to you, but there's nothing here that ties these beads to this letter opener. And, more importantly, there's nothing to indicate any foul play was committed."

Darcy slumped into her chair. She'd thought for certain that Kaitlin would see the beads for what they were—proof, tenuous that it may be, that Eddie had been murdered. So much for collaboration with the police.

Then, she rallied. "I know. You could check for glue traces on the beads and in those indentations. If they match, there you go."

The cop shook her head. "Which still wouldn't prove anything related to a crime. Good try though."

"What about this? You said there were fingerprints found on the handle. Can you use them to show how the handle was being held?" She got to her feet and thrust her right hand forward like she was stabbing Kaitlin with an imaginary pointed end directed at the cop. "Eddie was right-handed. If he really did kill himself, he wouldn't have held the letter opener so it was pointing away from him, like I'm doing now. It would have been awkward to hold the blade that way and then bring it back at himself."

She brought her hand back toward her, with the imaginary point first, as if she was stabbing herself. She opened her hand when it touched her midsection. Her palm was facing downward.

The cop crossed her arms. "Your point being? Pardon the pun."

"That if he was going to stab himself, he would have held the letter opener so its point was aimed toward him from the start, like this." Darcy pantomimed driving a blade into her midsection with the pointed end oriented toward her, then opened her hand to reveal her palm facing up. "See? There would have to be some kind of marks to show how it was being held when Eddie was stabbed. The orientation of the hand around the handle would be different depending on how it was held. And whether the sharp end started out pointed away from him or pointing at him."

"That's a good observation. Did you figure that out all by yourself?"

"A time or two I thought about taking my own life with a knife. I may have even practiced to make sure I got it right."

"Hmm." Kaitlin checked the paperwork. "The report doesn't say which way the prints are oriented. We'd have to do some additional analysis to test your theory."

"Does that mean you'll do it?" Maybe Kaitlin was finally coming around.

"I don't know." The woman's phone beeped. "Our time's up. Thank you for coming. I promise I'll talk to the other officers who were on the scene. If we can establish a compelling reason for the additional analysis, we'll proceed."

Darcy dropped her hands to her sides. Kaitlin could dance around the issue until the cows came home. She was right and the Detective-Sergeant couldn't bring herself to admit it.

Fine, she'd carry on with the investigation solo. The trip hadn't been fruitless. Far from it, in fact. The least Darcy could do was to wrap up the encounter on a positive note.

"Thanks again for your time. At least I got lucky you haven't gotten rid of the letter opener yet. Would have been hard to test my theory without it. Know what I mean?"

"Sorry to burst your bubble but it wasn't luck."

"What do you mean?"

"Let's say that with you sticking your nose into things, the department thinks it's best to hold onto all the evidence collected at the scene. Just in case."

"In case I might be right?" Hope sprung up inside Darcy, like daffodils pushing up through the soil as the weather warmed up.

"I wouldn't go that far. But if you do come up with evidence indicating a crime took place, which I think is highly unlikely, the department wants to have all material evidence on hand."

"You don't consider the beads material evidence?" She tried to keep the disappointment out of her voice but couldn't. On the other hand, that bloom of hope was holding steady. If the police weren't going to rule out foul play quite yet, that had to mean Darcy wasn't carrying on a fool's errand. Right?

"I'm afraid not. Look, I appreciate what you're trying to do. I really do. With your relationship with Mr. Maxwell, the department wants to be respectful to you. But, if we get reports that you're bothering people, we won't hesitate to take steps to bring this campaign of yours to a halt."

"Fair enough. Can I keep the beads?" She would put them to use someplace else.

"Be my guest." Kaitlin got to her feet. "Let me walk you out."

Bowed, but not beaten, Darcy returned to the record store. Hank and Peter had the store looking spotless. Evidently, they'd concluded their Miles Davis/Bob Marley dispute peacefully. With the sales floor in good hands, she retreated to the office. She needed to finalize arrangements for the bands performing on Record Store Day.

She also wanted time to regroup and figure out her next move.

An hour later, she emerged from the office.

"Peter, got a project for you." She handed a piece of paper to him. "This is the RSD performance schedule. The outside shows are at the top. The ones on the mini stage by the office are at the bottom. Think you put your rad art skills to work and come up with something cool? I want to hand it out with every purchase."

The young man's eyes lit up. "Oh, yesi. This will be fun."

Darcy was so tickled with the young man's reaction, she refrained from commenting about his use of the Caribbean slang term. She understood the meaning behind the expression, which sounded like *yes-aye* to her Midwestern ears. She wasn't sure if it was appropriate for him to use it, though. She made a mental note to speak to his grandmother about it since the matriarch of Peter's family was giving a talk about the history of reggae music on RSD.

"Good. I need something by the end of the day Friday. That will give us a week to hand them out. Now, if y'all will excuse me, I have an errand to run. Be back in an hour."

"Is everything okay?" Hank put a hand on Darcy's arm. "You're running yourself ragged. I'm worried about you."

She gave both of them her best smile. It was one she'd worked on a lot during the Pixie Dust days. Back then, when she used it, it was a fake as often as the real thing. Now, it was one hundred percent genuine, through and through.

"There's no need for either of you to worry. I'm fine. The store's fine. I need to make a quick trip to turn up the heat on Eddie's murderer."

Chapter Twenty

Darcy's parting comment to Hank and Peter had been made in jest. But only in part. Without support from the Detective-Sergeant, all she could do was take what she knew in her heart about Eddie's murder and keep unearthing evidence to prove it. Like flipping over an album and finding out the best song is on side B.

Easy peasy.

As if.

As she walked down the street, Darcy's situation wasn't complicated. The beads in her pocket were the key to a locked box that held the answer to the riddle of who killed Eddie Maxwell. Her fear, though, was that once the box was opened, all she'd find was another, smaller box with another clue hidden inside.

While she waited for traffic to clear at the intersection of Delaware and Madison Streets, she rolled her shoulders a few times. It was a surefire way to rid herself of some stress that had accumulated during the visit to the police station. It was an exercise she'd been doing from her first days behind a drum kit. In addition to relieving the discomfort, it also produced a sense of clarity.

Which she was going to need if she was going to get the Hobbit to fess up.

She jiggled the beads in her pocket as she took a step into the intersection. Her game plan was still a little fuzzy but was becoming clearer with each step toward The Magic Box, home for all of one's favorite board and role-playing games.

And murder weapons

"Make him sweat. Don't show your hand too early. Maybe he did it. Or maybe he made the letter opener for the person who did. That's what you need to find out."

Darcy took a quick look around. Nobody was near enough to overhear her talking to herself. The idea of being seen carrying on a one-way conversation didn't bother her. She looked like the countless souls who used pair of earbuds connected to their phones to chat with others.

What worried her was showing her cards too early in the game. So, she ended the conversation twenty feet from the store's entrance. Hopefully, way out of the Hobbit's earshot.

When she was ready, she straightened her spine to bring her up to her full five, nine height and grasped the door handle.

A few bars of the theme from *Star Wars* rang out when the door opened. She hadn't noticed it on her previous visit. The fact that she'd picked up on a new detail made her smile. Her detective skills were improving.

Unless the Hobbit had recently installed it. In that case, it was only a cool doorbell.

"Darcy Gaughan, what's shakin', sister bacon?" The Hobbit put a game box on a shelf, then wiped his hands on a rag. "Been putting some old stock out. Gets dusty. You know how it is."

"That, I do." She pulled the beads from her pocket but kept them hidden for the moment. "I was wondering if you could help me with something."

"Does it have to do with my 3D printer? If so, I don't have time to talk." He waved his hands in front of him to form an X, then turned away.

"Nope." She opened her palm. "Do these look familiar?"

The Hobbit did a double-take. Then his eyes narrowed for a moment. "Never seen them before in my life."

Liar. Darcy kept the comment to herself. It wasn't enough to know the man was a liar. Now she needed to use that against him to get even more information.

"Yeah. I'm not so sure about that. You see, they were found at the record store. After Eddie was stabbed to death." She drew close enough to him to see tiny drops of sweat above his brow. "What if I told you that the letter opener used to murder Eddie is missing two jewels from the handle? And what if I told you those missing jewels are in my hand right here?"

He looked around as he practically leapt away. Like he'd just stepped in a pile of dog poo and wanted to get away from it as fast as possible.

"I don't know what you're talking about."

He was going to dig in his heels and go the obfuscation route, then. Darcy could work with that. God knew she'd taken that approach with people trying to help her way too many times in the past.

"Let me enlighten you, then." She leaned against the sales counter and took a deep breath, using the silence to ramp up the man's distress. "Eddie adored his letter opener. He'd go on for hours about it if you gave him the chance. He kept it on his desk so people could see it. And enjoy it as much as he did."

"Your point being?"

"That it would be easy to take pictures of it. Then use those pictures as the basis of a 3D printed copy. It wouldn't be hard for someone with a little skill to give the blade a chrome finish. A photo of Elvis for the handle could be taken from the Internet. Copies of the jewels, the same as these ones, could be found at any craft store."

The Hobbit ran his palms along his shirt sleeves, leaving streaks of sweat in their wakes.

"So, what? You're trying to say I made the letter opener that was used to kill your boss?"

"I didn't say that." She waited a beat, just like she did with a song. "But you did."

"Oh, come on. You've got no proof of anything." He laughed but sweat had begun to trickle down the sides of his face. The man perspired a lot when he was under the gun.

"I don't?" She shook her head. "Dude, I met with the cops earlier today. These beads *are* the missing pieces from the letter opener over at the police station. What's it gonna be? Either you take the rap for murdering Eddie right now or you give up the person who hired you to make the copy."

He ran his index finger and thumb around his lips. She had him where she wanted him. Now, to see if he would call her bluff or raise the stakes even higher. As he continued some internal debate, she decided it was time to turn the pressure up another notch.

"If you want, I can call the cops. I've got Officer Rosengarten in my contacts." She held her phone out for him to see. She had the cop in her phone because of all of the trouble she'd gotten into in the past. That detail would stay under wraps, though.

"Fine, whatever." He dropped his hands to his sides with a huff. "I didn't do anything wrong. There's no way I'm taking the rap for anyone."

Darcy raised her eyebrows but kept the rest of her expression neutral. And said a thank you to the celestial powers that had made it so nobody else was in the store at the moment. Customers hanging around would have made it way too easy for him to blow her off.

Instead, as the man eased onto his stool behind the sales counter, she was about to get a key piece of information, like the bass track that she could layer on top of a drum track.

"Well?" She kept her phone in view to let him know she wasn't playing. "You made the murder weapon for someone. Who was it?"

"Okay, first off, I didn't make any murder weapon. We clear about that?" He held his tongue until Darcy nodded.

"About a year ago, I made a custom dagger for Heather Ewing. Looking back, I suppose it looked a little like Mister Maxwell's letter opener."

The revelation hit Darcy like a wall of off-key music. *Heather? A murderer? Can't be.* "Did she say what she wanted it for?"

"It was a gift for Claude. He's one of my regular D and D players. When he's Dungeon Master, he likes to show off a bit, get into character. He'd put it on a little display stand in front of him, so everyone knew who was in charge."

"Really?" Darcy didn't know much about role-playing games. Pretty much everything she knew came from the gaming scenes in *Stranger Things*.

"Don't act so surprised. Players really get into the spirit of game. Some like to dress for the occasion. It's not that much different from people who wear their favorite player's jersey to a ballgame."

"Fair enough. You said she asked you to do a custom job. Did she give you any specs? I mean, how were you able to make what she wanted?"

"She had pictures. Said Claude had been wanting something like it for a long time."

"Do you still have the pictures?"

"No. Gave them back to her when I finished the project."

Darcy nodded. It was all she could do. While she understood what she was being told, the words didn't compute. If Claude wanted something that looked like Eddie's letter opener, surely Heather would have mentioned it already.

Wouldn't she?

Darcy didn't want to assume anything. A lot of people still assumed she was an irresponsible wreck. They were wrong. She'd make the same mistake if she assumed Heather wasn't involved in Eddie's murder. After all, despite their recent brainstorming session, Darcy only had the woman's word to go on.

She scrolled through the pictures on her phone until she came to one that had the letter opener in it. "Is this what you made?"

To his credit, the Hobbit took a long look at the image. After a while, he frowned. "No. I mean the blade was about the same length, but the handle on the dagger I made was completely different."

"But you remember using beads like these," she placed them on the counter, "in the dagger you made. Is that right?"

"No. I have a whole stash of paint, glue, and other supplies for my print jobs. It's a lot of fun, actually. But I didn't add anything to the one I made for Mrs. Ewing."

"Okay. Do you remember Claude bringing the dagger with him when he was dungeon king?"

"*Master*. Dungeon Master." With a roll of his eyes, the Hobbit stood, using his entire five-fight height to let Darcy know he wasn't happy with her mangling the terminology.

"My bad. Dungeon Master. Do you remember seeing it?"

"Yeah, but that was a while ago. The D and D group meets once a week. They take turns being the DM, so someone only plays that role once every six weeks or so."

Darcy was about to ask another question when the familiar *Star Wars* melody interrupted them. A couple of guys walked in, deep in conversation. They waved as they went straight to the back room.

"That's some of my *Magic the Gathering* players. They have a game starting in fifteen. I need to see if they need anything. I take it we're done here?"

"Sure. Absolutely." Darcy stuck out her hand. "I appreciate you being straight with me."

"Good. Maxwell may not have been my favorite person, but he wasn't a bad dude. Helluva way to go. That ain't right."

"On that point, I agree with you one hundred percent." Darcy was effusive in her thanks to the Hobbit on her way out the door. The information she'd wrangled out of him was better than a gold record.

On her walk back to work, she reviewed what she'd learned. It was helpful but, as she'd feared, she was faced with another box that needed to be unlocked.

The most logical person to have that key was Heather.

She pulled up the woman's number on her phone. As she hit send, she was faced with a critical question. Was Heather Ewing, Eddie's old friend and neighbor, friend or foe? The woman answered the call before Darcy could decide.

It was time to go all in. "Heather, I wanted to say thanks again for your help the other day. I have some things I'd like to run by you. Are you available tomorrow?"

Darcy wanted to meet right that minute, but she'd promised Hank and Peter she'd return in a timely fashion. She couldn't take off for hours at a time whenever she wanted. Shirking her duties to Marysburg Music was not an option.

"Sure. Do you want to swing by the house on your way to work?"

Darcy opened her mouth, then clamped it shut. What if Heather was the murderer? Just because she told the Hobbit the dagger was for Claude didn't make it so. Besides, what did she *really* know about the woman? Heather had been married to Claude for decades but clearly had feelings for Eddie.

Was she a master at hiding her true feelings? And then had it become a case of Hell hath no fury like a woman scorned? Claude came across as a bit of a buzzkill. Maybe Heather had decided enough was enough and made her previously amorous feelings known to Eddie.

And he'd rejected them.

She was probably as familiar with Eddie's letter opener as anyone outside of Darcy and the man himself.

"Darcy? You still there?"

"Oh, sorry about that. Had a brain fade." Which for people who knew the old Darcy Gaughan, was something of a regular occurrence. "I can't make it in the morning. How about tomorrow afternoon? It's supposed to be nice weather. We could meet at six at the shelter at the park. The one by the trees." If Heather was a murderer, Darcy wanted to be near things that she could use for cover.

"Um." There was a tiny hesitation. "Okay, I suppose that should work. I'll see you then."

Until Darcy knew the lay of the land better, like whether or not Heather was a murderer, there was *no way* she was meeting her on the woman's turf. Neutral territory was way better.

She was betting her life on it, after all.

Chapter Twenty-One

For Darcy, the problem with arranging to meet a suspected murderer in twenty-four hours was that it left gobs of time for anxiety to build. It was like with each beat of her heart, a suffocating crowd of people squeezed in on her, step by step, until she had trouble moving, breathing, even thinking.

It also meant a night in which she tossed, turned, paced the bedroom, and counted sheep backward from one hundred to zero. Twice.

In short, by the time Darcy's alarm went off at seven, she'd already showered, gone for a stroll to the deck with Ringo by her side, and downed a mug of Irish Breakfast tea while she reviewed her case notes.

"Hey, Ringo. Time to get out of bed." She pressed a key on her phone to silence the alarm.

In response, the scraggly tomcat rubbed his partially shredded ear with his paw, stretched his spine until he resembled an inverted letter U, and trotted toward the house.

"I didn't mean it literally," she called over her shoulder, prompting the cat to stop midway between the deck and the back door. He seemed to be staring at a squirrel chirruping away in a nearby oak tree. No way it could be the case that the cat was listening to his human housemate.

She covered a yawn with her fist as she went back to her notes. During the night, she'd moved all of her notes from the investigation to an app on her phone. It was an act that helped her feel like she had some control over the situation. While she sipped the caffeine-infused drink, she kept studying the information, certain there was a clue there she simply hadn't yet seen.

A freshening breeze off the river made her shiver. She pulled her hoodie tighter around her head and blew on her fingers. Even though the sun's rays were only beginning to warm her surroundings, Darcy had enjoyed the brisk temperatures and the wildlife's melodious chattering. The time on the deck had calmed her frazzled nerves, which in turn had opened her mind to consider the case's myriad potential permutations.

After sleeping on it, or not sleeping on it, really, Darcy had stripped away questions, suppositions, and theories until she was left with a handful of scenarios.

In the first one, the Hobbit made the dagger and sold it to Heather. She modified it to look like Eddie's letter opener and murdered him with it in a case of unrequited love. It was the simplest solution. And Darcy hadn't been able to verify the woman's alibi yet.

In the second scenario, the Hobbit made an exact replica of Eddie's letter opener at someone's behest. That person used it to murder Eddie. This gambit was more complicated than the first. On the other hand, Darcy could totally see Todd hiring the Hobbit to create the murder weapon and then holding something over him to keep his mouth shut. Maybe that's why they'd been arguing the other day.

In the third scenario, Heather lied to the Hobbit. She sold or gave the dagger, after remodeling it into letter opener form, to someone else to murder Eddie. Like Rafe. Even more complicated than the first two.

In the fourth scenario.... She threw her hands up in surrender. There were still too many schemes. And still too much unknown.

Her brain was running around in circles faster than an Olympic sprinter. Which meant she needed someone to talk to.

A little bit later, Darcy pulled to a stop in front of Perfect Pastries. She took a moment to savor Rusty's quiet rumble. Liam had done a masterful tune-up job. In addition to the engine's new low, throaty growl, the blasts of noxious blue smoke from the tailpipe were gone. The manual transmission shifted as smooth as a jazz percussionist moving from instrument to instrument, too. She'd worry about the cost when the credit card bill arrived.

At the moment, she had other priorities.

It was a little after eight when Darcy entered the café. The place buzzed with the hustle and bustle of the morning rush. A line of customers waited to pay for to-go orders of coffee and a doughnut or other yummy pastry. Every stool at the counter was occupied, mostly by workers in heavy boots and dungarees who'd recently finished their overnight shift at the local auto parts manufacturing plant.

Jenna nodded to Darcy as she speed-walked by, laden with a massive serving platter that was holding six mouth-watering breakfasts. "A two-seater by the window opened up a minute ago if you don't mind wiping down the table and chairs yourself."

At any other dining establishment, Darcy wouldn't have known how to respond to such an informal greeting. At Jenna's place, she knew exactly what to do. She grabbed a clean rag from behind the counter, wetted it down, and did what she was told.

Then she made herself a cup of English Breakfast tea. She would have helped herself to a blueberry scone but thought messing around with the pastries was one step too far. Instead, she asked Jenna for one when the woman had a chance. No rush.

While she waited for the scone, she sipped her liquid rocket fuel and returned her notes.

"There's got to be a way to eliminate some of these people."

"What's that, hon?" Jenna placed the pastry and a glass of water on the table.

"I'm struggling with the case. I feel like keep running into brick walls. Don't suppose you can spare a few minutes to help a woman in need?"

They took a look around the restaurant. Since Darcy had sat down, a few tables had opened up and three stools at the counter had been vacated. The busiest part of the morning rush seemed to be in the past.

"Give me five and I'm all ears."

A bit later, after filling Jenna in, Darcy shrugged. "And that's what I've got. Even after everything I've learned, I still don't know who did it. And that's got me freaking out because I don't know what to do or say when I meet Heather tonight."

Jenna took a sip from her water bottle. Her gaze remained focused on Darcy while she drank. Eventually, she dabbed at the corner of her mouth with a paper napkin.

"I'm amazed at all you've learned. And I'm more convinced than ever that you're right." She gave Darcy's hand an encouraging squeeze. "Believe in yourself. You're close. I can feel it."

"Thanks, but close doesn't get the job done. You know that thing about horseshoes and hand grenades." She let out a frustrated growl. "My biggest problem is that I can't confirm anyone's alibi. Todd says he was at his lake cottage, Claude and the Hobbit were at Selena's but later in the evening, Jasmine says she went home after work, Heather says she was at—"

"Wait a minute. What did you say about Jasmine?"

"She told me she went home after work and read a book. I'm sure she's lying I but can't figure out why."

Jenna smiled. All of a sudden, the woman across from Darcy looked like a barracuda revealing its rows of razor-sharp teeth moments before going in for the kill.

"I believe I can help you with that. Jasmine didn't go home and Todd wasn't at his cabin."

"Then where were they?" After a few moments of silence, the implication hit Darcy like a roar from the crowd. "Holy smokes. They were together? But they split up, like four years ago. He's remarried, for crying out loud."

"Yes, but at least the night someone took Eddie's life, they were together. I know because I saw them."

Jenna paused for dramatic effect. No doubt a product of her involvement in Marysburg's community theater group.

"Todd recently bought a house in my neighborhood. He's renovating it so he can rent it to college students. I was taking Bruno for a walk, this was about nine, and I saw Jasmine walking down the driveway from behind the house. She was in running gear and took off without noticing I was there."

"Go on." Darcy was literally on the edge of her seat.

"I was curious, so I crossed the street to get a closer look. Todd's BMW was parked in the driveway. Well, I figured that was as good a time as any to encourage Bruno to take a potty break. While he did his business, the lights in the house went off and the car, with Todd behind the wheel, pulled out. This was about ten minutes after Jasmine left."

"Wow. Talk about *Your Cheatin' Heart*."

"I know, right? Sorry I didn't mention it before. I figured they might be hooking up again and I didn't want to be a gossip. It never crossed my mind it would matter to your investigation."

"It's matters, all right. The question is how long they'd been there, though." Darcy drummed her fingers on the edge of the tabletop.

"Maybe, maybe not. All you really need to do is tell one of them that you know they lied to you. Then you put the pressure on to get them to fess up about how long they were together that night. Promise them you'll keep their little secret. I know I'd fess up if it took me off a list of murder suspects."

"I don't know if I have time to track both of them down before I see Heather." Darcy downed the rest of her tea. "I'll go after Todd. With the trophy wife in his life, I'd bet he has a lot more to lose than Jasmine if their secret got out."

Jenna gave her a fist bump. "I like the way you think, girl. A touch of deviousness in the pursuit of justice. Text me if you need anything. I have a feeling you won't, though."

* * *

Darcy was working on payroll when Hank knocked on the office door. "Things are quiet out front. Do you mind if I skip out for a coffee?"

"Nope. I can do this work out there as easily as I can back here." With her laptop under her arm, Darcy walked with Hank to the sales floor. "Hey, before you go, I'd like to run something past you."

"Yes?" He cocked his head to the side and put his hands behind his back.

"Don't worry. It's not bad. I was thinking of asking Charlotte if she'd be interested in becoming store manager. You know, take over some of the things I did since I'll be doing things Eddie did." She shuffled her feet while she tried to figure out the right words to say next.

"I know you've always said this job is fun for you. You've been here longer than she has, though. And I really value your opinion." She shrugged. "And everything else you bring to the table. If it's a problem for you, say the word. What do you think?"

He looked away for a moment. When his gaze returned, his eyes were watery. And he was grinning.

"I think that's an excellent idea. I also appreciate you talking to me. You're the boss. You don't need my approval, though."

"Maybe not. Your support means the world to me, though. And with Char as manager, I can officially make you Chief Audio Consultant."

"Has a nice ring to it. What would I be doing in this new position?"

"Same thing you've been doing. Except at fifty cents an hour more. I wish I could offer you more than that—"

"But, like you said, I work here because I like it. I don't need the money. Still, thank you." He gave her a formal bow. "Now, if you don't mind, your Chief Audio Consultant needs caffeine."

By the time Charlotte arrived for her shift, Darcy's cheeks were aching from her non-stop smile. It had done her soul good to focus on work for a while. She was ready to spread more good news before returning her attention to Eddie's murderer again.

Darcy and Hank had worked out how she was going to offer the new position to Charlotte. It was going to be a challenge to keep a straight face during the performance.

The woman was hanging up her jacket in the office when Darcy came in behind her and closed the door.

"Char, I need to have a word with you." She covered her mouth with her hand, like she was thinking about something serious, to hide a grin.

"Sure. What's up?"

"We can't keep going on like this." Darcy let out a long sigh and stared at the floor. "Now that things have settled down a bit, I've decided to make some changes."

The blood drained from Charlotte's face. "Have I done something wrong? Whatever it is, give me a chance to fix it."

"I'm sorry. This isn't something you can fix. Sometimes, we have to accept what happens in life."

Tears were welling up in Charlotte's eyes. It was time to end the practical joke.

"Which is why I hope you can accept a two dollar an hour raise."

"Accept," her mouth opened, but no sound came out. "Wait, two dollars an hour? What?"

"To go with your new position as store manager." Darcy's smile grew from ear to ear. "Surprise! What do you think?"

Charlotte sat as still as legendary bass player Bill Wyman for a while. Her brows, which had been furrowed, shot up as she jumped to her feet.

"I think you are the meanest boss ever for pulling that trick on me. I thought you were firing me."

"Yeah, sorry about that." Darcy took a moment to chew on a thumbnail. "I guess it was kind of mean. Forgive me?"

"Well." Charlotte cracked a smile. "Since you apologized. Yes, I forgive you."

"Awesome. So, how about the job?" She put her hand on the door handle, ready to announce her the store's new manager.

"No."

Darcy froze while she tried to make sense of the simple, two-letter answer. Sure, maybe the joke hadn't been in the best of taste, but it was still a joke. Had she misread the situation?

"Look, Char. I really am sorry. It looks like I took the joke too far. That's on me. Please, don't let a stupid mistake on my part ruin things. We want you here. I need you here."

The woman gave Darcy a long, cold stare so intense that it made her want to crawl under the desk. Then Charlotte let out a huff and crossed her arms. After a few more seconds that felt like hours, Charlotte let her arms drop down to her sides.

And she broke out into a grin.

"Gotcha!" She laughed. "Two can play at that game, Boss. I forgive you and I accept the job. Let's go sell some music before Hank gets nosy."

As she slipped through the doorway, Charlotte put her arm around Darcy and gave her a squeeze. Then she skipped over to Hank to give him the good news. While the two were chatting in animated tones, Darcy fetched a bottle of non-alcoholic champagne she'd hidden in a cooler behind the desk and three HotBox Pizza cups.

"How about a celebration? Char, since I'm in your doghouse, you get the biggest pour." Once the cups were filled, Darcy raised hers. "To the best folks a woman could hope to work with. May the good times keep rolling."

They clinked amid a chorus of "Cheers."

A customer stopped flipping through the Taylor Swift albums to see what all the fuss was about. Charlotte immediately scrounged up another cup, brought him the last of the champagne, and got into a deep discussion with the man about which T-Swift album was the best.

Darcy leaned against the counter with a satisfied sigh. She caught Hank staring at her. "What?"

"Oh, nothing much." He chuckled. "Only that you did really good today. Eddie would be proud."

"Even with the prank that misfired?" Her cheeks got warm at the mere thought of how horrifically wrong things had gone.

"Forget about it. I'm pretty sure Charlotte has. And if she hasn't, that means she'll have a great story to tell the kids next time they work."

"Thanks for the warning. It gives me time to come up with a way to tell my side."

They shared a laugh, but then Darcy's jovial mood changed as a troubling thought came to mind.

Waiting a day to get together with Heather meant Darcy had given the woman more than enough time to go over the story she wanted to tell. And make changes to it until it sounded perfect, like a tune from a Bruno Mars album.

Would that actually come to pass? She'd find out soon enough.

Chapter Twenty-Two

Darcy was bagging a customer's purchase, the debut album from Black Pumas and a vintage LP by soul legend Al Green, when the appointment reminder on her phone went off.

"Hot date tonight?" Charlotte gave her a quick elbow to the ribs. On any other day, Darcy would have slapped her arm away. Today was a day to cut her new manager a lot of slack. The woman was in a great mood. There was no need to spoil it.

"I wish." Darcy rolled her eyes. Oh, how she wished she had something so much more pleasant, even a date, on her schedule.

On the other hand, she hadn't been out on a date, like a real one with the potential of romance, since before she got sober. Which had been totally fine with her. Like so many things in Darcy's post-rehab life, the goal had been to focus on her own mental health. That meant putting relationships, and the emotional roller coaster ride that so often went with them, on the shelf for a while.

"Well, I think Liam would be a good catch. He's interested in you, you know." Charlotte winked at her.

"Oh, come on. Liam's a buddy. Nothing more."

"You sure?"

"I am absolutely certain. Sure, he's easy on the eyes, but he's never made a move on me. If he was interested, he would have by now."

"If you say so." Charlotte shrugged. "I wouldn't be so sure, though. Give yourself some credit, girl."

"Okay, fine." Being agreeable was the easiest path of resistance at this point. Besides, Darcy had other things that were far more important than her nonexistent love life to focus on. "If he ever asks to meet for a cup of coffee, I'll say yes. I'm not going to hold my breath, though. And neither should you."

"Okay, okay." She put her hands up in surrender. "Can I ask where you're off to? You know, in case I have to, in the role as store manager, confer with you about something."

Despite the anxiety-induced knot growing at the base of her neck, Darcy laughed. "God love ya, Char. You are a persistent one. If you must know, I'm meeting with Heather Ewing at the park. The Hobbit claims he made something a lot like the murder weapon for Heather a while back."

"Jinkies. You don't think she's the murderer, do you? She's always so nice when she comes in here."

"I hope not. Now, I can't help wondering if she was playing me the whole time we were brainstorming in the office. To see how much I knew. That's why I want to meet her in a public space."

"If she is the killer, is it wise to go alone? Couldn't you at least let the cops know what you're doing?"

"I appreciate the suggestion. The good Detective-Sergeant might be coming around thanks to my letter opener holding demonstration. Still, she still isn't convinced Eddie was murdered. I'm afraid if I tell her what I'm doing, she'll stop me in my tracks. My meeting with her the other day actually went okay, all things considered. I don't want to screw that up." She straightened up. "No. This needs to be a solo project."

"You're the boss." Charlotte pointed to the clock on the wall. "But, if I don't hear from you by closing time, I'm calling the police. End of discussion. I have spoken."

* * *

Ten minutes later, Darcy pulled into a parking spot at the park. A blue minivan was parked at the far end of the lot by the playground. There were no other vehicles to be seen. If Heather had already arrived, apparently she hadn't driven. The hairs on the back of Darcy's neck rose to attention as scenarios ran through her head.

What if Heather arrived on foot so nobody would know she was here? And what if she'd made that decision knowing that Darcy was going to confront her? Would she try to take Darcy out?

Heather seemed like a lovely person, but what if that was a cover, like the helmets the guys from Daft Punk wore to hide their identities? If a confrontation got out of hand, who would the police be more likely to believe? Would they buy the story of the grief-stricken, recovering alcoholic who was obsessed with finding someone to blame for the death of the man who literally pulled her from the gutter? Or would they believe the woman who recently retired after working in the high school attendance office for twenty-five years?

It didn't take a genius to figure that one out.

"Doesn't matter, Gina. Only the truth does." Darcy tapped the Gina Schock photo. The drummer for the Go-Go's was Darcy's hero. She often talked to the photo when she had nobody else to confide in. The ritual gave her strength.

She had a feeling she was going to need every bit of strength she could muster in the upcoming minutes.

The shelter was a few hundred yards away from the parking lot. Freshly laid crushed gravel crunched under the soles of Darcy's Chuck Taylors as she made her way there. Squirrels dashed through the inch-high grass, sprinting from one tree to another. A bird chased another one, the pair making amazing twists and turns in mid-air before their race took them too far away for Darcy to keep track.

Despite the adorable wildlife, the shelter loomed larger with every step she took.

It seemed like decades ago that Darcy had met Hank and Charlotte under the same metal roof to tell them about Eddie's demise. At that very same picnic table, a lone figure sat. The individual was hunched over like they were reading something.

With each breath the knot in Darcy's midsection pulled tighter. Voices began whispering taunts in her head.

You have no clue what you're doing. You're way out of your league, girl. You failed your bandmates in Pixie Dust and you're going to fail Eddie.

"Stop it." Darcy came to an abrupt halt as the words escaped her.

The person in the shelter must have heard her. They looked at her, then waved.

It was Heather.

The woman rose and smiled wide as Darcy stepped from the gravel path onto the structure's concrete pad. The tin roof blocked out the evening sun's warming rays. A chill ran down her spine. Whether it was because of Heather or the drop in temperature, Darcy couldn't tell.

After exchanging greetings, the women sat, one on either side of the picnic table. They were like opponents with an imaginary chessboard between them. Instead of *The Queen's Gambit*, this was *The Drummer's Gambit*.

"What's on your mind? Are you making progress looking for Eddie's murderer?"

Darcy tugged at the collar of her jacket. This was the second time Heather had mentioned Eddie's death in terms of murder, rather than suicide. Was that mere semantics?

Or did the woman know for a fact that Eddie had been killed?

"Some." She placed her palms on the table. The smooth wood steadied her. "I was talking to Sean O'Sullivan the other day. He had some interesting things to say."

"Oh, really. Such as?" Heather leaned forward. Her eyes were wide and practically glistened with interest. Or was that excitement?

Time to put up or shut up. It was easy for Darcy to confront people she didn't like. Jasmine, Todd, Rafe—if Darcy never spoke to them ever again, it was okay with her. It was different with Heather. The woman had always been kind. She'd always been a ray of sunshine in the store. The thought of wrongly accusing her of murder made Darcy's stomach, which was already in knots, do somersaults.

"Well, he said about a year and a half ago, you asked him to make a custom ornamental dagger with his 3D printer."

Heather leaned back as her gaze narrowed a touch. She tapped the tabletop with her right middle finger. The air seemed to be sucked from the shelter as Darcy waited for the woman's response.

Then she tilted her head to the side. "That's true. I'd forgotten about that. It was a ceremonial dagger for Claude to use when he played Dungeons and Dragons."

That meant the Hobbit's story checked out. At least so far.

"But Darcy, you can't possibly believe it was used to murder Eddie. The thing's plastic. There's no way it could be hurt someone."

Maybe in its original form. Darcy kept that thought to herself. Now wasn't the time to escalate the situation.

"Do you know if Claude still has it?"

"Look." Heather's cheeks got red as she pointed a finger at Darcy. "It's no secret Claude didn't like Eddie. That doesn't mean he's a murderer. If you ask me—"

"That's exactly what I'm doing. The Hobbit seems to think that someone, with the right skill set, could have modified the dagger and turned it into a murder weapon. All I need to do is take a look at it and then I can take it off a list of potential murder weapons. Easy peasy, see?"

Despite her hopes, it might not be so easy. If Claude still had the dagger, then yes, case closed on that path. If he didn't, then Darcy was opening up a whole can of nasty, slimy, wriggly worms.

"Oh." The righteous indignation Heather had built up escaped like the air out of a balloon that had been pricked. "I see what you mean."

Darcy took a moment to let her emotions settle. "Do you know if he still has it?"

"I don't. A while back, he told me it got broken at one of his game nights. That was months ago."

"And he didn't say anything about trying to get it repaired or replaced?"

Heather shook her head. "No. He told me he threw it away."

It sounded entirely plausible. The world wasn't perfect. People broke things all the time. Goodness knew Darcy had broken more than her fair share of things over the years, from drumheads to whiskey bottles.

Still, something niggled at the back of her brain. Something about the explanation was lacking. Then it hit her.

Where was the proof?

Darcy's heart rate ticked up a notch as she thought back to her drinking days. Countless times, she told her tour manager she'd thrown out any liquor that was close at hand. And too many times, that had been a lie. She'd hidden some in a flask under her mattress or in a small bottle in a shoe.

No. It was like an action movie, where the villain appears to die in a fiery explosion, but nobody bothers to look for a body. Not even to make sure all really was well. Then the bad guy turns up again to wreak more havoc. Unless Darcy could see for herself that the dagger was broken beyond repair, she had to assume it had been modified and used to murder Eddie.

"Does Claude have any of those little figurines for his board games? The kind you can paint yourself?" Darcy was thinking of the ones the Hobbit sold. If Claude had a stash of art supplies...

"A few. He'll bring one home a new one every now and then. He said the other players had their own figures, so he might as well start doing it, too. I think it's good for him. Gives him something creative to do."

"Uh-huh. Do you know how long he's been doing that?"

Heather pushed a few strands of gray hair that had gotten loose in the breeze behind her ear. Was she thinking? Or stalling?

At last, she shook her head. "I don't know. Seems like he brought the first one home around the time I gave him the dagger. I remember him saying something along the line that the guys loved the dagger and he said his next step into full out D and D lifestyle was to start using his own custom-made game figures."

"Do you know where Claude is right now?"

"He's at home." Her gaze darted from side to side. "I don't understand. What's with the fixation with his gaming supplies?"

Darcy got to her feet. She needed a moment to think about her response. Everything she had was still circumstantial. Well, like the old saying went, history favored the bold. Especially when hard, irrefutable evidence was almost within her grasp.

"I'm sorry, Heather. I don't think Claude's dagger got broken some night at gaming. I think he told you that, but he actually modified it and then used it to murder Eddie."

"What?" Heather shot to her feet. "That's insane. Why would he do something like that?"

There was a rustling in the tree line a few yards from the shelter. A figure emerged.

"Because he'd had enough." The figure had a man's voice.

It was Claude. He had a gun in his hand.

It was pointed right at Darcy.

Chapter Twenty-Three

"Get down!" Darcy dove for cover behind a picnic table as a shot rang out. It might have been her imagination, but she would have sworn she heard the buzz of the bullet as it whizzed by, only inches from her ear.

With more adrenaline dumped into her system than she'd ever experienced onstage, she crawled to Heather. The poor woman was standing, still as a statue. Darcy pulled her down as a second shot made a metal *twang* as it ricocheted off one of the steel support beams.

"Heather, look at me." Darcy took the woman's head in her hands and held onto it until they made eye contact. "You need to get out of here. Right now. He's after me. Not you.

"As soon as I make a break for it, he'll follow. Once he does that, call the cops, go home, and lock your doors."

Without waiting for a response, Darcy turned and broke into an all-out dash for Rusty. An image of Olympic sprinters came to mind, and she tried to keep low. It meant less wind resistance while also giving Claude a smaller target.

Her thigh muscles began to burn as her feet pounded the gravel path. Darcy was in decent physical condition, but she was used to walking and skateboarding. Too terrified to check to see how close Claude was to her, she kept her legs and arms pumping, sending out a plea that her heart wouldn't explode before she reached the jeep.

She was almost there when her right leg cramped up. With a cry of agony, she tumbled to the ground in a cloud of gravel dust. Tears ran down her face as she rolled over, her calf a molten rock of pain. As she struggled to get back up, she took a look behind her. Claude was marching toward her. His figure, and especially the pistol in his hand, loomed larger with every step he took.

"Frack you," she shouted at the man as she forced herself into a standing position. Sweat poured off her as she righted herself and limped toward her beloved vehicle.

"Twenty feet." Her breaths became labored with each lurch forward. "Come on, girl. This is nothing compared to rehab."

Ten feet from her goal, she stumbled, scraping her hands on the gravel. The pain signals from her palms dumped another dose of adrenaline into her bloodstream. Her head was pounding, but she got back up and in a final burst collapsed against the jeep.

"Thank the spirits above." She drew in a breath, then bounced on her good leg once, then again before launching herself into the driver's seat. As the engine rumbled to life, Darcy stole a look at the path.

Claude was nowhere to be seen.

Her breaths sped up as she spun around in her seat, looking for him. Before the panic attack could take full hold of her, she spotted him.

He was jogging toward a truck parked in a corner of the lot. Had it been there when she arrived? It didn't matter. Whether Claude had followed Heather and laid in wait to see what happened was irrelevant. What mattered now was he was only a few paces from his vehicle.

The chase was about to begin.

Darcy pressed down on the clutch, shoved the manual transmission into reverse, and...promptly stalled the engine. The cramp was easing, but she had almost no feeling in her right foot. The foot that she needed to operate the gas and brake pedals.

She keyed the engine again and managed to get moving the same time Claude got into his truck. With her teeth gritted against the pain in her leg, her palms, everywhere really, Darcy shifted into first and headed for the park's exit.

With Claude hot on her tail.

"God, I'm in a car chase straight out of a detective show." Despite the worrisome numbness in her foot and the stinging sensation radiating up her arms from her hands, she let out a laugh. It was better than breaking down in tears.

Until she knew what Heather's status was, going straight to the police station was out of the question. For all Darcy knew, Heather's role in the drama currently playing out had been to lure Darcy to her demise. If husband and wife were working together, they'd no doubt claim any story Darcy told the cops was nothing more than a conspiracy borne of desperate delusion.

No. She needed to finish this solo.

She sped up to beat a yellow light, hoping to put some distance between herself and her pursuer. A glance in the rearview mirror, along with the startling honking of multiple car horns, dashed those hopes.

Claude wasn't going to let anything as trivial as a yellow light keep him from his prey.

As she slowed to take a right-hand turn onto Concord Lane, she decided. If Claude wanted a showdown, it would be on her turf.

"Let's go, girl." She hit play on the car stereo. As "Bad Reputation" blasted through the speakers, Darcy floored it. It was time to show the man who was boss.

Darcy piloted the jeep toward the cabin, skirting Downtown Marysburg where traffic would slow her down. With the accelerator floored, commercial buildings quickly gave way to neighborhoods filled with tidy sidewalks and picturesque homes. The houses became more spread apart with each revolution of the jeep's wheels. She coasted through a bend in the road then floored it again.

This was a race she couldn't afford to lose.

As a stand of sycamores flashed by, Darcy's heart raced like she was playing a drum solo before a sold-out theater. Strangely enough, the pursuit was exhilarating. Even with the massive silver grill of Claude's rig looming in her mirrors, she'd gained a key advantage—familiar surroundings. That is if Claude didn't take her out by ramming her or with a lucky shot while they were moving.

As Joan screamed about not caring about her bad reputation, Darcy blew through a four-way stop. She'd always considered it an optional one anyway.

The moment the cabin, in all its ramshackle glory, came into sight, Darcy sucked in a lungful of air, counted to five, then blew it out. The deep breath and sight of home sweet home cleared her mind.

The flight reflex had done its job. Now, it was time to fight.

She kept her foot on the pedal until the last possible moment, then slammed on the brakes, and yanked the steering wheel to the right. The jeep tilted to the side as she took the abrupt turn on two wheels. The passenger-side tires returned to the earth with a thud, rattling Darcy's teeth, as if to tell her, "Enough already."

"Thank the goddess Stevie Nicks for wide tires," Darcy told the photo of Gina. The stunt driving had kicked up an impressive dust cloud that was obscuring her view of Claude. As she skidded to a stop behind the house, she hoped it was enough cover to get her into the house safe and sound.

The nanosecond she leapt from the jeep, though, an all too familiar crack broke the silence. *The gun.* She dropped to her knees and scuttled around to Rusty's front end, keeping it between her and Claude.

She pressed her back against the jeep's grill, sucking in deep lungsful of air. *Think, girl, think!*

It was a twenty-foot sprint to the back door. Under normal circumstances, she could be there in seconds, have the door unlocked in a few more, and be inside before someone could say Rock and Roll Hall of Fame three times fast.

These weren't normal circumstances.

Darcy glanced at her palms. They were stained red and white from gravel dust and numerous cuts and scrapes. While she forced her breathing to slow down, her mind registered a new source of pain. This one was coming from both legs. Her jeans were stained a dark red color at the knees.

"I've got a killer after me. My hands and knees are covered in blood. I can barely feel my right foot. The house may as well be a million miles away. Still better than rehab." She laughed. "What does the Klingon dude from Star Trek say? 'It's a good day to die.' Not today, friends."

A car door slammed, bringing Darcy out of her reverie.

"Stay calm, Darc. Call the cops and keep the jeep between you and him." Darcy reached for her phone. It wasn't in her back pocket. Fighting back a full-blown panic attack, she checked all four pockets. No luck.

"Darcy? Come out, come out, wherever you are," Claude said in a sing-song voice. "Love that line. Robert De Niro makes such a great bad guy."

She crept around to the passenger side of the jeep. If he was going to waste his breath with movie quotes, she'd take advantage of his arrogance. She popped her head up high enough to look inside the jeep.

Her phone was nowhere to be seen.

Figuring it must have tumbled onto the floor sometime during her daredevil driving, she grasped the handle. Right when she was about to open the door, another shot rang out. Reflexes took over, and she crouched back down, covering her head with her arms in the process. A heartbeat later, the gunshot was followed by the nerve-jangling sound of glass shattering. A nanosecond later, she was showered with the remnants of her passenger side window.

She let out a string of curse words. Real ones, not made-up ones from Battlestar Galactica. They were out before she realized it. If there'd been any doubt in Claude's mind where she was, those doubts had to be gone now.

Fine. It was time to give the psychopath a taste of his own medicine.

She brushed off the debris, thankful the tempered glass had shattered into countless harmless pieces instead of big, sharp shards that could have pierced the skin.

"Hey, when this is all over, I'm gonna bill you for replacing my windows," she shouted.

There was a method to her taunting. If she could get him to respond, she'd get a sense of where he was. That would help her make a move based on his location. She'd used her hearing in a similar fashion back in the Pixie Dust days when she wanted to get past a group of fans and onto the tour bus without being seen.

Then a question popped into her head. How many shots had Claude fired at her? Three or four, maybe five? The man was a lousy shot, but how many bullets did he have left? She could take him in a battle of fisticuffs.

If she could get him to run out of bullets.

Darcy tossed some gravel down the driveway, away from the house. A second later, another shot rang out. Dust was kicked up where the bullet embedded itself near the gravel's landing spot.

She took advantage of the distraction and made a run for the house. Her hands trembled as she yanked open the screen door with one hand and dug her house key out of her pocket with the other. Claude shouted something that barely registered. She ignored him, intent on getting indoors, where it would be safe.

She hoped.

Another gunshot came too close to ignore. Her key ring slipped through her fingers as the bullet hit the wooden back door with a mighty *thwack*.

"Enough." She grabbed a folding camp chair that was by the door. Ringo liked to sun himself in it when Darcy worked in the back yard. She wasn't going to sit in it, though.

"You murder my friend, shoot out the windows of my jeep, and now shoot at my house. I am *so* done with you."

Darcy let out a ferocious roar and charged at Claude. With the chair in front of her like a shield, she bore down on the man. Her sudden change of tactics appeared to catch him off guard. He shielded himself with his hands instead of firing at her.

Once she was a few feet away from him, she swung the chair at him like a baseball bat. The chair contacted his upper arm. It broke into two pieces. The part not in Darcy's hands helicoptered away as the man fell to the ground from the force of the blow.

His grip held firm on the firearm, though. He pointed it at Darcy before she could hit him with the remainder of the chair. Time slowed to a crawl as he squeezed the trigger on the pistol. She had time to notice that it was a small semi-automatic, barely larger than Claude's hand.

Darcy prepared herself for a loud bang and then a blast of searing pain in her midsection. There was no way he would miss her from two feet away.

Instead, the only sound that came from the gun was a harmless *click*.

Chapter Twenty-Four

Darcy looked at her belly. Instead of seeing a bloody hole, she found herself to be one hundred percent intact. If a little grimy.

"Holy Mother of all Drum Solos, I'm not dead." Her voice was barely louder than a whisper.

It was loud enough for Claude to hear, though.

"Not yet, girl." He ejected the clip in the gun and reached into a pocket.

Her fight response had expended itself, so the flight instinct took back over. With nothing more directing her motions than a primal desire to survive, she kicked the gun out of Claude's hand, scooped it up, and made a hobbling dash to safety.

In the wrong direction.

By the time Darcy took time to collect her wits, she was on the deck. She turned around. Claude was bearing down on her, his face a grotesque parody of a snarling tiger. He had another clip of bullets in his hand.

But she had the gun in hers.

It had a cheap feel to it. Now that it was empty, the weapon wasn't much more than a harmless chunk of metal. She sensed that if Claude got too close, though, she could whack him upside the head with it.

He stopped short of the deck, breathing heavily as he glared, wild-eyed, at Darcy.

"Time to give up, girl. There's nowhere for you to go." He stepped onto the deck, narrowing the space between them to ten feet.

"Maybe. Maybe not. I could always swim for it. Besides, I've got your gun. What are you going to do with those bullets? Throw them at me really hard?"

"Ha. Credit where credit's due. That was funny." He took another step closer. "I've lived near the conjunction of this creek and river my whole life. You try jumping in, all you're going to do is get yourself caught in sunken tree limbs or hit a submerged rock. If those don't get you, the current will."

"Save your breath. I'm a good swimmer." Darcy moved toward the deck's edge to show she wasn't afraid to back up her words with action. In all honesty, the thought of jumping into the water to escape terrified her. Claude was spot on about the conditions in the water. She wasn't going to admit that, though.

Instead of escaping, Darcy needed to stall him. If Heather hadn't called 9-1-1, somebody must have done it to report car chase, or the shots fired. If so, the police would arrive soon enough.

If someone called them.

"In that case, let's find out." He took another step closer but stopped when Darcy raised her hand holding the gun.

"Where's Heather? Is she okay?"

"She's fine. I told her to go home and wait for me there. And stay off the phone. When I get home, we're going to take a long drive out west and then south. Just the two of us."

Relief coursed through Darcy. Despite the awful predicament she was in, she was happy to hear the woman was out of danger. There'd been enough death and destruction already.

Claude must have sensed Darcy's moment of relaxation. He leapt at her, grabbing for the gun. She tried to step out of the way, but his hold on her wrist was too tight. As one, they fell to the wooden surface of the deck.

The gun slipped from Darcy's grip. Claude lunged after it, but only managed to give it a nudge. It skittered away, coming to a stop on the edge of the deck. As he made another move for it, Darcy grabbed at his foot. He tumbled head over heel into the water.

"Help!" He splashed around in a panicky attempt to grab hold of one of the posts supporting the deck. "I can't swim."

For a second, indecision immobilized Darcy. Should she help Claude get out of the water or fetch her phone, call 9-1-1, and then give him a hand? Or should she simply walk away and leave the horrible man to save himself? Or let the water take him away?

Claude flailed around in the water, then started to go under. Apparently, the man really couldn't swim.

An image of Eddie propelled her to the deck's edge. She grabbed Claude's hand with one, then both of hers, and pulled with all her might. At first, he fought her.

"Stop fighting. I'm trying to save you." Darcy called him a few unsavory names as she hauled him around a corner of the deck toward a sun-bleached rope ladder.

Once there, she kicked the ladder into the water. She hadn't used it since the previous summer, so she had no idea whether the anchor bolts would hold after being exposed to the elements all winter.

"Let go of me and grab the ladder." She released Claude and held her breath. It was all up to him, now.

Darcy exhaled when he grabbed the rope. After a few moments of flailing around, his feet appeared to find a lower rung. He wrapped his arms around the ladder as he tried to catch his breath.

After a few more moments, he pulled onto the deck and lay there gasping for breath with a dazed look in his eyes, like a certain drummer Darcy could recall who'd had one drink too many and taken a tumble.

Before he had a chance to recover, Darcy pulled up the ladder and wrapped it around his legs, fashioning it into a knot of sorts.

"What the...?"

"You're a murderer." Darcy gave the knot a final tug. "And an attempted murderer, too. You think I'm going to let you get up and walk away? I don't think so."

"What in the world is going on?"

Darcy spun around in response to the questioner. It was Liam. His mouth was open in an exaggerated O and his brows were arched as high as she'd ever seen him.

"Am I glad to see you." She rushed to her friend and wrapped her arms around him. "I caught Eddie's killer."

"You what?" He guided Darcy into a chair while keeping an eye on Claude. "I don't understand."

"Call the cops. Now. I'll explain while they're on the way."

Liam did as he was told without asking any more questions. It was one of the things Darcy loved about the guy. He knew when to roll with it. It was something they'd developed over the years. Something Darcy had earned.

He trusted her.

Once the call had been placed, Darcy and Liam dragged the partially immobile Claude into the chair. Darcy had wanted to leave the man where he was, but Liam overruled her.

"Having him hogtied might look bad when the cops get here. Besides, if he tried to make a break for it, I'd catch him before he got ten yards. Ain't that right, old man?"

Claude looked away and grunted. "I got nothing to say to the likes of you."

"That's okay. I'll talk for him." Darcy planted herself in front of Claude, her feet spaced hip-width apart. She crossed her arms and stared at the man. The sun was to her back. Making him squint as he looked at her was one final way to cause him discomfort.

"You killed Eddie Maxwell because you thought he was having an affair with your wife, didn't you?"

"You're crazy. I don't know what you're talking about." Claude dropped his chin to his chest. His denial lacked conviction, both in body language and in his words.

"Let me spell it out for you then. Feel free to stop me if I get something wrong. Life was good for you and Heather until Eddie moved next door. You didn't like his parties. Same as the Grinch, you didn't like all the noise, noise, noise. Then, Heather started having such a good time at them. That's when he became the neighbor from Hell."

"So? They were loud, a nuisance. I'm an early riser. Those parties of his made it impossible to get to sleep. And I needed my rest. Especially the nights before going on shift at the fire station. Lives depended on me getting a good night's sleep."

"Sure, I'll give you that. But then, she started spending time at the record store, too. Did you know, Liam, that over time, she became one of the record store's most loyal customers? And insisted on being taken care of by Eddie and not anyone else?"

"I did not know that." Liam scratched his chin as he studied Claude, like the man in the chair was a fantastical creature from an old monster movie.

Darcy nodded. "In fact, as the years went by, she spent more and more money, and time, with Eddie at good old Marysburg Music."

"Doesn't prove anything." Claude looked over his shoulder. If he was hoping for a rescue, nobody was coming. And there were no police sirens to be heard, either.

At least not yet.

"It does show that Heather really liked Eddie. She enjoyed spending time with him. She told me more than once that being around him made her feel twenty years younger." Darcy stared at Claude. "In fact, it got to the point that Eddie was able to give her one thing you couldn't. Joy."

"Liar." Claude lunged at Darcy. Before he was halfway out of the chair, Liam sprang into action and wrestled him back into place.

"Calling me names won't change the truth, Claude. Everybody loved Eddie, your wife included. Not in the way you thought, though. You became convinced that they were messing around behind your back, especially after his divorce. Because of that, you decided to take your revenge against him and destroy your wife in the process."

"How'd he do that," Liam asked.

"It was really pretty clever." Darcy told Liam about the dagger. "It never got broken during a *Dungeons and Dragons* game. He just told Heather that. Then he used his art supplies to refashion the dagger into a copy of Eddie's beloved letter opener.

"A gift from his wife was used to murder the man she was supposedly having an affair with."

"Holy cow." Liam's complexion had gone pale. "That is—"

"Bonkers?" Darcy laughed. "Believe me, I know bonkers. Did you ever talk to Heather about Eddie, Claude? Huh? Because if you had, she would have told you the truth. They were friends. Nothing more, despite your delusions. He never got over his ex-wife. That's one of the reasons he let Rafe live with him. To make Donna happy."

"You think you're really smart. I asked her. A bunch of times. She always denied it." The old man shook his head, flinging water all over Darcy. Then he straightened up in an attempt to regain some of his lost dignity.

"Why didn't you believe her?" Darcy head meant for the question to come out stern. Instead, it sounded like a mournful wail. One life was lost. Two more were damaged forever. All because the man refused to believe the woman he'd been married to for almost forty years.

"I trusted Heather." A tear ran down Claude's cheek. "It was Eddie I didn't trust. I never meant to hurt him. I only wanted to let him know enough was enough."

Darcy and Liam exchanged a glance. He nodded, as if say, *You brought us this far. Bring it home.*

"What happened?" Darcy crouched down in front of him. Her knees screamed in protest, but she wanted eye to eye contact. Plus, she wanted to get the story out of him now, in case he clammed up later.

"You're right. I went to the record store that night. I'd had a couple of drinks at Selena's and was full of liquid courage. I was going to have it out with him once and for all. You were right about the dagger, too. Took me six months to get it exactly right. I only worked on it when Heather was out of the house, to make sure she didn't find it."

"It was a convincing copy. I'll give you that," Liam said.

Claude shrugged. "Wasn't that hard. All I had to do was go to pictures of it Heather posted on Facebook. She bought that Elvis story hook, line, and sinker."

"What happened when you went there?" Maybe it was her imagination, but Darcy could almost make out the faintest wail of a police siren.

"I'd called the store earlier in the day. Gave Maxwell a fake name and said I had a record collection I wanted to sell to him. I arranged it so I'd show up after everyone else was gone. I convinced him to leave the front door unlocked even thought we were going to meet after hours.

"When I got there, I went straight to his office. Wanted to catch him off guard. I pulled out the fake letter opener and grabbed the real one. Didn't even take the time to take my gloves off." Claude let out a groan as he looked at the sky. "All I meant to do was scare him. I took the real one to make him think I wasn't kidding around."

"But something went wrong, didn't it?" Darcy put a hand on Claude's knee.

The man was a murderer. He had a tortured soul, though. She might not be able to forgive him for a long time. She could empathize with his pain, though.

"He tried to get me to calm down. He said they were only friends, but if it would help, he'd talk to her. Put some distance between them."

"But that wasn't good enough, was it," Darcy asked. The sirens were growing louder.

"I told him he needed to stay away from Heather. No friendship, no nothing. When I told him that, he started to get up out of his chair, real sudden like. I guess my reflexes took over and before I knew it, I'd stabbed him."

"Then you arranged for it to look like he stabbed himself. And you took the real one with you. What'd you do with it?"

"It's at home. I stashed it with my art supplies."

As Darcy looked over Claude's shoulder, a Marysburg police cruiser, running full lights and sirens, rolled to a stop behind Claude's car. She stood proud and tall as Detective-Sergeant Rosengarten approached. Never again would she lower her gaze before her nemesis.

The officer drew her gun and approached slowly. Liam's message must have really gotten her attention. "Got a report about an attempted murder. Someone want to enlighten me?"

Darcy put up her hands to make sure the police officer wouldn't mistake her for a threat.

"Yeah, this guy," she nodded toward the gun, which was still resting on the edge of the deck, "tried to shoot me. He's also Eddie Maxwell's murderer."

"You can't be serious." Kaitlin kept her gun drawn as she joined them on the deck. "Why don't you tell me what's really going on. You first, Liam, since you're the one who made the nine-one-one call."

Liam gave Kaitlin a full report of everything he'd seen and heard since arriving on the scene. When he was finished, Darcy filled in the rest, from when she met Heather in the park to when Liam had appeared out of the blue.

"Don't anybody move." Kaitlin keyed her microphone to request backup. When she was finished, she holstered her gun. "Mr. Ewing, you're not obligated to say anything. Do you want to respond to what Mr. Simmons just told me, though?"

"No." Claude leaned forward and put his face in his hands. "I'm so sorry." Then he broke down in tears.

While Kaitlin dealt with Claude, another officer arrived and took statements from Darcy and Liam. While Liam gave his report, Darcy stared at the older man, who was now in handcuffs. Something kept niggling at the back of her brain.

Then it came to her. Kaitlin had Claude halfway to her cruiser when Darcy caught up with them.

"Hey, Claude, did you take the collectible Beatles record, too? That's worth a lot of money. The store could really use it back."

The man stopped. After a second, he shook his head.

"It wasn't me. Talk to the Majors kid. When I was waiting to go into the store, he showed up and went inside. He was only there for a minute, then he came back outside with something under his arm. Maybe he took it."

Darcy stood, too shocked to move, as Kaitlin led Claude the rest of the way to the police car. It wasn't until the officer maneuvered him into the back seat that could get her head around what she'd learned.

Darcy turned to Liam. "Did you hear what I heard?"

"Yep." He joined her in the yard. "Two mysteries solved in the span of a few minutes. Not bad, Sherlock."

"Crazy, huh?" She fished a black band from her pocket and pulled her hair into a ponytail. "I can't believe that just happened."

"Which one." Liam smiled. "Catching Eddie's murderer or finding out who stole the Beatles record?"

"Both, I guess. Holy Mother of Drummers, what an insane day." She stared at her friend for a moment. "By the way, where'd you come from? I mean, don't get me wrong, I appreciate the assistance, but how'd you know where to find me?"

"A little birdie called and hinted you might be getting into some mischief."

"Charlotte." Despite the gravity of the situation and her head-to-toe aches and pains, Darcy laughed. "Should have known. I'll have to figure out a way to return the favor."

"Don't tell her I said this, but she was worried sick about you. When she told me what you were up to, I went to the park. You weren't there, so I figured you must have been there and were already gone. When I didn't see your jeep at the police station, I figured you were either at Ewing's house or here."

"Glad you picked this place." She leaned against him. Complete and utter exhaustion was taking over. Despite that, she caught a whiff of his shampoo. It was a woodsy scent. She liked it.

"I am, too." He put his arm around her. "Never played the knight in shining armor coming to the rescue the damsel in distress before. It was kind of cool."

"God, you are such a dork." She gave him a soft punch to his midsection. "I did *not* need rescuing. You did a good job of arriving right on time to assist me, though. Good job. Five stars."

"Any time, Darc."

He helped her into the house. Once she was settled on the couch, he got a couple of bottles of water from the fridge. Along with one bottle, he handed her two small, round tablets. "Take these. It's only ibuprofen. I have a feeling you're gonna need some painkillers."

"Thanks, dude." She downed the pills and drained the bottle. "We made a pretty good team out there, didn't we?"

"That we did." He cleared his throat as he ran his fingers down Ringo's spine. "Maybe we could, you know, do the teamwork thing a little more often. Maybe when the consequences aren't so dire."

Darcy's mind went back to her conversation with Charlotte earlier in the day. Had the woman put a bug in Liam's ear or had the right time simply arrived? It didn't matter. Darcy was battered, bloodied, and bruised.

She was also read to take him up on the offer.

"Sounds good. There's a new Mediterranean restaurant in Muncie I've heard is really good. We ought to check it out. I'll even let you buy."

Chapter Twenty-Five

Darcy spent most of the morning after catching Eddie's murderer at the police station. First, the officer who interviewed her the evening before took her formal statement. After that, Kaitlin insisted on reviewing the statement with Darcy in minute detail.

When the digital clock on the wall behind the cop's desk turned to *10:45,* Darcy rose to her feet.

"I need to get to work. We've gone over that thing three times. Can I go now?"

Kaitlin looked up from the page she'd been studying. She was frowning. After a couple of tension-filled moments, she flicked her fingers in the direction of the exit.

"Yeah, get out of here. I know where to find you."

Darcy started to leave. Before she got far, she turned on her heel and returned to Kaitlin's desk. She placed her hands on the desktop and took a deep breath.

"I get it. You don't trust me. I caused you a lot of grief in the past. But that was then. I've been clean and on the straight and narrow for half a decade. And I caught Eddie's Maxwell's killer when you were happy to call it a suicide."

"And?" Kaitlin rose to her feet. "What do you want? A cookie?"

"You can't bring yourself to say it, can you? No, I don't want anything. Knowing Eddie's murderer is behind bars is enough of a reward. A simple thank you would be welcome, though."

All of Kaitlin's bravado seemed to fall away from her, like a tree losing its leaves until the only things left were bare and vulnerable branches. Darcy's salvo had been a little heated, but darn it, she'd gotten her life together and she'd been good. And done good, too.

And she'd made sure Claude Ewing didn't get away with murder.

Eventually, Kaitlin shook her head and chuckled.

"You're correct. I don't trust you." She stuck out a hand to shake. "But you got this one right when I didn't. Thank you."

"You're welcome." They shook, then Darcy made for the door before she said anything that might ruin the moment.

She reveled in her feeling of accomplishment, though it was tinged with a heavy dose of sadness. Sadness at the loss of her friend and mentor, Eddie Maxwell. Sadness for a kind woman, Heather Ewing, who lost a friend and would be separated from her husband in such short order. And yes, even sadness, for Claude Ewing, that his inability to trust his neighbor led to such an awful outcome.

In the end, though, Darcy had stayed true to her heart, ignored the naysayers, and did right by Eddie. That had been her goal. And she'd met it.

It was something to be proud of.

Darcy hadn't been proud of herself often in the last decade. It was a feeling she welcomed. Because she'd earned it.

After a quick stop at Renee's to grab a donut and a tea to go, she arrived at the record store. What she found there was mind-boggling.

A line of customers waiting to enter extended down the sidewalk and around the corner. White vans from two different Indianapolis television stations were parked in front of the store. Their satellite dishes were raised toward the sky.

With a knot tightening in her belly, Darcy greeted the waiting customers. They responded by giving her a round of applause.

"What's going on," she asked a regular customer named Todd Robinson, who was holding the door open for her.

"It's the town showing our local superhero their appreciation for a job well done." He gestured for her to go inside. "After you."

The scene inside took Darcy's breath away.

The aisles were filled with customers who'd paused their shopping to turn their attention to her. Charlotte was stationed near the store's front picture window. She nodded to Hank, who promptly lowered a needle onto a record album. As the strains of "Kind and Generous" by Natalie Merchant came over the speakers, the crowd broke out in applause.

A lump formed in Darcy's throat, and she blinked to fight back a fresh flood of tears. She held it together until Char gave her a hug. Then she let the floodgates go and held onto her friend like she never wanted to let go.

When the applause died down, she exchanged a few words with her new store manager, then turned to the gathering. Everyone had their phones out, ready to take her picture. And record her saying a few words.

"I, uh, haven't been in front of a crowd this big since my Pixie Dust days, so I'm a little out of practice."

"You're doing fine. In more ways than one," a man in the back said in a jovial tone that got the crowd laughing.

The owner's voice stepped to the side so Darcy could see him. It was a gray-haired gentleman in his late fifties. He was holding hands with a bespectacled woman who was dabbing at the corner of her eye with a tissue. It was Brad and Helen Gaughan.

"Mom? Dad? What are you doing here?" Even though Darcy's up and down relationship with her parents had improved in recent years, it was still very much a work in progress. Like Aisling, they lived near Chicago, a three-hour drive away. Spur of the moment visits never happened.

"Same as everyone else here. We want to show our support for Marysburg's newest hero. You were saying, though."

"Right. Thank you all for being here. Eddie Maxwell loved this town, and especially this store, with all his heart. This place was his dream come true. I'm gonna do everything I can to keep that dream of celebrating music alive." She pointed toward the crowd with both hands. "And y'all can help by buying lots of records, so I'll let you get to it."

There was another round of laughter, then Darcy waded into the crowd to exchange hellos and accept words of thanks. There was an awkward moment of silence when she made it to her parents.

Her mom ended it by giving her a tight hug.

"Liam called us last night to tell us what you'd done. You're a real hero, Darcy Jo," Helen said through her tears. "We know we've waited too long to tell you this, but we're so proud of you. Of the road you've traveled to become the amazing woman who's standing right here, in front of us."

Brad put an arm around her. "And how honored we are to get to call you our daughter."

"Thanks. It means a lot. I'm sure Eddie would have appreciated it, too."

Hank appeared at Darcy's side. "I'm terribly sorry to interrupt, but there's someone in your office who'd like a word with you, Boss."

Intrigued by Hank's vague report, Darcy excused herself and wound her way to the back of the store. Her jaw tightened when she saw who was waiting for her.

"Hello, Rafe." She closed the door and took her seat behind the desk without breaking eye contact. Between the silence and her glare, the man started fidgeting.

"I have something that belongs to the store. I found it at home last night."

He unzipped a backpack to reveal the framed *White Album* that had gone missing the night Eddie died.

Darcy kept silent until Rafe handed it to her. Once it was in her possession, she breathed an inward sigh of relief. She wasn't going to let the guy off easy, though.

"Found it at your house? I have it on good authority that you were witnessed leaving the store with it under your arm the night your step-father was murdered."

He flinched at the word *murdered*.

"I didn't know anything about that. I swear. I came here that night to ask for some walking around money to get me by until payday at the library. When he said no, I got mad and took the record. Figured I'd sell it on eBay."

Darcy crossed her arms. She wanted to lash out at Rafe. How could he be so unfeeling toward the man who had given him a home, taken care of him? And his only thoughts had been all about himself.

Yelling at him wouldn't bring Eddie back, though. Instead, she shrugged.

"Why should I believe you?"

"Why would I bring it back if I was lying? Besides," his shoulders sagged, "after I found out what had happened to the old man, I knew the record would be too hot to sell. And then when you showed up at the house the second time, I thought you might know something. I didn't want to go to jail over that, especially after I found out about the inheritance. Why take a chance on throwing that away? Know what I mean?"

He raised his head until his gaze matched hers. "Besides, aren't you supposed to be into the whole forgiveness thing after rehab and all that?"

Darcy sighed. Then, she let out a little chuckle. Warped though it might be, she could see where Rafe was coming from. She also had to admit, even begrudgingly, that he had a point about forgiveness.

"You're right, dude. It is better to forgive, so I forgive you for taking the record. I also want to thank you for bringing it back. That took guts. I hope this is the start of a productive tenant-landlord relationship."

"Yeah, about that." He scratched his chin. "I've been thinking about Meadows's offer."

Darcy's heart sank. She'd become so focused on the investigation the past few days that she hadn't thought about much of anything beyond that and Record Store Day. "Yes?"

"I don't want to be a landlord. Too much of a hassle. Todd's a jerk, though. I talked to some people and found out that he lowballed me. Big time. It makes me mad. I know I'm not a hard worker, but I'm not stupid."

Unsure of where Rafe was going with the conversation, Darcy resorted to a simple nod.

"His offer proves he thinks I'm stupid. To be honest, Meadows was a jerk to the old man, too. Since he's been gone, I've been learning how much he did for people, especially me."

"He always had your best interest at heart." It was true. Eddie had used that exact sentiment when he talked to Darcy about his challenges trying to mentor Rafe.

"Yeah, I'm beginning to see that now." He leaned forward. "That's why I've got a proposition for you. What if I sold the building to you?"

Darcy's mind reeled. The offer was music to her ears. It was also an unbelievably sudden change of direction.

"Okay, gotta admit, that's not what I expected you to say." She raised her hands to stop Rafe, who had opened his mouth. "I'm totally interested. Before we get too far down that road, you need to know the rent payments the store paid were way below market value."

"I don't care about that. We both know there's no way you can get a loan to buy the building. Not right now. How about this? I sell the building to you at the price Meadows offered to me. You keep making the same monthly payment, except now it will be like a mortgage instead of rent. You'd also have to pay all the utilities."

Numbers ran through Darcy's head. She was no accounting expert, but if Rafe was being straight with her, the proposition was definitely doable, especially with a former accountant as her store manager. It was too early to get her hopes up, though. Caution was needed.

"I appreciate the offer. It's really generous. I gotta ask, why not just sell to Todd and walk away with a big, fat wad of cash?"

Rafe laughed. It had a gentle tone to it. One that Darcy couldn't recall hearing ever before. Was a new Rafe Majors emerging, like a cicada after its seventeen-year hibernation? If so, Darcy liked it so far.

"I was talking to my mom the other day. She said without the old man around, I had no choice but to grow up. That I needed to figure out a way to make a steady income. I figure getting a monthly payment from you does two things for me."

"What's that?"

"It will help me learn to live on a budget. If I got a big check from selling the place to Todd, I'd probably end up spending it on a lot of stuff I don't need."

"That's a good point." Darcy's heart was beginning to flutter with hopefulness. Rafe seemed to have given his proposal a lot of thought. "What's the other one?"

"By selling to you, I get to keep it out of Todd's hands. Nothing beats stickin' it to the man." He laughed again. This time it was long and loud.

Like a victory laugh.

Darcy didn't want to be a vengeful person. Emotions like that were toxic and she didn't have room in her life for that kind of stuff. Still, it wouldn't be the worst thing in the world to see Todd Meadows knocked down a peg or two.

"Rafe, I believe we have a deal." As they shook hands, she joined him in the laughter.

* * *

The day flew by. Between TV and radio interviews, a generous group of customers that were in the mood to show their support with their dollars, and the non-stop text messages and emails, the only times Darcy was able to catch her breath were during a couple of quick trips to the office.

She was in no mood to keep the store open late, though, so when eight o'clock arrived, she gently, but firmly let the remaining customers know it was time for them to make their final selections and depart.

The moment the final customer was out the door, she flipped the lock and let out a loud *"Whoop, there it is!"*

All four members of her team stopped what they were doing in mid-task to look at her.

"Something on your mind, Darcy," Hank asked from behind the cash register.

"Yes. Gather round, friends." Darcy held her arms out wide and motioned then toward her with her fingers. Once they were all together, she draped one arm around Hank and the other around Charlotte.

"I've got some amazing news. Rafe Majors and I had a little chat earlier today. We've agreed to work together so I can buy the building from him and keep the record store here for the long-term."

Izzy's and Peter's jaws dropped in unison. The young lady was the first to recover. "Does that mean Mr. Meadows isn't buying it from Rafe after all?"

"That's right." Darcy giggled and recounted her conversation with Eddie's stepson.

"Can you trust him?" Charlotte asked. "I mean, he sponged off Eddie and stole from the store."

"He sounded sincere, so I'm choosing to give him the benefit of the doubt. Kind of like Eddie gave me the benefit of the doubt when he hired me. I remember during rehab, one of the counselors told me 'We all have the capacity to change.' When I was given the chance, I changed. Now, it's my turn to do the same for someone else."

"I like the sound of that." Hank gave Darcy a hug. A moment later, it turned into a group hug.

"I love y'all." Darcy wiped a tear from her cheek. She had shed countless tears over the course of the day. They'd been tears of joy. And she'd been happy to let them fall.

"Marysburg Music forever, yesi!" Peter queued up an upbeat reggae tune on his phone and led the group in a conga line as they danced through the store.

After all Darcy and her team had been through, it was the perfect way to get the party started.

* * *

Ten days later, Darcy took a final look at the store. Everything was in place. She nodded in satisfaction. Then she gathered her team together, which had a few new faces, given the enormity of the day.

"Welcome to Record Store Day, everybody. I'd like to give a shout out to our special guest stars for today—Liam, Rafe, Aisling, Brad, and Helen."

After a polite round of applause, Darcy glanced toward the front of the store. The customers waiting outside, some since the night before, had been well behaved. Based on the growing noise level, they were getting restless. She had a few more things she wanted to say before they opened the door, though.

"Today's going to be a long day. It will also be an amazing one and you'll have a lot of fun. The musical performance starts in an hour, so be sure to take a minute to give our artists a listen." She swallowed. "One last thing.

This is the first Record Store Day in Marysburg Music's history without Eddie Maxwell at the helm. He was like a mother eagle, teaching and guiding us so we'd be ready when it was time to fly. It's time to spread our wings and make him proud."

Darcy jogged through the group, her group, exchanging high fives with each of them. Every single person had a smile on their face and radiated positive vibes. It was going to be an amazing day.

The future of Marysburg Music, and Darcy Gaughan, was going to be like a bright, bright, sunshiny day, indeed.

Acknowledgements

I can't thank Todd Robinson, owner of Luna Music, enough for his willingness to share what it's like to run a real-life record store. Please be sure to support independent record stores. They truly do celebrate music of all sorts, every day of the year.

About the Author

J.C. Kenney is an Amazon and Kobo bestselling author. Record Store Reckoning is the first novel in The Darcy Gaughan Mysteries. He is also the author of The Allie Cobb Mysteries. When he's not writing, you can find him following IndyCar racing or listening to music. He lives in Indianapolis with his wife, two children, and a cat. You can find him at www.jckenney.com.

SOCIAL MEDIA HANDLES:

Facebook - https://www.facebook.com/JCKenney1/
Instagram - https://www.instagram.com/j.c.kenney/
Twitter - https://twitter.com/JCKenney1
Goodreads - https://goodreads.com/jckenney
BookBub - https://www.bookbub.com/authors/j-c-kenney
Amazon author page - https://www.amazon.com/-/e/B07C7K4WH1

AUTHOR WEBSITE: https://www.jckenney.com/

Also by J. C. Kenney

The Allie Cobb Mysteries

A Literal Mess
A Genuine Fix
A Mysterious Mix Up
A Deadly Discovery
The Dead of Winter